W9-BDV-552

"You're a knight in shining armor, aren't you? Ready to save the damsel in distress."

"If you'll let me."

Sam chuckled. "Evan, trust me, I'm not a damsel and if I did need saving, I'd do it myself. Just be there on time. I'll pick out the outfit I want you to wear." She started to walk away toward her own car. That sleek ice-blue Mercedes that reminded him of her.

Evan scowled. "I'm not some damn doll to be dressed up," he called after her.

"No, you're a client who I want to make sure is dressed and looking appropriate for his first public appearance."

"I don't like red!" he shouted even as she was opening her car door.

She waved back. "I don't care."

Yeah, Evan thought as he watched her drive away, hiring her was both the best and worst decision he'd ever made.

Dear Reader,

Well, this is it. The final book in The Bakers of Baseball series. It has been so much fun writing these books. I know I'm going to miss Minotaur Falls and baseball.

I have to confess I absolutely love baseball movies. In my opinion you don't even have to love baseball to love baseball movies. These books have been my tribute to every baseball movie I have ever loved.

In this final chapter, we meet Samantha and Evan, who were introduced in *Scout's Honor*, and being able to take their story from one book to the next was also a thrill. Sam and Evan don't have the easiest time finding their way to a happy ending, but of course it wouldn't be a story if they didn't!

I hope, if you've read the series, you've enjoyed the Baker women as much as I have. I love to hear from readers, so please feel free to contact me at www.stephaniedoyle.net, on Facebook or on Twitter, @stephdoylerw.

Stephanie

STEPHANIE
DOYLE

—

Betting on the Rookie

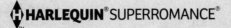

HARLEQUIN®SUPERROMANCE®

If you purchased this book without a cover you should be aware
that this book is stolen property. It was reported as "unsold and
destroyed" to the publisher, and neither the author nor the
publisher has received any payment for this "stripped book."

Recycling programs
for this product may
not exist in your area.

ISBN-13: 978-0-373-60960-4

Betting on the Rookie

Copyright © 2016 by Stephanie Doyle

All rights reserved. Except for use in any review, the reproduction or
utilization of this work in whole or in part in any form by any electronic,
mechanical or other means, now known or hereinafter invented, including
xerography, photocopying and recording, or in any information storage
or retrieval system, is forbidden without the written permission of the
publisher, Harlequin Enterprises Limited, 225 Duncan Mill Road,
Don Mills, Ontario M3B 3K9, Canada.

This is a work of fiction. Names, characters, places and incidents are
either the product of the author's imagination or are used fictitiously,
and any resemblance to actual persons, living or dead, business
establishments, events or locales is entirely coincidental.

This edition published by arrangement with Harlequin Books S.A.

For questions and comments about the quality of this book,
please contact us at CustomerService@Harlequin.com.

® and TM are trademarks of Harlequin Enterprises Limited or its
corporate affiliates. Trademarks indicated with ® are registered in the
United States Patent and Trademark Office, the Canadian Intellectual
Property Office and in other countries.

Printed in U.S.A.

Stephanie Doyle, a dedicated romance reader, began to pen her own romantic adventures at age sixteen. She began submitting to Harlequin at age eighteen and by twenty-six her first book was published. Fifteen years later, she still loves what she does, as each book is a new adventure. She lives in South Jersey with her cat, Hermione, the designated princess of the house. When Stephanie's not reading or writing, in the summer she is most likely watching a baseball game and eating a hot dog.

For Wanda

PROLOGUE

"RICHARD, TELL ME again you didn't do this thing."

Samantha sat behind the desk in her office and continued to read the Tweets on her phone even as she waited for the person in front of her to prove he couldn't be guilty of what he'd been accused.

She knew Richard. She'd followed him his entire college career and was the first to call him when he committed to the NFL draft. She'd sat down with his family, she'd talked to ex-girlfriends, former teachers. Everyone had glowing things to say about him.

Who didn't love Richard Stanson, the all-American quarterback?

Samantha prided herself on having a small close-knit clientele. These weren't just people she represented; they were people she *knew*. Her entire business model was built on the idea that trust was the number one component of each and every relationship.

They had to trust her with their careers, their compensation, and she had to trust that she was working for the right people. Good people who understood what it meant to be not just an athlete, but a professional. It wasn't just about the money for her. It hadn't been since she'd left Barkley Partners to go it alone.

She wanted to be an agent on her terms. She wanted only the best kind of clients, and she wanted to make sure she did right by all of them.

Richard had been one of her first major wins. Everyone wanted him, but he chose her because he said he trusted her the most. He'd legitimized her agency. He'd legitimized her.

If an all-American quarterback didn't have a problem with a woman as an agent, then who would?

"Sam, I didn't do it."

Samantha closed her eyes. He looked so earnest. Sometimes she forgot he was only twenty-six. Still, in many ways, just a kid playing a game.

"Come on, you have to believe me," he said again, putting his hands on her desk. He had immediately flown to Chicago when the story had been about to break. He said it was because he wanted her to hear his side first, and he wanted to do it in person, so she could see his face when he told her.

Too late about getting to her first.

Social media was already beginning to tear down America's quarterback. Guilty before even having a chance to say he was innocent.

Samantha's phone had been buzzing frantically all morning. His sponsors would want constant updates. She didn't blame them, not when the man whose face was on so many of America's favorite products had just been accused of hitting a woman and knocking her down a flight of stairs.

"I've been with you for four years," he told her. "You know what kind of person I am. You have to."

Samantha stopped reading the Tweets and set her phone aside for now. She looked into his eyes, really looked into them as she tried to evaluate whether or not he could be that good a liar.

He sounded innocent. He looked innocent.

In the four years he'd been her client nothing like this had come out before. But in the past seven months of him dating Juliette, the supermodel, things had been different. Their relationship at best could be described as intense. At worst volatile. Several of their verbal arguments had been caught on camera outside various nightclubs.

Samantha had at one point suggested that maybe they weren't a good fit. Richard had shrugged it off and just said that they were working through their issues. The next thing Sam heard, they were engaged. When he'd called to tell her that news, he'd promised Sam that they were better. More relaxed as a couple. He seemed so certain she was *the one*. That their love was the *real thing*.

Would a man who loved his fiancée hit her?

Sadly, Sam knew the answer to that question all too well.

"People are reporting hearing shouts in the stairwell before you opened the door and called for help."

"We were drunk," he insisted. "Yes, we were loud and obnoxious before it happened. I've got no excuse for that, I can only tell you it's the truth. Hell, that's why she fell. And I was too drunk to catch her before she went down."

It wasn't the most unreasonable story.

They had left the hotel bar late at night and decided to take the stairs to their room on the second floor. They had been drunk, clearly loud enough for people in the hotel lobby to have heard them. Juliette had tripped in her four-inch-high stilettos, fallen, hit her chin on the stair railing and knocked herself out cold.

The concierge had opened the door to the stairs, only to find Richard picking up his out-cold fiancée with a severe red mark already forming on her face. He did the next logical thing and called the police.

Only, Juliette had revived by the time the police got there and backed up Richard's story. No formal complaint had been filed, and the police left the hotel.

However, someone in the lobby, who must have realized who Richard was, had apparently snapped a picture of the quarterback with his unconscious fiancée in his arms. From there it was nothing more than a few reTweets to social media obliteration.

"You need to let me get out there. Let me tell them my side of the story. They'll believe me. Hell, they will believe Juliette."

No, Sam thought. *They won't. Not when a woman is about to marry a man who is about to become the highest paid NFL quarterback of all time.*

"You're not saying anything," she told him. "I'll hold a press conference in the large conference room downstairs. I'll tell them everything you said exactly as you said it and let them ask me their questions. If you and Juliette are seen together, I think it will just lend more credence to a false accusation. Besides, her face must be a mess. I'll handle it."

"I knew you would believe me," he said, smiling and nodding. "I knew you would never think that of me."

"Just one last question." Samantha had gone over the series of events Richard had detailed for her, coupled with the police report and the story she'd heard directly from the concierge at the hotel. One thing hadn't sounded right.

"Why was her shirt ripped?"

"What?"

"Her shirt, the concierge said a bunch of buttons were at the bottom of the steps, and it looked like her shirt was ripped in front."

Richard shook his head. "Maybe when I reached for her, I grabbed her shirt from behind?"

"Maybe?"

Richard groaned. "Come on, Sam. I already told you. I was drunk. Freaking blitzed. It happened in a second. One minute she's standing next to me, the next she's at the bottom of the steps."

It all came down to trust.

Did Sam trust Richard or didn't she?

THE NEXT DAY Sam stood in her conference room, which was filled to capacity with press. ESPN had sent a film crew, and it was clear they were disappointed only Sam would be speaking.

"Richard Stanson is innocent. I'm not saying that as his lawyer or his agent, but as his friend. He is the victim in this case. The victim of a picture taken out of context by a person who didn't have all the facts."

"Can you tell us the facts as you understand them?" one reporter called out.

Samantha laid out Richard's perfectly reasonable explanation for the events of a few nights ago.

"Now, this doesn't excuse him from overindulging—Juliette, either, for that matter—but it doesn't make him the monster he is being portrayed as..."

Sam stopped talking, because she could

feel an immediate change in the room. Phones were buzzing. Everyone was shifting to look at their messages.

No one was paying any attention to her.

That meant bigger news was breaking.

Good, she thought. The quicker they moved on to the next story, the sooner they would leave Richard alone.

"So if that's all your questions..."

"Ms. Baker," one reporter said, stopping her. "A last question. Have you seen the video?"

"I'm sorry?" Sam could feel the heat in her cheeks. "What video?"

"The video from the stairwell. Turns out there was a camera just over the door."

A video shouldn't matter. A video would just prove Richard's innocence. Then, why was her gut turning over?

"Excellent," Sam said. "I'm sure any video will corroborate my client's story."

No, she thought. She could see it in their faces. The glimmer of excitement as the story was about to get even worse. Which, of course, made the reporting of it better for all of them.

"Sam," said another reporter, a woman Sam had given any number of interviews to in the past. "You're going to want to see the video before you say anything else."

So Sam did. She took out her phone, also buzzing like crazy with texts, and pulled up YouTube, which was showing a video of Richard Stanson clearly ripping the shirt off his girlfriend and then punching her in the face only to watch her unconscious body fall down four steps to the floor.

CHAPTER ONE

Six months later...

SAMANTHA STARED UP at the house and wondered maybe for the thousandth time why she had felt like this would be a good idea.

Talk about starting over.

Returning to Minotaur Falls seemed like as good a place as any to reboot her life. After all, this was where she'd been raised, and that had worked out pretty well...

Until it hadn't.

If she was going to stay in the Falls, in her old hometown, then her old home seem appropriate, as well. It had been empty these last years since Duff had died, and Scout had followed her husband, Jayson, to Arizona. Scout was thrilled with the idea of someone actually living here. As if the empty house reminded her of the fact that their father was dead. Which of course would make Scout profoundly sad.

Wow. Had it been almost two years since Duff passed? Some days Samantha felt the grief as if she'd just lost him. Other times it seemed far away, as if those months of reconciling with him, only to then lose him, were a dream from another time.

Back then Sam hadn't really allowed herself the chance to grieve. There had been Scout to deal with. Samantha had felt it necessary to put her emotions aside to focus on her youngest sister. Scout and Duff had been inseparable through life. There had been worry amongst the family that Scout might not mentally survive his loss.

They should have given Scout more credit. After all, she was pretty tough. Just like Duff raised her to be.

No, no one would have guessed that, of all the Baker girls to lose their grip on their mental faculties…that it would have been calm, cool—practically icy—Samantha Baker.

It was only a small meltdown.

But now you're back.

Sam's phone buzzed. It used to go off at all hours of the day in a constant stream of incoming calls and texts but had suddenly gone quiet. Now when it buzzed, it was actually a surprise to her.

"Hello?"

"Are you home yet?"

Scout. Only Scout would refer to this house as Sam's home. Sam hitched her very expensive handbag over a shoulder and made her way up the porch steps.

"Yes, I'm here."

She shook out her key ring and identified the one to the house. Pressing the phone between her shoulder and her ear, she unlocked the door and let herself in.

Two years away, and yet nothing had changed. The only thing missing was Duff's favorite chair. Scout had moved that out to Arizona with her.

"Sandy from down the street has been cleaning it for me once a month. I know it's a ridiculous waste of money, but I just can't let it go," Scout was saying as Sam set her bag down.

"It looks like it's in really great shape." She took a moment and glanced around the place. No dust, no smell to suggest the air was musty. Just a fresh and clean house, much like it had been the last time she'd been here.

Much like it had been when Duff was alive.

Sam braced herself for the pang of sadness and let it roll over her. Despite her and Duff's troubles, the love had always been there. She'd never considered what a hole his absence might mean in her life.

Duff was always supposed to be there.

He was supposed to be here now, telling her that she could do this. She could get back on the horse and get her career back. Her life back.

"Well, it's a perfect hiding place to lick your wounds for a while. Just ask me."

"I'm not hiding," Sam said immediately. "I'm not licking wounds. I'm staging a comeback. That's totally different."

"Fine, but listen, if you need me to come home and hang with you…"

"I don't need anyone," Sam said, cutting her off. There was no room for sympathy and hand-holding. Yes, she'd had a setback. A significant one, but nothing she couldn't overcome with some hard work and belief in herself.

"Wow." Scout chuckled in her ear. "That, my friend, was a very good impression of me. But let me remind you… I did need people. So again, I'm only a phone call and a flight away."

"It's the middle of the baseball season, Scout."

"And you're my sister, Sam."

Right. As important as baseball was to the Bakers, family was even more important.

"Understood. Really, it's not like I'm curled up in ball crying my eyes out." She had been, but that had been over a month ago. Now she was back.

She hoped.

"The only thing I need from you is prospects."

Up-and-coming baseball players were Scout's bailiwick. Sam figured she only needed one solid prospect to sign with her to show everyone she was down but not out.

Someone who would be okay signing with an agent who had loudly and fervently supported a man who'd turned out to be an abuser.

Sam's stomach rolled, and she wondered when the self-disgust would stop. When she might consider forgiving herself for trusting Richard Stanson.

No one had believed her, of course, that she'd actually trusted him.

Then again, no one had thought she would be so stupid as to stand in front of a room filled with reporters announcing that her client was the victim if she'd known there was video proof.

Richard had known about the video. He'd seen the camera and had paid the hotel security person two hundred thousand dollars to erase it. Apparently that hadn't been enough.

She'd lost all of her female clients first. No one wanted to be associated with someone who would support a man like him. She couldn't blame them. Then, her male clients had started to drop her, one by one. Some had been afraid of guilt by association. Others had simply had a concern about her judgment.

In the end she'd been left with Richard, who she'd severed ties with immediately.

He and Juliette were in counseling now. The wedding was still planned for late August.

"I've got one, but I'm not sure how you're going to feel about this."

Sam focused on what Scout was saying. She needed to start putting the past behind her and work on her future. This was about rebuilding, not tearing herself down just because she'd made a mistake and believed a man who lied to her.

Twice. You've made that mistake twice.

"Who? Give me a name," Sam said, not acknowledging her own thoughts.

"Okay, remember Evan Tanner?"

The name sent a bolt to Sam's stomach. It wasn't disgust. Not fear or anxiety. If she had to label it, the closest she might have come was lust, but even that didn't seem right.

She'd met Evan two years ago when Scout had picked him out as a draft prospect for the New England Rebels. At the time, he'd been a twenty-seven-year-old former college football player who had just taught himself the game of baseball so he could coach a high school team.

Evan Tanner had cost Scout her job with the Rebels; he'd been such an unlikely pick. But there was one thing Scout knew better than anyone, and that was baseball and baseball players. He'd ended up being drafted in the third round, but that was the last Samantha had heard about him. Which made sense if he was bouncing around in minor ball.

Players didn't make it on to Sam's radar until they hit the majors.

"Vaguely," Sam said, because she in fact remembered him vividly. There had been something about him that made it hard for her to look away. It wasn't just his straight-up good looks or his golden brown eyes. There had been something so *nice* about him. And when she'd given him her full ice princess shutdown when he'd flirted with her, he hadn't seemed the least put off or intimidated.

Everyone quaked at her ice princess face.

"Well, guess what? He just got traded to the New England Rebels organization. He's going to play for the Minotaurs, and while that's just their minor league team, the talk is he'll be playing in The Show by the All-Star break."

That made Sam's jaw drop. "You're kidding me. The team that fired you over even suggesting this guy, and they traded for him?"

"Please, you know baseball. A lot of short memories when it comes to this kind of stuff. Especially given Evan's talent. I'm sure Reuben had no problem spinning his way out of that even a little bit. And it's not like Evan has a say in where he goes. He's got to take his chances as they come. He's blowing it up big-time in the minors, hitting over .350. Once they call him up, he's going to need an agent. Someone ruthless, too, if he's going to negotiate with Reuben."

Great, Sam thought. Her first shot at a real client, and it had to be Evan Tanner.

"Plus, Evan owes me. I put in a good word for you, and it's a done deal."

"No word!" Sam snapped. "First, I'm going to investigate the hell out of this guy, and when and only when I decide he's worthy of my services, then I'll do the work of landing him. It has to be that way, Scout. I can't be taking on pity clients. That won't accomplish anything."

"Okay," Scout said, relenting. "No word from me, but it's not like he doesn't know who are you. You can't help that."

Would he even remember her? Nearly two years seemed like a lifetime ago. A few conversations, some flirting on his part. Ice princess on hers.

Of course he would know her by name. He would certainly know about the scandal. But that was an obstacle she was going to have to overcome with any potential client.

I made a mistake. I believed a man. But

*give me one more chance, and I swear I'll
never make that mistake again.*

She was going to have to work on her
pitch.

"The Minotaurs are traveling now, so he'll
join the team on the road. But he should be
back in the Falls by the end of the week.
That should give you plenty of time to do
your research."

"Thanks, Scout. This could be the break
I need."

"No problem, and if you do sign him,
please, give the New England Rebels hell
for me. Take every penny out of their pocket
you possibly can."

Sam smiled. "That I can do."

Sam ended the call and suddenly felt a
thrill of excitement. This was it. She was
back in business and on the prowl for a new
client.

Maybe she would get lucky. Maybe she
would see him again and realize he wasn't
as remotely nice to look at as the last time
she'd seen him. Because it wasn't the great-
est idea to be attracted to a potential client.

Yes, she was sure her memory was exag-
gerated.

After all, at the time, she thought he'd

been one of the most handsome men she'd ever seen.

That had to be wrong.

EVAN TANNER WAS pulling into the Minotaurs' baseball field parking lot with his father still talking through the speakers in his truck. It was a new truck, red with black interior. Something he had absolutely no need for but had always wanted.

As a high school teacher and coach, it had been a pipe dream. Conservative used cars had been more his style. Now, he could afford this truck easily. Something he acknowledged was completely jacked—getting more money to play a game than to teach kids. Because he could swing a bat and hit a ball. Life was crazy sometimes.

"You're going to think about what I said."

"Yes, Dad."

"I mean, it's time, son, we're talking about the big leagues."

"I know, Dad," Evan said, trying to be as patient as he could. After all, his father couldn't help it, he was just excited for him. The reality was that this next climb into the majors was going to happen…it was just a question of when.

"I worry about you getting taken advantage of because you're not the prototypical baseball player."

Evan understood that. There was no doubt the Rebels would lowball any contract they offered him, given his significant age. At least his baseball age.

No, Evan knew an agent was necessary. The hard part was going to be finding the right one. Someone he could trust. Whose first concern was what Evan wanted, not how much money was in it for the agent.

"I promise. I will start looking. Hey, I'm here now. I want to drop my stuff off in my locker and get set up before the game tomorrow."

"Play sharp."

Evan smiled. That's what his dad always told him. Not play well or hard, play sharp. It was his dad's way of saying to use all his abilities. Not just his physical ones but his mental ones, as well.

"Got it."

"Oh, and one last thing… I wasn't going to mention it, but it seemed odd…and I guess I thought you should know. Kelly called me."

It took a second for the name to register. "Kelly? My ex-girlfriend, Kelly?"

"Yep. She said she was wondering how you were doing and decided to call to catch up. Mine was the last number she had for you. She wanted to know why you weren't on Facebook."

Evan grimaced. Because he hated the idea of social media. Because of things just like this. Kelly was part of his past. A long-ago past. There was no reason they needed to be internet friends. He hoped she was doing well but felt no need to catch up with her.

"Anyway, I wasn't sure I should tell you. The timing...well...let's just say it's suspicious."

Evan understood his father's concern. It had been Evan's decision after college not to try and make an attempt at a pro football career. That had ultimately ended the relationship between him and Kelly. She seemed so convinced he would be drafted despite his size and that, by not at least trying, he was walking away from a future that would be radically different than that of a schoolteacher.

Kelly hadn't wanted to be the wife of a schoolteacher.

Evan would never forget her saying those exact words to him. They deserved better, she had said. It had devastated him and destroyed them as couple. Only months before, he'd actually been thinking about proposing.

Although he couldn't imagine there would be any way she might know what was happening with him now. They weren't from the same hometown, having met in college. She was from Florida originally, if he recalled. As far as Evan was aware, none of their mutual college friends knew that he was now playing baseball. Certainly no one knew he was as close to the majors as he was.

Because he wasn't out there on the internet talking about himself every day.

"It was probably just a coincidence. Don't worry about it, Dad."

"I'm not worried. You've got too good a head on your shoulders to get distracted by Kelly, of all people. You know, I never liked her."

"Yes, Dad. I remember."

"Okay, son…well… I'll see you soon. You'll call me the minute you get called up, and no matter where you're playing I'll be there."

His dad, now retired, had spent the last year following Evan around the country to various different minor league ball clubs.

Including all the way to Puerto Rico when Evan had played fall ball last year.

Evan had always encouraged his dad, a widower for over ten years now, to find a hobby other than his son. His father had never listened.

Now there was a very real chance before the season was over that his father would be watching Evan at his major league debut game. Evan felt goose bumps at the mere idea of it.

Stay cool. You're not quite there yet.

"Love you, Dad."

"Love you, too, son."

The call ended, and Evan sat in the truck for a moment to appreciate this time and this moment. The stadium where he had tried out loomed in front of him. The bull situated over the entrance seemed like a fierce thing under the new summer sun. He'd made it to Triple A, one step away from The Show. The irony that he was back here where it all started wasn't lost on him, either. Karma, it seemed, had a sense of humor.

Scout Baker, a New England Rebel scout at the time, had seen something in the swing of a high school baseball coach. Her belief in him had cost her her job. But her belief in him was what had told him he should continue trying. So he had.

Now he was one step away from fulfilling a dream of being a professional athlete. Something he thought he'd left behind after college.

Evan got out of the truck and grabbed his equipment bag from the cab in back. It was an off day, so the lot was barely filled. Probably mostly with just the support staff who ran the park and the general manager.

Maybe that's why the ice-blue Mercedes caught his attention. Or more likely the woman leaning against it.

Sleek body, long heels, blond hair that just hit her chin. And even though he couldn't see them from this distance, the prettiest blue eyes he'd ever seen.

He would have known her anywhere. He wondered if she might look at him and guess that she had starred in several of his fantasies over these past months. If it would somehow be written on his face that he had dreamt about taking her every way a man could have a woman.

"Samantha Baker," he called.

He could see that startled her a little. They'd only shared a few casual conversations not quite two years ago. Maybe he should have forgotten her.

He hadn't. Not even a little bit.

She straightened and came walking toward him. He could hear the distinctive click of her no-doubt very expensive heels hitting the pavement. A woman on a mission.

"Evan Tanner," she said, holding her hand out. "It's good to see you again."

He nodded and then slowly took her hand. It was small in his, and he held it for a second too long.

"What brings you here?" he asked, even though he had a pretty good idea.

"You," she said succinctly. "I took a chance you might want to come down to the stadium before your start tomorrow, so I've been camping out here."

"That's some serious dedication."

She flashed a smile. "A long time ago I told you that if you moved through the ranks, I could offer my services. Here you are on the cusp of stardom with a contract that's expiring. So here I am."

"You said you could or could *not* offer your services. You claimed you were very exclusive," Evan reminded her.

"I am," she said, raising her chin. "I've

done a pretty thorough background check on you. You're the kind of client I'm looking for."

It was a shame, Evan thought. A real shame that someone who looked like her could be so completely disgusting on the inside.

What made it worse was that even though he knew what she was, standing here in the hot summer sun of a baseball parking lot, she still looked so cool and sophisticated he wanted to take her on the hood of her fancy car. Pull her blouse out of her pants and push his hands through her hair. Kiss her, until her lips were red and swollen.

"Sorry, Samantha. I'm not sure what kind of client you're looking for. But I know what I'm not. That's someone who would ever hit a woman or cover up for someone who did. So, no, I don't think I'm your type."

He watched her body jerk at the verbal assault. Then he watched as she quickly hid behind a mask of indifference. As crazy as it was, it made him think that this was how she might react if he had physically hit her. Which made him feel less sanctimonious and more like an ass.

"Hey, listen, I'm sorry. It's just…"

"No, I understand," she said quickly. "You don't believe I didn't know about the cover-up. Most people don't. The clients I take on will have to believe me. Just like I will have to believe in them. Sorry to have wasted your time."

She turned and quickly walked away, and with each step Evan felt a twinge of regret. Maybe he should have at least asked to hear her side of things. Hell, he owed that much to her sister, Scout, if nothing else.

He was about to open his mouth and call out to her, when she turned around in an elegant move and started walking backward. A feat he admired in such high heels.

"Oh, and Mr. Tanner...good luck dealing with the Rebels. I understand Reuben is a remarkably fair man to work with and will assuredly want to compensate you accordingly."

She smiled, and it was the smile of a wolf.

"Your loss."

She gave him a jaunty salute and then did the pirouette thing again and was once more walking away.

His loss.

His loss, indeed.

CHAPTER TWO

"I'LL HAVE THE contracts drawn up, and you won't regret it. We're going to do amazing things together, Evan."

Evan listened to the pitch of the agent on the phone and inwardly groaned. They were all the same. Speaking to him as if Evan had agreed to anything. It seemed to be a thing with agents. As if they could talk over until you simply cowed to their wishes.

Cowing wasn't Evan's style.

"I told you before, Donald, I'm not doing this over the phone. You want to sign me, you're going to have to come out here and meet me. I'm not trying to play prima donna here. I just want to sit down across from you and get to know you a little. I would come to you, but I'm in the middle of the season, as you know."

There was a soft sigh on the other end of the line. Clearly the man wasn't happy, but Evan wasn't budging. Signing with an agent was a big step in his career, and he wanted to make sure he made the right call. The only way to do that was to get a sense of the man face-to-face.

Or person. If he decided to go with a woman. So far, only one had made an offer, and he'd flat-out turned her down. What bothered him was that he'd been regretting that decision ever since. On many different levels.

"Let me see what I can do with my schedule. I'll be in touch."

Don ended the call quickly before Evan could reply. He wished he could've told the man not to bother. Evan wasn't feeling it. He tossed the phone on the coffee table in front of him and stretched out on the couch. He had another hour before he needed to be at the ballpark, and he planned on relaxing until then.

As the old man on the team at twenty-nine, he figured he needed to give his body every chance to rest he could. Spending some time listening to agents give him their pitch wasn't physically taxing, but it was starting to become mentally challenging.

He simply hadn't connected with Don the way he wanted to. There was something too slick about the guy that didn't rub right. At least on the phone. The truth was, he hadn't liked any of the men he'd met either in person or over the phone. All of them had talked to him like he was a sucker at a used car lot buying a car for the first time.

Telling him how much he didn't know about the business side of baseball. Throwing numbers around like they meant nothing. None of them really cared what he wanted for his future career.

As Evan had made his way through small ball and minor ball, he'd come to understand that his particular athletic talent to hit a baseball was unique. Ultimately he'd started thinking about his future and what making it to the majors might mean. He'd always thought when that time came, Samantha Baker would be his agent.

He knew her reputation. He'd liked the idea of being with a boutique agency where he wouldn't be one in a crowd. Plus, he knew her personally. It was crazy, but despite the brief time they'd spent together nearly two years ago, he'd felt a connection to her. A sense that if she took him on as a client, she would always have his back.

That was, until he'd watched her stand

up in front of crowd of journalists and call Richard Stanson a victim.

A victim!

Yes, Evan had wanted someone who would have his back. But he wanted that person to also have a modicum of integrity. Sam Baker, despite what he thought he knew about her, apparently didn't.

His phone rang again, and Evan considered letting it go to voice mail. Then he heard his father's dire warning in his ear about needing to get this done, so he picked it up again assuming it would be Donald wanting to schedule a sit-down.

"Are you an idiot?"

It took him a second to register the female voice on the other end of the phone.

"Scout." Evan smiled. "How the hell are you doing?"

Scout was the woman he owed everything to, and he'd made it a point to stay in touch. Out of both gratitude and having a serious baseball person in his life to guide him through the ropes of small ball. No doubt she was calling to talk about the irony of him being traded to the Rebels.

"I'm great, but you're an idiot."

"You know I didn't have a choice to come

here. It's not like I could ask for a no-trade clause as part of a minor league contract. I have to go with the team who wants me, but I agree it's a little crazy that I'm back here with the Rebels."

"I'm not talking about that! I'm talking about the fact you had a chance to sign with Samantha, and you didn't. Are you a fool? Don't you want to make money as a professional athlete, or are you one of those purists who only plays for the love of the game?"

Evan was no purist, but what the hell was he supposed to tell Scout? That he didn't want to sign with her sister because she lacked character? That she was the kind of woman who would look the other way when confronted with domestic abuse, something that was intolerable to him?

"She didn't know," Scout said, reading his mind. "That's what you're thinking, and that's why you walked away. But you know me, and you know I would never lie about something like this. Samantha would *never* have supported a creep like that if she knew he'd been abusive to women. You have to trust me on this."

"Scout, you know I want to believe you, but that video…"

"She didn't know about the video. Saw it the first time when the rest of America did. Richard paid a large sum of money to make it disappear, and no one, not even the police or the NFL, had seen it. Certainly not Sam. Look, you know what kind of people I am. Surely you've heard stories about Duff Baker and the type of man he was. Do you honestly think Sam could be so different from us?"

No. He hadn't thought it possible. Until the evidence was there in front of his face. Only now Scout was telling him a different story. Maybe he shouldn't have been so quick to judge. Maybe he at least owed it to Sam to hear her side of the story.

"Okay, I'll talk to her."

"Good. Oh, and do me a favor. Do not mention that we had this conversation. Got it?"

Not really, but he wasn't going to argue with Scout. He owed her too much. "Got it."

EVAN KNOCKED ON the door of the Baker home and thought about the last time he'd been here. He'd come knowing he'd cost Scout her job, but instead it had been Sam who'd opened the door. Sam, who'd been sporting a considerable black eye at the time. He remembered the way his gut had tightened at the thought of someone hitting her. Hurting her. He'd had an almost crazy urge to find who did it and hurt him back.

Then she'd told him it had happened as a result of squabbling sisters, and suddenly the idea of cool and pretty Samantha getting into a brawl with her sister made her a little more human.

Unexpectedly Evan wondered if she would even bother to open the door to him. If she was innocent, then he'd been kind of a jerk. He was about to turn and leave when he heard the steady drum of sneakers hitting the sidewalk coming to a stop, and he knew he didn't have to worry about her shutting him out.

Sam Baker looked like a hot, sweaty mess. A damp T-shirt over a sports bra, skintight running shorts and legs that were tan and toned, covered in a sheen of sweat. Her hair was pulled back into a short stubby ponytail.

Nothing icy about her now.

Like every time he laid eyes on her, regardless of how she looked, he felt it deep in his gut.

Evan shifted his feet and wondered again if coming here was a bad idea for an entirely different reason. He wasn't sure it was a good thing to be thinking about licking the sweat off his potential agent's neck.

One thing he knew, he'd caught her off guard. He could see that in the way she had brought herself to a sudden stop with her hands crossed over her chest even as she tried to regulate her breathing. Why he liked that, he wasn't sure. Maybe catching her off guard was the only way to get the upper hand with Samantha Baker.

"Hi," he said. The lamest opening ever, but he had to start somewhere.

"What are you doing here?"

"I wanted to talk."

"I wanted to talk the other day, and you told me to get lost."

That pretty much summed it up. "I think maybe I was wrong. I was judging you based on something I saw on television, and I realized that's not fair. I would like an opportunity to hear your side and decide for myself what kind of person you are."

Arms still crossed over her chest, she looked away and shrugged. "Why bother? Surely there are any number of agents who are aware of the trade that just happened and have been in contact with you."

"I don't like them," Even said as honestly as he could. "They're all trying to sell me something. That's not what I want."

"What do you want?"

"I want someone who I trust will fight for me. Someone who will have my back. Someone who will listen to what I want, rather than tell me what they think I should do. I'm looking for a partner."

She looked at him and nodded. "Okay. Then, let's talk."

SAM WALKED UP the front steps of her porch silently cursing that he was seeing her like this. Beyond looking terrible, she was fairly certain she smelled, too. This was not how one conducted business. This was not how one gained the upper hand in a negotiation. She considered telling him she would make an appointment for another day, but if she let him go, who was to say he might not find another agent he did like?

There were good people out there. Sam knew a lot of them. They weren't all scumbags and car salesmen.

"Can you wait down here while I take a quick shower?" she asked even as she was opening the door to let him inside. There was just no way she could talk to him feeling this rattled. She needed tools, her clothes, her sophisticated cool style.

"Is that a real thing for a woman?"

"Oh, he's funny and a sexist," she quipped. "I'll only be two hours. That's not very long, is it?"

He smiled and took a seat on the couch in the living room. "I'll wait."

He said it like he meant she was worth it, and that did funny things to her insides. She jogged up the steps, happy to be out of his sight and hopefully sense of smell, and headed directly for the bathroom, stripping her clothes off along the way.

As the hot water washed over her, she had this crazy thought that she was upstairs naked, while he was downstairs waiting for her. Knowing she was naked and wet. Knowing that all he had to do was climb the steps and open the bathroom door…

"Stop thinking about him like that," she mumbled as she turned off the water after a very quick five minutes.

Ten minutes later, she was dressed in pants and a pale pink blouse, her damp hair pulled back into a sleek knot, and her professional demeanor now fully in place.

When she came down the steps he stood.

"Can I get you something to drink? A beer or something?" Actually, Sam had no idea what type of alcohol was in the house. She only drank white wine, but the fridge down in the basement always used to be stacked with a variety of beers.

"No, I've got a game tonight. I only have a little less than an hour before I have to head to the field."

Sam nodded, his point taken. "Then, sit, and I'll get down to it."

Sam pulled a small, delicate chair over, so that she was directly across from him.

"The Montreal Robins traded you to the New England Rebels for their closer. The Robins have a shot at the play-offs this season, while the Rebels are iffy at best. So they are probably already looking to next year, and they consider you the best any play-off-bound team had to offer. Your batting average is currently .359, but don't expect to keep it that high when you face off against major league pitching, although even if it falls off a little, it's still quite good. Plus, not only do you hit consistently, you also hit for power. A natural three- or four-hitter in the lineup."

"I get it. You looked up my stats. What I

want to know is what happened between you and Richard Stanson?"

Samantha bristled at that but continued. "I spoke to your father, of course. Naturally, he had only glowing things to say about you, but I get the sense there is a deep well of pride when it comes to you. I also spoke with Michelle Lowell."

"My high school girlfriend?"

"She also had nothing but good things to say about you. Even though you were the star quarterback on the team, she said you were always very humble, which is rare in a stud athlete. Then there was Megan Craig, the teacher you worked with at your former job. She was a little cool with me, of course, having recently been dumped by you, but when pressed about your character, she couldn't really say anything negative. I'm still trying to get in touch with your college girlfriend, Kelly Lawson. She seems to have moved around the country a bit, but I'm sure I will eventually track her down..."

"Hold up, hold up," Even said, raising his hand. "You did all this research on me? I'm not the one who did anything wrong."

"I'm not the one who did anything wrong, either," Sam said coolly. "The research I did on you, I also did on Richard Stanson. I can only work with what people tell me, and Richard failed to tell me that in recent months he'd grown violent with his fiancée. Had he told me, I would have immediately reported him to the police for assault. I would have counseled Juliette to seek therapy for accepting that assault and still maintaining a relationship with him. When I went before the press I only had the word of a man who I had known for four years who had no previous history of violence, if the women in his past were to be believed. So I trusted him."

"You were wrong," Evan said solemnly.

It took everything she had, but Samantha kept her chin up. "I was wrong."

"I believe you didn't know."

"I believe what Michelle and Megan said about you as a person. But I'm still going to speak to Kelly when I find her."

"She won't say anything different. I loved Kelly. I would never hurt her."

He sounded so sincere, Sam thought. Like he absolutely believed what he said. Except Richard had said the same thing about Juliette, and Don had at one point said the same thing to her.

"You'll have to forgive me," Sam said. "I find I'm a bit cynical these days."

"Right. I guess you can't believe anyone anymore. Makes what that bastard did even worse. Knocked around his girlfriend and then shattered your trust in the process. I don't know how a person lives with that."

Sam smiled humorlessly. "Richard was suspended for four games. He'll be playing again next fall, and last I heard his new agent landed him a deal that will make him the highest-paid quarterback in the NFL. He and Juliette are to be married in August. They seem to be living just fine."

"And you lost your business."

"I lost my clients," Sam corrected him. "I'm the business. I'm still here. Not going anywhere."

Evan seemed to study her as if he was making his own decisions.

"I'm not going to sell you anything," Sam told him. "I'm not going to beg you to sign with me. I'm just going to tell you a few simple facts. You've got a contract that expires at the end of the season. The Rebels, if they are smart, will wait until they call you up to the Bigs to see how you perform, before they even consider making you an offer. But it's a risk they take. If they wait too long and you succeed, there will be other bidders. If they move too fast, and you don't pan out…"

"That's not going to happen."

Sam looked at him straight on and saw it in his eyes. Not confidence or arrogance. Instead, she saw determination.

"You wouldn't be the first stud minor league player not to make the transition to the majors."

"It's. Not. Going. To. Happen."

Sam shrugged. "Either way, you're going to want to play this to your best advantage. Let's face it, you're twenty-nine. This next contract is likely to be your one and only big money deal. If you sign with me, I'll make sure together we make the most of it."

Evan huffed. "I'm making almost two hundred thousand dollars right now. That's more money than I thought I would ever see in my life."

Sam got up and moved to sit next to him on the couch. It was a staged maneuver meant to infer intimacy between the agent and client. A bonding process. Only with Evan she felt stilted. When he looked at her, looked at how close she was to actually touching him, she could feel him stiffen.

Neither of them were comfortable sitting this close. It was a flag in Sam's brain, but she refused to acknowledge it.

"You understand what happens next, don't you? If you get called up this year, when the negotiations start...we're talking millions. If you're as good as everyone says you are... we're talking multiple millions. I know it sounds crazy, but you would be amazed at how many people have a hard time adjusting to that kind of life change. I could help with that, too. With the transition you'll need to make."

"All part of the service, huh?"

"Yes," Sam said simply. "I don't just handle one contract and we're done. If you do this thing with me, then I become part of your life, and you become part of mine."

Even looked at her hard, and for a second, just a second, she might have thought that his gaze lingered on her mouth.

Another flag she was choosing to dismiss.

"Yeah." He finally nodded. "That's what I want."

Sam held her hand out and suppressed the shudder that went through her when he engulfed her in his handshake.

It was going to be fine, she thought. So

what if he was handsome? So what if her thoughts strayed into dangerous territory when it came to him? In the end she was a professional and a woman who had complete control over her actions. She simply wouldn't let whatever this thing between them was get out of hand.

"It's a deal?" she asked as he was still shaking her hand.

"It's a deal."

CHAPTER THREE

Crack.

Sam knew the moment she heard the sound that Evan had hit the ball out of the park. She watched as it sailed over the left field wall. Duff used to say it was the sweetest sound in the universe, right after the sound of any one of his daughters laughing.

The Minotaurs were taking batting practice before the game, and Sam found a certain amount of contentment sitting in the stands and just watching players swing a bat. She probably hadn't actually watched a game since...

Since the last time she'd watched Evan play.

Then she'd been fascinated because she'd rarely seen such a display of raw talent.

"Sure. Talent. If that's what you want to tell yourself," Sam muttered.

"Am I interrupting a conversation with

yourself? Because I can come back later. I know how important they can be."

Sam startled and turned to see a woman just a few steps up from the seat at the end of the aisle. Sam stood and reached out her hand. "You're Jocelyn Taft."

"Jocelyn Taft Wright," the woman replied, taking Sam's hand in a sure and confident grip.

"Oh, yes. Sorry. I forgot."

Jocelyn jerked a shoulder. "Call me sentimental, but I like the other name better. With mine and my husband's together. May I join you?"

Sam couldn't see any reason to object. Jocelyn was the Minotaurs' owner. The two women sat next to each other, both staring down on to the field. While Sam had dressed again professionally in pants, blouse and heels, being here as an agent, Jocelyn was infinitely more casual in a pair of shorts and a T-shirt. Which Sam could tell, just by the quality of the material, still probably cost as much as Sam's outfit.

"What can I do for you, Mrs. Wright?"

"Oh, please, call me Jocelyn. Everyone around the park does. And we're vaguely connected through Scout. How is she these days?"

"Happy. In love."

Jocelyn smiled. "You know I'm responsible for that. I invited her to my wedding, just so she would have an opportunity to ask Jayson out. And I made sure she was in a killer dress."

Sam laughed. "Uh, yeah, but then he left her and broke her heart, and she wasn't the same for four years."

"Until he came back and mended her heart, and they lived happily ever after," Jocelyn said in a put-on hoity tone. "I still think it counts as a match in my favor."

"If you say so," Sam said coolly. She wasn't going to argue with a woman as powerful as Jocelyn Taft Wright.

"So you know who I am, right? I have this inbred desire to make money all the time."

"The way I understood it, you gave away most of your money to charity."

"I did." Jocelyn smiled mischievously. "Which of course I'm glad I did, but it didn't seem to kill my desire to make more. That's where you come in or, more accurately, your client."

Sam watched Evan take another swing. She watched another ball sail out of the stadium. It was just batting practice, so the pitches were basically softballs, but he certainly had a sweet swing.

"What are you thinking?"

"I want to do a little meet-and-greet with some of the press. He's been playing with the team for a week, and everyone knows he's bound for the majors. I want to milk ticket sales as much as I can while he's here. More people will come out to a game if they think they're seeing the next big thing, so I need to let everyone know I've got it."

"There's press in Minotaur Falls?"

"My husband would be very offended to know you thought so little of his struggling gazette."

Sam winced, remembering Jocelyn's husband essentially was the local sports media, but she could see from Jocelyn's expression, she wasn't truly offended.

"Sorry," Sam said anyway. "I'm just used to a bigger market."

"That's fine. I would imagine we might attract more than just a few local sports people. After all, he's a unique story. Late bloomer, just coming to the game. And he's way better-looking than Robert Redford."

Sam smiled at the movie reference. "Remember, Robert Redford had been a baseball player before the evil woman seduced and shot him. So Evan is even more unique than him."

"Either way, he'll pique the interest of enough people to get some sports coverage on television, and that will bring the people to my stadium, which will make me a very happy woman."

Sam looked at her. "You really do enjoy it. Making money, even when you have all you could need."

Jocelyn shrugged. "'Fraid so. But I look at it this way...the more Pete and I have, the more good we get to do. It's a win-win for everyone."

"Okay, I'll see what I can do to set something up. You would want this to happen in the next few days, I imagine." After all, it was anyone's guess when the Rebels would decide to bring him up.

Jocelyn winced. "Uh, yeah. But here's the thing—I would appreciate it... I mean, this is a small town. Everyone knows everyone else's business. Certainly anything having to do with the Bakers..."

Sam nodded, Jocelyn's unsaid message sinking in. "You don't want me there. You're afraid my bad press will rub off on him."

Jocelyn turned to Sam, and it wasn't hard at all for Sam to see the tough business-woman she must have been to have succeeded so well. There was steel behind her eyes. "Look, I've had a chance to talk with Evan a few times. He's as squeaky clean as they come. The fact that he hired you to be his agent tells me there is probably more to your story than what most people have heard. So I get that you might be wrapped up in a scandal you didn't choose and weren't responsible for, but unfortunately too many people around here know you and your story. I hope you understand I'm doing this for his sake."

At that Sam laughed harshly. "See, you've already told me the truth, Jocelyn. You're not doing anything for Evan's sake. You're doing this to sell more tickets. And you don't want someone who might have turned a blind eye to domestic violence anywhere near your squeaky clean poster boy. It's business, and I do understand. I won't be anywhere near the cameras. Now, if you'll excuse me, I have a sudden craving for a hot dog."

It was a thing with her. Sam always wanted food when she was pissed. She stood, but

Jocelyn remained seated, essentially blocking her path out of the aisle.

"You had no clue, did you?"

Sam didn't have to ask what Jocelyn was talking about, and she realized that question was probably going to haunt her for the rest of her life. Or certainly the foreseeable future.

"Nope."

"Men," Jocelyn muttered.

"Not all men," Sam said, nodding her chin toward her squeaky clean client on the field. "At least, we have to hope, right?"

Jocelyn turned her knees to the side, and Sam left her behind in search of that hot dog. She wasn't quite as pissed anymore, but that didn't mean a hot dog wouldn't taste damn good.

EVAN CAME OUT of the stadium freshly washed and feeling amazing after a solid game. He'd gone three for four, with a home run. The team had won, and overall the mood was jovial in the locker room.

Sure, he was getting a lot of grief about when he was going to get *the call*. His ascent to The Show seemed all but inevitable. He could see some jealousy in the younger players around him, too. Guys who maybe thought they were more deserving, because they had been playing the game longer. Evan wouldn't let that negativity touch him. He wasn't getting ahead by keeping anyone else down. He was simply playing his game his way.

He stopped when he saw Sam leaning on the hood of his truck. Much like that first time he'd seen her again, only then it was on her car. Leaning against his truck like that only made her hotter.

Clearly, her ability to knock the breath out of him was still alive and well, despite telling himself nearly every day since they had shaken hands that he needed to stop thinking about her as a woman.

She's my agent. A sexless creature entirely.

Then she stood straight, and he took in her cool expression, long legs and slim high heels and snorted.

There was no way, as long as he still had his penis attached to him, that he could look at Samantha Baker and not see her as flat-out sexy.

He'd wanted her the first time he saw her almost two years ago. Had she given him a glimmer of an opening back then, he would have asked her out.

But she hadn't. It never occurred to him to wonder why that might be.

"Do you have a boyfriend?" he blurted out as he dropped his equipment bag in the back of his cab.

He could see he'd startled her—it seemed he was always doing that—because it took her a few seconds to come up with a suitable response. Which made no sense, because it was a yes or no answer.

"Why are you asking?"

Evan shrugged. "No real reason. Just curious about you. Like you said, you're part of my life now."

She crossed her arms over her chest and eyed him warily before saying, "No. I don't."

"What about when I met you? Did you have one then?"

She cocked her head to the side. "I see. Trying to understand why I didn't fall at your feet when you smiled at me the first time?"

Evan smiled a little bashfully now. "Yup."

"Sorry to wound your ego, but, no, I didn't have one back then, either. My last relationship ended with a broken engagement.

I haven't been all that eager to get back out there since."

"Had your heart broken?"

"Something like that."

"Idiot."

Sam quirked a single eyebrow. She really was an icy creature. Unless she was all hot and sweaty from jogging, that was. Evan tried unsuccessfully to suppress that memory.

"I meant the guy. For having you and then losing you."

There was an emotion in her eyes that made him sorry he'd brought the topic up. Like he had poked at an old wound and suddenly made her pain resurface.

"Are we done discussing my love life? We have important business to go over."

"Must be important if you were willing to stay through the whole game rather than just call me later."

Sam shifted her feet a little. "Well, you were having a good game, so it wasn't hard to watch. Given you're my only client right now, you're entitled to the VIP treatment."

Evan couldn't say why, but he knew she was lying. She'd stayed to watch the game because she had wanted to, not because of their business. He was fairly certain that this thing he felt, it went both ways. No doubt she was as uncomfortable about it as he was. Instead of calling her on it, he backed off.

"Okay then, what's so important?"

"Jocelyn Taft... Wright. Jocelyn Taft Wright, you know, owns the team and the stadium. She wants to capitalize on your time with the Minotaurs. She thinks a small press conference to talk about your journey here might sell some tickets."

Evan shrugged. He wasn't exactly thrilled with the idea. He already had a minor issue with jealousy among the guys. He didn't want to exacerbate that with more attention focused only on him. It didn't seem right in such a team sport. Then again, he had to be practical. This was his career, after all. He was going to have to start thinking about these things.

"It's a good idea," Sam said. "You've got a unique story, and we need to take advantage of that. I've been trying to think of some sponsors who might be interested once you're called up and hopefully start hitting home runs. Someone who wants to advertise a product along the lines of...it's never too late..."

"Sam." Evan stopped her. "That's fine. Whatever you think is necessary."

She nodded. "Good. Jocelyn will set everything up. You just need to show up and look pretty for the cameras."

"That won't be too hard with you standing next to me."

Sam shook her head, and again Evan could see something beyond the icy façade. Another flash of pain. He felt it in his gut, too. The mere idea of causing her pain bothered him. He wanted her to be safe behind those icy walls she'd constructed for herself. Even as much as he wanted to be on the other side of them.

"I won't be there. Jocelyn doesn't want to risk your image being tarnished with me on the scene. Keep in mind she's trying to sell tickets to families."

"Seriously? You're standing there telling me she's ashamed of you."

Sam got a little stiffer. "It's a fact we'll need to deal with. We should probably prepare an answer if anyone actually questions you about your decision to hire me as your agent."

"How about the truth? You didn't know

Stanson was a lying douche bag, and you're a damn good agent."

Her lips quirked. "You might want to refrain from using the word douche bag in front of television cameras."

"I'm serious, Sam. This is bull you have to pay for that guy's actions. Let me tell people what really happened. Maybe no one will believe you if you say you didn't know, but if other people hear it from those who respect you…"

Sam shook her head. "I'm not the story. You are. Remember that. It's not going to hurt you to have me one room away."

"I don't like it," Evan said stubbornly.

Sam smiled, genuinely smiled for maybe the first time since he'd met her, and it took his breath away.

"You're a knight in shining armor, aren't you? Ready to save the damsel in distress."

"If you'll let me."

Sam chuckled. "Evan, trust me, I'm not a damsel. If I need saving, I'll do it myself. Just be there on time. I'll pick out the outfit I want you to wear."

She started to walk away toward her own car. That sleek ice-blue Mercedes that reminded him of her.

Evan scowled. Because she was so casually telling him what to do or because she was leaving him, he wasn't sure.

"I'm not some damn doll to be dressed up," he called after her.

"No, you're a client I want to make sure is dressed appropriately for his first public appearance."

"I don't like red!" he shouted even as she was opening her car door.

She waved back. "I don't care."

Yeah, Evan thought as he watched her drive away, hiring her was both the best and worst decision he'd ever made.

CHAPTER FOUR

"IT'S RED," EVAN SAID, looking down at the shirt in his hands.

It was two days later, and they were alone in the team manager's office, while Sam could hear the press assembling in the small room next door.

Sam smiled. She couldn't even say why she'd done it. Sure, red would look awesome against his tanned skin and golden brown eyes, but there were other colors that would have worked just as well. The truth was, she had wanted to tease him a little. See his reaction, which really wasn't very professional of her, but she couldn't help it.

"Trust me," she said. "It will look great."

He grumbled as he started unbuttoning the shirt he was wearing. Sam watched his fingers for a few minutes, enthralled with how they moved down his body, button by button. He was wearing a white tee underneath. There was no reason he shouldn't have been able to change shirts in front of her, but she found herself turning around anyway. Better to avoid the show.

"So, about the interview, you know how this works, right?"

"I'm pretty sure they ask me questions, and I answer them."

After what she imagined was enough time to take one shirt off and put another one on, Sam turned around. He was straightening the sleeve around his wrist.

"I'm going to get you back for this," he told her, looking down at himself in self-disgust. "I hate red."

"I'm trembling in fear," Sam said, although she couldn't help but wonder what his form of retribution might look like.

She handed him the tie she had picked out, and he looped it around his neck. "Now remember this next part is a little bit of a performance. I want to make sure you're aware an audience is listening to everything you say. You have to be careful. In some respects, you want to keep a shield up between you and the audience. A layer of self-defense. You don't want to say anything too pointed or something that might attract people's negative opinion. However, the more candid you are, the more they will warm to you."

"You want me to be guarded, but also candid."

Sam beamed. "Exactly. Be yourself. Just don't give them everything."

"You understand what you're saying right now makes no sense."

"Trust me, it will make perfect sense when you watch it back on TV later."

"Are you going to watch?"

Sam pointed to the television. She had agreed not to be in the room with him, but she'd asked Jocelyn for the TV here so she could at least watch and assess her client's performance.

"Every step of the way. I'll be able to give you notes after."

"Swell. Notes on being candid."

"You're in a whole new ballpark now. Get it…ballpark?"

He winced. "Wow, that was bad."

She punched his shoulder. "It was funny."

"It was not even close to being funny."

"I'm a funny person," Sam insisted and then watched as he burst out laughing.

"I'm sorry, honey, but funny is not the first word that anyone would assign to you. Smart, cool, sophisticated…terrifying. Funny might be somewhere down here." Evan held his hand to his knees.

Then Sam did something she was pretty sure she hadn't done since she was five years old.

She pouted.

She could feel it. Her bottom lip pushed out as she crossed her arms over her chest. She would have harrumphed, but she had some pride. Girls who pouted did so to get something from men, and Sam didn't need anything from a man. Samantha Baker didn't pout.

Except she was pouting now. And apparently her pouting only made him laugh more.

"Oh, honey, I'm sorry," he said as he walked over and pried her hands away from her body so he could hold them. "You're right. You are funny. You are being super funny right now."

She wanted to punch his arm again. She wanted to…

The door to the room opened. It was Jocelyn, "Hey, Evan, you're up."

"Right. One second."

The door closed, and he turned back to

Sam. "Seriously, I wish you were in there with me."

"You'll be fine."

"You'll be waiting for me."

"Right here."

He nodded as if that gave him some satisfaction. Then he took a deep breath.

"Good luck," she told him. "Go kill it."

Then he was gone, and Sam settled in to watch the show.

After twenty minutes Sam wouldn't exactly call what he was doing killing it. More like…bombing big-time. He clearly was not someone who shone in the limelight. Which was strange given how utterly handsome he was and truly charming when he was talking to you face-to-face.

He should have been captivating.

Instead he seemed uncomfortable as he fidgeted in his chair while some female reporter from ESPN asked him what he predicted his batting average might be once he had to face off against major league pitching.

He stumbled around the answer, not really saying anything to indicate how good he planned to be. Which he'd already assured her was going to be very good. This was not a man without self-confidence.

Humility, that's what his high school sweetheart had remembered about him, and it showed. He didn't think he should be the one everyone was focused on, even though he was by far the best player on the team.

He's a good guy. A genuinely good guy.

Sam would have believed her cynicism was so deeply ingrained no man would be safe from it. That she would forever believe all men were hiding parts of themselves from view until some trigger revealed their violent darker side.

Evan Tanner, however, was proving to be resistant to her cynical belief. He was charming when he wanted to be, funny when he wanted to be. Yet when he'd believed the worst about her, he wasn't afraid to let her know that, either.

Through all their interactions she sensed a solidness about him. A forthrightness that was there for everyone to see. She couldn't imagine he had anything to hide. Certainly not a dark side.

He was the hero. Not the villain.

"Uh…no… I'm not involved with anyone."

Another female reporter was asking about his social life. Yes, that was something he clearly didn't want to talk about. Was he blushing?

Sam smiled. They would have to work on drafting some practiced answers to those kinds of questions. If he did what everyone was projecting and became a superstar, then he would need to be more relaxed with a camera in his face.

The smoother he was during interviews, the more chance he'd have to pick up sponsors. More sponsors meant more money. And that was the game Sam needed to play if she was going to show everyone she was back on top. An agent any athlete would want to have.

"You are currently being represented by Samantha Baker…" one reporter began.

Here it was. Sam tensed, and, as she watched, so did Evan. It was clear that he wanted to say something, in some way to stand up for her. It's who he was. He was built to be a knight.

But she'd told him when he agreed to do this, it was necessary to stick to the script.

"Yes, as many of you may know, Scout Baker was working for the Rebel organization as a scout when she found me coaching a high school baseball team. She invited me to a tryout camp, and, well, my life really hasn't been the same since."

Sam nodded. That sounded sincere. Real. Most likely because it was.

"Anyway I owe the Baker family a tremendous debt, and I'm confident that Samantha will do right by me."

There. It made perfect sense. A man could overlook scandal out of loyalty to the family. Sam hated that she had to set the narrative that way, that he had taken pity on her, but at least he would be perceived as squeaky clean despite her past.

"Are you at all worried about her questionable character and her collusion with her client to cover up an assault?"

Sam gritted her teeth. She had hoped for no follow-up, but this part was still scripted just in case. All he had to say was: *I'm not here to talk about my agent's past. I'm here to talk about my future in baseball.*

A perfect line that would pivot everyone back to the game and him and away from her.

"She didn't collude with her client on anything. She was lied to by a man she trusted to tell her the truth. And what really cranks my gear is that somehow it's like she's to blame for what that asshole did. This guy is a violent scumbag who hit his fiancée, tried to cover it up and then lied about it. Why is my agent to blame for that? I'm perfectly happy with Samantha Baker as my agent, and, no, I have no concerns about her character at all. Now, if we're done here?"

Evan stood so quickly he almost toppled over his chair. A few reporters were still firing questions at him, obviously wanting to feed on the sound bite he had given them.

Sam closed her eyes and sighed. He was going to make the ESPN highlights tonight by calling Richard Stanson a violent scumbag asshole.

At least it hadn't been douche bag. He'd at least taken her advice and avoided that one.

The door to the office where she was waiting flew open and then slammed shut behind her. Evan was already loosening his tie as he mumbled under his breath about more assholes.

"I'm not here to talk about my agent's past. I'm here to talk about my future in baseball," Sam said. "It's a great line. You know how I know? I wrote it for you."

He glared as if he were about to snap at her, too, then she could see he just released

his anger in a woosh of breath. As if simply
by looking at him, she had soothed the sav-
age beast. She had originally thought he was
a white-knight hero, but he wasn't without a
little temper, either.

"It's not right. Calling out your character like that. And sorry, but I'm not going
to stand for it. You've got to deal with that.
Okay? You're my agent now. I get to say
what I want about you when I want to. Got
it?"

At his intensity, Sam felt a swirl of something in her chest. Like she was being looked
after and cared for and protected. It wasn't
an uncommon feeling.

Of course she'd always had Duff.

Then there had been Bob, her mother's
husband and Sam's biological father. Something Bob hadn't known for eighteen years
of Sam's life because he'd been stupid by
dumping Sam's mother when he thought he
was doing the right thing by her. Bob had
wanted to fight her battles, too, like any
other father would, but Sam was an adult
when she met him. She'd been able to take
care of herself, even at eighteen.

Yes, Duff and Bob were two men with

flaws. But they were also two men who'd had her back.

Now Evan stood in front of her, and with him, she had that same feeling. Like no matter what, he would guard over her, snarling at anyone who dared to take a swipe at her, no matter how many times she told him she could save herself. Hadn't he called her terrifying?

Terrifying people took care of themselves.

She opened her mouth to tell him one more time he didn't have to save her. That she wasn't that kind of woman who needed rescuing.

Instead she nodded. "Got it."

He was looking at her warily, like he was waiting for more of a fight, but the truth was there was no point in arguing. She wasn't going to change his mind, and she wasn't going lie to herself and say there hadn't been some satisfaction in watching someone else defend her. Someone else besides her say she wasn't a liar.

"I'm going to be on Sports Center tonight, aren't I?"

"Yes," Sam agreed. "Maybe that's not such a bad thing. A little buzz never hurt anyone. And since you don't have a Twitter account, you're not going to know what all the horrible Richard Stanson fans are going to Tweet about you for calling out their boy."

"The fact that he still has fans… I mean, seriously, how do people reconcile that? How can you root for someone who you know has no respect for women?"

Sam frowned. "Because he wins. Don't get me wrong—we'll call him out for it, we'll talk about him for a couple of weeks, we'll even discuss domestic abuse and ways to help end it. But at the end of the day, people don't really care about their sports heroes' lives. They care about their own lives, and when their team wins, they feel good. That's all that counts."

"Doesn't make it right."

Sam walked over to him and brushed a little lint off his shoulder. "I told you before. Welcome to the Bigs, my friend."

They looked at each other, and Sam could feel a shift in the dynamic. She was standing too close. She had made an excuse to touch him. Had there been any lint really, or had she just wanted to get closer to him? So she could be near the man who wanted to rush to her defense.

The man who had made her pout.

He was looking at her now not as his agent but as a woman, and she could feel the answer to that look all the way to her toes.

Yes.

No.

She tried to be casual about how she removed her hand from his shoulder, but before she could fully escape, he'd circled his fingers around her wrist, trapping her.

"Are we going to talk about this?" he asked, his voice low and slightly gruff.

"Talk about what?"

Sam almost wanted to smile at how well she had pulled off that line. She was cool, casual and sounded completely unaware of anything he might be talking about.

"I want you."

Sam's jaw dropped. Who did that? Who just said the thing they were thinking despite the consequences?

"I get it. I know it's messed up. You're my agent and I want it to stay that way, but maybe it would be better, easier, if we talked about the elephant. Because I'm pretty sure this goes both ways."

Sam managed a weak huff. "That's awfully arrogant of you."

Evan shook his head slowly. "Not really.

You're trembling, and where my thumb is hitting your pulse point I can feel your heart racing."

Sam jerked her hand away, and Evan let her go.

"We need a plan. A way we're going to deal with it."

"I had a plan," Sam said. "I was going to ignore it. You were supposed to do the same. It's how adults deal with things they don't want to deal with."

"That seems silly, doesn't it?"

He was smiling, which made him look incredibly endearing. She wanted to slap his face. Maybe that would cure him of his desire. "Look, Evan, what did you think I was going to say?"

"I want you, too."

Like that was going to happen. Like she would just put herself out there and see how he reacted. Raw and vulnerable.

"I meant, what did you think talking about this openly would accomplish?"

He shrugged. Then sighed. "Honestly I don't know. Like I said, I don't want to lose you as an agent."

"Then you must know we can't possibly

have any romantic entanglement. Ours is a business relationship."

"Entanglement? You make that sound like a game of Twister. I'm not talking about just an entanglement. Yes, I get our business relationship makes things more complicated. And, yes, it makes sense to walk away from any kind of personal relationship."

Sam felt physically relieved. He understood. That was good. That would prevent him from making any more ridiculous comments.

"But it doesn't change the fact we still want each other."

Comments like that.

"Evan." Sam sighed. What in the hell was she supposed to do with a man like this? One who was just so out there with himself. Wasn't he worried he was going to get hurt? Because it's what she would most likely do. To protect herself she would lash out like a cat that has encountered an overfriendly dog who wants to play. A few swipes and the dog would walk away whimpering.

"Okay, look, I can see it makes you uncomfortable to talk about it. I'll drop it for now."

"Thank you," she said, feeling for the first

time since he'd started speaking she could take a deep breath.

"Here's the thing, though, Sam. I've learned a lot in the last few years since I first met you. I've learned you don't get anything in this world you truly want without taking some risks. While our situation might not be ideal, don't think it means I'm not going to try for it. For you. Because now I know what it means to take that risk and win. I'm not afraid."

He moved around her, and Sam turned to watch as he opened the door to the office and left. Happy that she'd been able to keep her mouth closed. Because what she had really wanted to say was...don't go.

Which of course was ridiculous. They were having dinner that night with Jocelyn Taft Wright and her husband, Pete. A thank-you from Jocelyn for Evan having agreed to the interview.

Today was Evan's off day, and really it was generous of him to give up his free time to do the press conference in the first place.

Sam took a few deep, calming breaths. All things considered, nothing too terrible had happened. Evan had confessed to wanting her, but she hadn't really done the same.

She hadn't been able to work up the steeliness to actually lie to him, so it was better she say nothing. Now she knew she would have to work much harder to keep a personal distance between them.

What made that so hard was that beyond wanting him, she actually just really liked him. She had an idea that maybe leaving Minotaur Falls was the smart choice. Distance would surely help the situation. Only it felt a little like cowardice, not to mention humiliating.

Hey, Evan, I want you so much I can't be in the same town as you for fear I'll give in and jump your bones.

No. Leaving was not an option.

"You'll get over it," she told the empty room.

KELLY LAWSON WATCHED from her car as the elegant blonde left the stadium and headed to her Mercedes. She couldn't help but feel a twinge of envy at the cool, sleek business suit, slim high heels and sophisticated haircut. All things she had wanted for herself, but nothing she could ever afford.

Not that she regretted for a second where all her hard-earned money had to go.

"Mom, I don't huh-understand why we're here if there's no game today. I huh-thought we were going to see a baseball game."

Kelly looked at her son, and her love for him overwhelmed her. He took a hit of his inhaler, and she schooled herself not to wince. The humidity at this time of year wasn't bad in upstate New York, but really they should be in the least humid environment she could find for him. Anything to make his breathing easier.

She reached over to ruffle his hair. "We are, Connor. Soon, I promise. I just wanted…"

I wanted to see him first.

"I wanted to make sure I had the right directions first. This is like a dry run."

She hadn't been prepared for the punch in her gut when he came out of the stadium. It had been so long since she had seen him, and now…now she was committed to doing this thing.

For Connor. For Connor she would do anything.

CHAPTER FIVE

"This was lovely of you to invite us to dinner," Sam said as they entered the restaurant. Minotaur Falls wasn't a mecca for fine dining, but this was by far the best restaurant in town.

"My pleasure," Jocelyn returned. "You did me a favor today. Pete and I appreciate it. This is the least I could do to offer my thanks."

"Not going to lie," Evan said. "I'm not a fan of the interview stuff, but anything to help the team."

Pete, Jocelyn's husband, studied Evan with a skeptical gaze. As if it was hard to believe he was truly that honest. Although Sam was beginning to believe that's simply who Evan was. What you saw was what you got.

I want you.

Yes, he was a man who felt very comfortable with the truth. Sam hadn't been able to get those words out of her head since he'd said them.

The two couples settled into a booth, Jocelyn and Pete across from her and Evan. Not that she was in any way part of a couple, of course. It was just the situation, that she and Evan were here with Jocelyn and Pete. Another couple. That the four of them were having dinner.

Enjoying each other's company. And laughing and having fun.

Not that you couldn't have fun on a business dinner, of course. However, Sam needed to remind herself she was here only in a business capacity. Yes, she might have taken special care with the dress she picked out. Yes, she might have changed three different times before settling on the black jersey with the plunging back, and, yes, maybe she had been more than a little thrilled when Evan had called earlier and offered to pick her up.

This way she could have some wine and relax, as Evan didn't drink during the baseball season. When she'd asked him why, he'd told her he didn't like to have his senses compromised in any way.

Sam thought it sounded reasonable, but

there had been something in his voice when he said "senses" that made her think of sensuality and that made her think of things she shouldn't be thinking about.

Accepting his offer of a ride was in many ways a test for her self-control. Of course he could pick her up. Absolutely he could open the door for her. Yes, she could sit next to him in the cool confines of his truck without there being a hint of intimacy.

Yeah, right. Then how come you can't keep from looking at how close his thigh is to yours in the booth?

"So, Evan, are you more nervous or excited for your debut start in The Show?" Pete asked as soon as the waiter had left with their drink orders.

Evan opened his mouth and then abruptly closed it.

Knowing instantly what he was afraid of, Pete held his hands up. "I'm not on the job right now—no notepad. This whole dinner is officially off the record. Tonight I'm just Jo's husband."

Evan nodded, and Sam wanted to praise him for at least realizing he needed to be cautious any time when speaking to a reporter. He was learning.

"Then the answer is nervous," Evan said with a small chuckle. "Not about playing. I mean, that will happen. I'm nervous about my dad being there. Knowing he's watching. I don't want to let him down. He's pretty excited about this whole thing."

"Fathers can be terrifying," Pete agreed.

"Tell me about it," Sam said without really thinking. "I happened to have two. A baseball legend and a former Navy Seal. Maybe that's where I get my ferocious side from."

Evan looked at her quizzically, and she realized he didn't know her particular story. Jocelyn and Pete did because of their relationship with Scout, and it wasn't as if there was anything to hide anymore with Duff having passed.

"My mother and her current husband, Bob, knew each other many years ago," Sam explained. "He left to go on a military mission and broke up with her before leaving. For her sake, of course."

Jocelyn snorted. "Men can be so frustrating that way."

"Anyway, my mom didn't know at the time she was pregnant with me. Duff, when he met my mother, fell in love with her immediately. He stepped in and married her and accepted me as his own. It was only after Bob reconnected with my mom years later that I learned the truth."

"Wow. That must have been a sucker punch," Evan said.

"A little bit. I was eighteen and probably not as mature as I should have been about it," Sam mused. "Duff had insisted on keeping it a secret from me, and that kind of created a rift between us. Fortunately we got over it before the end. And now I get Bob, who is pretty terrific, too, if just a little bit scary sometimes with the things he can do. Just ask Scout if anyone behind a locked door is safe when Bob is in the house."

The group chuckled, and the somber mood was lifted.

"Speaking of one of your fathers," Jocelyn said. "You know how hard I had to fight to get the statue of Duff Baker for my stadium."

"Yes, and I'm glad you won." Sam turned to Evan. "Two other teams wanted to honor Duff with statues. But we felt like this was home, and if there was going to be a statue, it should be here."

"Without the Baker girls' support I don't know if I would have pulled it off, but it's coming along really well. We're planning the unveiling during the All-Star break in July. This way Scout and Lane will be able to fly back to the East Coast. It's going to be a major event, and, best of all, the seats will be packed!"

"My wife, ever the sentimentalist." Pete laughed and got an elbow to the ribs for his efforts, even though it was clear to see Jocelyn took no offense.

The food was delicious, and, after her second glass of wine, Sam thought how nice this was. She couldn't remember the last time she'd spent an evening like this. Sure, they talked some baseball, but not really in the context of work. No, there was no getting away from the fact that this was just an enjoyable social night out. Last time she had a night like this...probably wasn't since Donald.

Only now, thinking about her time with Don, did she realize she usually felt sick to her stomach anytime she remembered him. But she didn't feel sick tonight. There was none of the shame and humiliation. None of the hurt.

It was like he was gone. Finally gone after all this time.

One hard crack of his hand against her face with an intent to inflict pain. Maybe it shouldn't have meant so much. Or had such an impact on her life. Yet it did.

Sam would be thrilled if that night no longer held any power over her. That she was finally ready to let it go and move on.

"Hey there, did we lose you?" Evan nudged her with his elbow.

Sam blinked. "Sorry, woolgathering."

"I was just wondering if you were taking on any more clients," Jocelyn asked.

"That's the plan, but for right now, Evan is my one and only." In a somewhat spontaneous moment, Sam reached over and grabbed his chin to give it a little shake. "Look at this moneymaker. Is that not the face of the next Captain America?"

"Maybe that's your opinion because you like it so much," Evan murmured.

She did like his face, she thought, as she pulled her hand away from his chin, letting her fingers linger over the hint of stubble that had grown since he'd shaved.

She couldn't look away.

Suddenly it was just the two of them in the booth, with the electricity arcing between them.

Sam forced herself to break from his gaze and smiled way too widely. "Dessert, anyone?"

She turned to look for their waiter, desperate for the distraction. Instead of the young man who had been waiting on them all evening, a woman Sam would put in her late twenties was heading to their table with a young child in tow.

Sam could hear the boy, maybe six or seven, wheezing a little.

"Kelly?" Evan said. As if she was the last person he might expect to be here in this time and this place.

Sam turned to look at his expression and she could read his confusion.

Kelly. Kelly Lawson. His college girlfriend?

"I'm sorry to do this to you, Evan. I've been trying to find you and ran into someone down at the stadium who said you were here with the owner and…"

"Kelly, what are you doing here? I haven't seen you in seven years. My father said you called him the other day. I had no idea why."

"I needed to find you," she said again. Then she pushed the little boy in front of her. "Evan, this is Connor."

"Hi, Connor," Evan said with a small wave and a smile. Like the scene happening in front of all of them was completely normal.

It was when Sam looked over to Pete and Jocelyn to get their reaction that it started to click in. The couple was exchanging a look that said what was about to happen next was not going to be good.

But it couldn't be bad, could it? After all, this was Evan Tanner. Kelly was the girlfriend Sam hadn't been able to get in touch with. But Evan had said she would have nothing but good things to say about him.

Because he had loved her.

"I'm really sorry, Evan. I'm really sorry to do it this way, but I have no choice."

"Spit it out, Kell," Evan said, his voice a little flatter.

Kelly crouched down so that she was at eye level with her son. "Connor, could you go wait for Mommy in the lobby? Stay by that man with the menus. I won't be long."

The child did as instructed without protest, and Kelly clearly waited until he was out of earshot to say what she wanted to say.

"Connor...he's your son. He's your son, and he's sick. I need your help."

Yep, Sam thought. That sounded about right for her luck.

Captain America turned into a delinquent baby daddy right in front of her eyes.

"I think we'll skip dessert," Sam said in the void of silence.

"WHY ARE YOU doing this, Kell? You need help, I'll help you," Evan said, trying not to look at the kid who was sitting in the passenger seat of the cheap sedan Kelly said was her car. Equally, he was trying not to look over at Sam who was patiently waiting, leaning against the hood of his truck. He was, after all, her ride home.

"It's the truth, Evan. Do the math. We were together that last semester in college at the end of May, and Connor was born in January. The thirteenth to be precise."

"And that's it? I'm supposed to believe, because the numbers sort of work, that you chose—after learning you were pregnant—to keep the baby, never tell me and wait seven years before dropping this bomb on me. Sorry, it doesn't compute. First of all, you were adamantly pro-choice. If you didn't want the baby, you would have aborted it."

She shrugged and pushed her long dark

hair, much as he remembered it, back over her shoulder. "What can I say? All that changed when I realized I was pregnant. I didn't want an abortion. I wanted a baby instead."

"Fine. Then why didn't you tell me?"

"Well, for one thing, I didn't want to be told to kill my own child!"

Evan struggled for patience. He'd forgotten that, with Kelly, there was always a little drama.

Actually, a lot of drama.

"That's horseshit," he said between clenched teeth, desperate to keep his voice down, so that Connor wouldn't hear anything. "I would have been one hundred percent supportive, no matter what you decided. If you had decided to keep him, then I would have damn well married you, and you know that, too."

"Right. I did know that," she said tightly. "Except you knew I didn't want to marry a schoolteacher."

"So you chose to cut me out of *my child's* life until when? You'll forgive me if the timing of your announcement isn't a little suspicious. I'm not exactly a schoolteacher anymore, am I? When did you find that out?"

She had just enough shame to look away from him, but she seemed to get over it quickly.

"I'm not going to lie about it. I was listening to these two guys at the diner where I work talking about this over-the-hill baseball player who was actually going to make it to the major leagues. Then I heard your name… I mean it couldn't have been a coincidence. You were always such a good athlete at whatever you did. So I looked you up. I'm here now because I heard you were traded, and that sometime soon you're going to be playing for the Rebels. That means a contract and big money, right? I mean, that's what she's here for, isn't it? I know who she is. She's Samantha Baker."

Kelly pointed to Sam, but Evan didn't look over at her. He wasn't ready to see what was sure to be disdain. Disdain for him. He could only imagine what she was thinking about him right now.

"Yes, that's what she's here for," he said, resigned to the idea that any shot he had tonight of making out with Samantha Baker in his truck when he dropped her off after dinner was probably dead in the water. Not that it was a great shot anyway, but a man had to have home.

She had a predisposition of mistrust. There was no universe in which she was going to believe him. Not unless he had absolute proof.

"He's sick, Evan. He's so sick," Kelly whispered, a hiccup in her voice.

He didn't know if she was telling the truth about Conner being his son, but there was no question she was telling the truth about this. He'd heard the kid wheezing, and it was evident there was a problem with his lungs.

"What's wrong with him?"

"It's asthma. Which sounds like not the worst thing, right? Some kids have asthma, they need an inhaler once and a while. Not Connor. It's unrelenting for him. Sometimes he has these fits…he has to be hospitalized for days. He can't run or play. A walk through the grocery store can be too much for him on a bad day."

"I'm sorry, Kelly. I am, but…"

"I have this crappy health insurance, which only lets me see the doctors in my HMO. They're doing the best for him, but I want more. I want the best in the country, and for that I need money. Serious money."

Evan looked into the car again. The kid was playing some game on Kelly's phone. He looked slight. Like a stiff wind could blow him away.

My son? Is it possible?

He walked around to the passenger door, opened it and squatted down on his haunches to be able to look at the kid at eye level.

He held out his hand. "Hey, Connor, I'm Evan. I'm an old friend of your mom's."

"H-hi." The boy shook hands, and Evan listened as the kid took each breath. He shouldn't be able to hear breathing, he thought. It should just happen.

"What are you playing?"

Evan expected him to say Candy Crush or one of those bird games.

"Trivia Crack."

"Know a lot of stuff, do you?"

The boy nodded. "I'h-m b-hest at sports. I know everything about them."

Evan smiled. "That's a lot to know."

"Mom said we're going to see you play a real game soon."

"Absolutely. I'll set you up with tickets. The best in the stadium."

"Cool."

"Cool."

"Huh, are you my m-hom's boyfriend now?"

Evan shook his head. That was an expectation he wanted to eliminate immediately. Nothing could have repaired their relationship after she told him being a schoolteacher wasn't enough for her.

Her possibly withholding his son from him for seven years…that was beyond unforgivable.

"No, like I said, your mom is an old friend of mine. We went to college together a long time ago. That doesn't mean you can't be my new friend."

"Oh-kay. I don't really have h-a lot."

Evan stood and ruffled the kid's hair. It was dark like Kelly's. In fact there wasn't a thing about the boy that reminded him of himself. Not his hair or his nose or his eyes. It was all Kelly. Not that that meant anything.

The kid went back to his game; Evan closed the door and returned to Kelly.

She had her arms crossed over her chest and was sneaking guilty peeks at Sam who seemed to be keeping a steady gaze on the two of them. Like she was watching a play.

Or a circus.

"I need some time to think about this, Kell."

"He's a little boy who needs help. What's to think about?"

Evan couldn't argue with that. "Let me set you up with some tickets for our next home game. It's in two days. Then we'll talk after about what we're going to do."

Suddenly she smiled. Like a hundred-pound barbell had been removed from her shoulders. "You said what *we're* going to do. I knew it, Evan. I knew I could count on you. You've always been the best person I've ever known."

"Yeah, I was such a great guy you waited seven years to introduce me to my son," Evan said, disgusted. "Give me your number and I'll be in touch."

Kelly took his phone and punched in her contact information, then handed it back to him.

"You'll do the right thing, Evan. I know it. You always do."

After moving Connor back into his booster seat in the backseat, she got behind the wheel and drove out of the restaurant's parking lot. There weren't many cars left. Probably only those of the staff who were still cleaning up.

Evan was left with no choice but to walk back to his truck.

And Sam.

Damn, they'd been having a nice time tonight. The way she had touched his face, the way her fingers had lingered. It had taken everything he had not to kiss her right then and there, forgetting Pete and Jocelyn and everyone else in the restaurant. He'd never felt anything like it before. A need for her, not just a desire.

"I offered to call a cab," he said. Checking his watch, he could see it was nearly midnight. Way too late for a sick kid to be out. Evan should have sent them both home instead of demanding answers immediately.

"I know," she said, running her shoe around the pavement in front of her. "I didn't have to wait. I could have called one myself. Somehow I thought you might need someone to talk to."

"As my agent or as a friend?"

"Are we friends?" Sam asked him.

He felt a lump in his throat and had to swallow around it. He was starting to see what was happening. What this sudden news, one sentence really, was going to do to his life. Potentially change how everyone he knew thought about him. Good guy to deadbeat dad. Worse, deadbeat dad to a sick kid.

What the hell was his father going to say?

Sam was the one standing in front of him, though.

"I wanted that. I wanted a lot of things, actually."

"Fine," Sam said smoothly. "We're friends. Now, tell me what's going on."

"What's going on? Well, I think I just met my son."

With that he could feel tears in his eyes, and he looked away. He'd never cried in front of a woman in his life. Hadn't cried much since becoming a man as far as he could remember. The day his mom died.

He felt her hand on his shoulder, and it didn't help. In fact her empathy only made it worse.

"My dad is going to be so disappointed in me," he choked out.

"Come on. Give me the keys. I'm driving. We're going to go back to my place, and we're going to break a rule."

Seemed like an odd proclamation, given the situation, but nevertheless he felt a spurt of unexpected hope. It must have shown on his face.

"Sorry, no. Not that rule," she said, patting his arm. "You're going to drink during the season."

CHAPTER SIX

SAM POURED THEM both a glass of white wine—it was the only alcohol in the house, it turned out. The downstairs fridge had been completely cleaned out of beer. She walked back to the living room with the two glasses and handed him one.

"White wine? Seriously?" Evan took the glass, resigned. "You saw tears in my eyes… is that it? You think less of me as a man now."

Sam snorted and joined him on the couch. "Yes, I saw you have an emotional reaction to being told you are the father of a seven-year-old boy and have dismissed you from my list of manly men. The wine is all I had, and besides, it will make you sleepy, which you're going to need tonight."

Evan looked down at the glass in his hand. "I can't believe this is happening to me. I really can't. When everything seemed to be going so right. This is like the worst thing

I could have ever done. I had a child, and I wasn't there for him. For seven effing years."

"Well, that's your first problem. Right now it's all emotion. You need to take a large step back and evaluate the situation from a distance and with some objectivity and clear thinking."

He looked at her like she was crazy, and Sam didn't blame him. Underneath her calm exterior she was filled with so many emotions. Not the least of which was anger on his behalf. She couldn't imagine what he was going through.

Which meant she had to put a lock on her feelings. This was about him, and it had nothing to do with her.

One thing for certain, though, Evan hadn't known about this child. The sheer shock factor was proof enough. He was not some deadbeat daddy who had skipped out on his son. He hadn't known his son had existed. So it's not like she could get judgmental about a father walking away from his responsibilities when he didn't even know he had them.

What kind of woman did that? What kind of woman kept a secret like that from a man like Evan?

If it was true.

"First, let's start with her story," Sam began, her legal background kicking in. "Why didn't she tell you she was pregnant?"

"She said she knew I would marry her, and she didn't want to be married to me."

"I find that hard to believe."

Evan looked at her, and she cocked her head as if he was an idiot. "You're smart, you're handsome. You had a teaching degree, and you already told me you loved her."

"Yes, well, Kelly only loved me, the football player. She was pissed I wasn't going to at least try and be drafted. She didn't want to settle for life with a schoolteacher. It's why things ended between us." Evan sighed and drank his wine. "This tastes like cold sour water."

"I know. Isn't it delicious? Right there I have my first suspicion. Yes, you had decided to walk away from football, but if you had found out you had a baby on the way, a chance to make maybe even the league minimum, she might have had a stronger argument to persuade you to try. You being you would have been more motivated than ever to make a team. Doing whatever you had to do for her and your kid."

Evan stared at her. "Is that really what you think? Is that the kind of dad you think I might have been?"

Sam didn't have to search her thoughts for long at all. "Yes, I think it's exactly the kind of father you would have been."

"I dated Kelly for a year and a half, and I've known you for two weeks."

"Your point?"

"How do you know you're right about me? Because Kelly obviously didn't see what you see in me."

Kelly was a fool. Or shallow or too immature to recognize what a good man Evan was.

Or maybe he was right, and she was once again trusting her gut to make decisions about a man which might be entirely false. She had been wrong about Donald, wrong about Richard. What made her think she might be right about Evan?

He's one of the good ones, baby. I know it.

The thought that drifted through her consciousness seemed like something Duff might say. Maybe that's who she needed to trust.

"Am I right? What would you have done

if Kelly had come to you and told you she was pregnant?"

"I would have moved heaven and earth to make sure she and my child had everything they needed."

"So, don't you think it's odd Kelly didn't even consider telling you the news and seeing what you might have done?"

"Maybe she didn't love me enough."

"Maybe. But a twenty-two-year-old woman with no job who just found out she's pregnant... I'm not sure she gets to have that luxury."

Evan closed his eyes, and when he opened them again he was a little more focused. "You think he's not mine."

"I'm thinking the timing of your eventual rise to the majors is a little bit too suspicious."

"She was honest about that at least. Said flat-out she's here for the money, but it's not for her. The boy has asthma. Apparently really bad. Life-threatening bad. She wants to help him. I can't knock her for that. Any mother would."

"I get that. But you can loan an old friend some money to help out her sick kid. You'll have that luxury when you get your contract.

You don't have to take on the responsibility of also being that boy's father. Especially if he's not yours."

"Do you honestly think she would lie about that?"

It would be a horrible thing for a woman to do to a man. Especially a man as trusting as him. Kelly would know how he'd react to the news.

"I think you need to arrange for a paternity test," Sam said. "I'll handle it. Very quietly, under the radar, so as not to attract attention. If it's positive we go from there, but if it's negative, you get your life back. If she's telling the truth, there is no reason to hide anything."

Evan sighed and drank the last of the wine in one solid gulp. Then he made a face as if he'd eaten a lemon. "Don't ever serve me that again. I mean, like, even if I'm wounded badly and you have to cut off my leg with a saw... I would prefer water."

"I'll keep that in mind if I ever need to cut off your leg. You'll let me arrange things? I'll reach out to Kelly to get a sample of the boy's DNA. I believe we just need a swab of the inside of his cheek. Nothing invasive."

Evan stood and folded his arms over his

chest. "This isn't going to look good for you, is it? If the media finds out you're arranging for a paternity test for one of your clients. They're going to think you're representing scumbags again."

"You're not a scumbag."

"I'm not a scumbag," Evan said. "I'm not. I never would have…he's a cute kid. He wheezes a lot, which is scary. He plays Trivia Crack instead of Angry Birds. And he doesn't have any friends. He broke my heart."

Sam heard it in his voice: the physical pain of thinking this child might be his and he'd never been there to raise him, to play with him, to be his friend. To love him.

"I need a few days. I told Kelly the same thing. I think I just need to let this all settle in before I start making decisions."

Sam nodded. "That's fair. Just know I'm here when you need me."

Evan turned to her. "I thought you were going to fire me. Figured you would think I was some disgusting jerk who knocked up a girl and walked away."

It hurt a little. The accusation. Because the truth was it had been her first thought before she had a chance to process Evan's disbelief. Before she considered everything she knew about him. Out of the gate she had thought the worst. She seemed conditioned to consider the worst about people now. That wasn't a happy thought.

When she had seen his face, though, it became obvious he had known nothing about Connor until that evening. And then everything she knew about him had screamed at her that he was a good and decent man.

She needed to stop letting the past impact her present. Especially with him.

"Yeah, well, I'm taking a chance you're not that guy, and I think I'm right."

"Thanks for this. I needed you."

The words did funny things to her insides. Sam stood and set her glass down on the table in lieu of responding, because she really didn't know what to say.

"Not the wine, though. That was just cruel."

She laughed on cue, and the tension of the moment was broken.

"I have to call my dad," Evan groaned. "That is not going to go well."

"Your dad sounds like the supportive type. He'll be there for you."

"That's what I'm afraid of. He has a tendency to want to rush to my rescue. The perils of being a single dad for so many years, I think. The truth is he never really did like Kelly. Thought she was a bit of a flake, so this is not going to go over well."

Together they walked to the front door. Evan opened it and paused.

"What if he's mine?"

Sam touched his arm. "Evan, please, be careful. Because you also have to consider— what if he's not? You let yourself fall in love with that boy and it turns out not to be true... I don't want to see you get hurt."

"Right. I'm going to kiss you on the cheek. I'm announcing that, because I don't want you to see me swooping in thinking I'm trying to take advantage of a situation. I want to politely say thank you for listening to me and offering me your advice. I also want to feel how soft those cheeks really are."

Sam held her breath when he kissed her. It was soft, and his lips might have lingered for longer than a thank-you entailed. As much as she was tempted to turn her head, just enough so that her lips would be in range of his, she didn't.

Because of all the rules that were supposed to be there between them, because of all the new turmoil his situation created. It made no sense to kiss this person now with romantic intent.

No matter how much she wanted to.

That was her cool and logical thinking, and sometimes Sam hated herself for it.

"Be safe. Talk to me about what you're doing. No matter what happens, we're going to have to be ready when this does leak to the press."

"You think Pete…"

"No," Sam said. "He was pretty clear about the whole night being off the record. But this is a small town, and you're a big deal in it. It won't be long before people start seeing you with Kelly and Connor and start asking questions. Plus, Kelly will likely use the press to help her case."

Evan sighed as if just remembering how mercenary his ex-girlfriend could be.

"I used to love her."

"I know," Sam said. "You told me."

"It's like, either way, it hurts. If she lied to me then or is lying to me now. Who does that to another person, someone they used to care about?"

"I don't know."

But Sam certainly planned to find out.

Kelly's arms were shaking by the time she bent to swipe the card through the door lock. Connor, as small as he looked, was still a significant weight to have carried from the car to their motel room. But she couldn't justify waking him up when it had been her fault they were out so late.

An ambush at the restaurant hadn't been her first idea, but she had started to second-guess her decision, and if she hadn't pushed ahead, she might have backed down and headed home. Except there was nothing for Connor back home. Nothing except the same treatment he'd already been receiving, which wasn't enough.

Not even close to enough.

She managed to get to one of the double beds just in time to lay him down before her arms gave out completely. Now he was sprawled on the bed still snoring, or his version of it, which sounded more like a broken whistle. She got him out of his shoes and shorts and pulled the comforter from one side of the bed to the other to cover him.

Then she checked the lock on the door and got into her own pajamas—which consisted of an old T-shirt and boxer shorts—

and crawled into the other bed. She was physically and emotionally exhausted.

But she doubted she'd be able to sleep. Not wanting to disturb Connor with the TV, she just shut out the lights and listened to him breathing.

In the dark she stared at the ceiling and didn't know how to feel. Triumphant, probably. After all, she'd finally done it. She had had a plan when she'd left Arizona; it had taken all her nerve, but she had executed that plan. Now it was time to sit and wait for Evan.

There wasn't a chance he could turn his back on Connor. It was not who he was. At least it's not who he had been back when she was dating him.

Looking back on her decision to leave him, it might be easy to think how completely stupid she had been. How foolish to let such a quality guy go just because he'd committed to a profession that was going to guarantee them a middle-class life. Heck, at least he'd had an idea of what he wanted to do. Kelly had gone through four years of college being a football player's girlfriend.

Maybe if she had focused, she could have worked toward a career that would have given her the life she always wanted. But she'd become pregnant, and all she cared about was a job that paid the bills with flexible hours, which for the past seven years had been waitressing in a number of different places.

No, she supposed she had blown it completely. After meeting guy after guy who wanted nothing to do with her sick child, she had learned the hard way that Evan had been unique.

At least she had grown up since then.

Kelly looked over at her son who was still whistling away as the air always seemed to struggle to get in and out of his lungs, and she knew *he* was the only thing that mattered. The only thing of value in her life was knowing he loved her, and she loved him back.

When she looked back at the end of her relationship with Evan, she remembered feeling so certain it was the right decision. She told him it was about his career choice, that she wanted something more out of life. But that hadn't been the only reason.

Being with a guy like Evan Tanner, she'd always felt obligated to live up to his expectations. In every conflict he took the high ground. Every decision he made was the right one. Every choice he was presented with, he chose wisely.

Finally it became too much for her. She wanted just once to see him fail a class, or hit a parked car but not leave a note, or even get stupid drunk to the point where he fell down.

The last few months they were together she'd felt like she perpetually wore a sign on her forehead that read *I'm not as good as this guy*. And everyone knew it. Living with that every day, she'd started to resent him.

She was a pretty girl with average grades who aspired to be a good wife and mother and not really much else. It didn't make her a bad person. It just didn't make her feel special enough to be Evan Tanner's girlfriend.

Certainly not his wife.

When he'd told her about being a high school teacher instead of a football player, it had been an excuse to walk away, despite how shallow it made her seem. After all, what was she supposed to tell him?

I don't want to be with you because you're too good, and every day you make me feel like I'm not worthy.

Sure, telling him she didn't want to be

married to a schoolteacher was mean. She'd
even felt a little good when she did it. She'd
thought maybe for one second he might
think he wasn't good enough for her, and
then he would know what that felt like.

Now here she was back in his life and
being not at all the kind of person a man
like Evan Tanner would expect her to be. No
moral compass or high ground was going to
get in her way.

She was going to use him for money. She
was going to jump on his fame with two
feet, and she was going to take everything
she could get from the deal.

She was going to use his goodness and his
honor against him. She was going to play on
every heartstring he had in order to get him
to commit to Connor and his well-being.

Did it make her a bad person?

Maybe.

But in her opinion it made her a hell of a
mother.

"Good night, Connor," she whispered to
her son. "Momma loves you."

CHAPTER SEVEN

"AND IN OTHER NEWS, sports agent Samantha Baker, daughter of legendary baseball player the late Duff Baker, is back in the spotlight with another bad-boy client. Baseball's newest phenom, twenty-nine-year-old Evan Tanner, who many think will be playing for the Rebels before the summer is out, apparently has had shocking allegations brought against him by a woman claiming to be the mother of his child…"

"Turn it off."

Evan looked over his shoulder to see his dad standing on the other side of the front door with a duffel bag over his shoulder.

"Dad, I told you…"

"Not to come, yes, I know. That was not going to happen. I took the early flight in and got a rental. Now, are you going to open the door to your father or what?"

Evan turned off the television and walked over to let his father inside. Nelson Tanner was just past sixty but didn't look his age. Evan had inherited his jawline and nose from his father. The rest of him, his father would say, was all his mother's doing. Still, for his age, he kept in shape, and in the over fifty-five community in the town where he lived he was considered quite the stud.

Evan knew this based on the number of casseroles his father had in the freezer anytime Evan visited.

Not that any woman since Evan's mother had been able to get him down the aisle. Casseroles or not.

"Dad, there is nothing you can do about this."

"The hell I can't. I'm going to talk to that girl and get the truth from her. You know I never liked her."

Evan had to chuckle. It had been the fifth time his father had reminded him of that since Evan had called to tell him what was happening two days ago. Had it really only been a couple of days? It had seemed like time had slowed to a complete halt and become this vacuum where the only thing he could think about was what was he going to do if Connor was his son.

His son.

"You're not going to talk to Kelly. I don't want her feeling pressured in any way that might result in her acting out. It's bad enough it's already leaked to the media. I don't need her doing TV interviews or something about how I walked away from her and my kid."

Evan strode to the kitchen and started making coffee mostly because he knew his father drank the stuff pretty much throughout the day.

"Speaking of which," his father said as he took a seat at Evan's kitchen table, "how did it leak? You said the reporter you were having dinner with wouldn't talk."

Evan shrugged. "It could have been anyone. It could have been the couple sitting at the table next to us or the booth behind us. It's not like it was a private moment. She was standing in the middle of a restaurant when she just shoved him at me. Poor kid. At least she had the sense to tell him to wait in the lobby before she dropped the bomb. She hasn't said one way or the other, but I get the impression she hasn't said anything to Connor about me. Or who I might be."

"Oh, no," Nelson interjected. "Don't you go that route. You are not to think of that boy at all. He is nothing to you."

"How can you say that?" Evan asked, hitting a button and waiting for the coffee to brew. "It was seven years ago. I can't remember a particular time when I wouldn't have used protection. Even if I always did, it could have failed. Condoms aren't one hundred percent. You have to face it as much as I do, Dad. I was having sex with Kelly nine months before Connor was born. He could be my kid."

Nelson snorted. "I don't believe that for a second. Not when she waited this long to tell you. Which means you can't either. Not until the proof is staring you in the face. Until then, that boy has to remain a stranger to you."

"He's a cute kid, Dad. Besides that, he's sick. I can't just treat him like he's nothing. He deserves more, regardless of who I am. He didn't do anything to deserve this."

"You know, I never gave her credit for being a smart girl, but I can see now I was wrong. She knew exactly how to play you. She didn't call you up. She didn't send you an email. Hell, she didn't even serve you with legal papers. Oh, no, she let you meet her son so you could see him and see that he was a real live person. You're too damn softhearted, and she knew exactly how to play you."

"He's a sick kid! If you can't be soft-hearted over a sick kid, then I'm pretty sure that makes you a bad person. Of anyone, he is the most innocent in this."

Nelson shook his head, clearly angry. "You need that paternity test, and you need it now. Because the more you walk down this path, the more invested in this kid you'll get. I know you, son. Your whole life you've always done the same. You collect the weak and wounded and take them under your arms like you're some damn superhero. While I previously always admired that quality in you, except for when it turned our garage into a zoo for small wounded creatures, I'm here to make sure you don't do that with this child. The stakes are too high. This boy is not your problem unless DNA says he is."

"If it's any consolation, Sam agrees with you. About the DNA I mean."

"Sam?"

"Samantha. My…agent. Remember? I told you about her. She wants to arrange the whole thing. Says I shouldn't have any contact with Kelly or Connor until we know definitively."

"She sounds like a smart woman."

She was. That fact that he hadn't heard from her in two days made him think she was smart enough to reconsider their working relationship. An agent trying to re-establish her reputation as someone who represented decent people didn't need to have a deadbeat baby daddy on her client list. Whether it was true or not, the perception would still be there.

"I wonder if she saw that news report on ESPN," Evan mused. "She doesn't need that right now. Just one more thing I messed up. She's trying to rebuild her reputation, and I'm hanging around her neck like an anchor."

"First of all, you didn't mess anything up. Kelly did with her lies. And if Samantha Baker is worth her salt as an agent, then she'll know how to handle this quickly and quietly. With the least amount of trouble."

The coffee done, Evan poured two mugs and sat down at the small table across from his father. He'd worn a perpetual scowl since he'd shown up, and Evan knew it was because he was mad at the world right now on behalf of his son. The two of them against everyone. Just like they had always been.

"I thought when I saw you again it would be at my major league debut. I'm sorry it's not."

Nelson put his hand on his arm. "I'm not sorry. I'm always happy to see you, son. We'll get this mess straightened out. You leave it to me and that fancy agent of yours."

Evan laughed. "I'm a grown man, Dad. I'll handle this on my own. Also, I don't know that I have a fancy agent anymore. It's been two days since I've heard from her."

"Trying to fire me already? That's a little premature. Wait until you've gotten your money."

The two men looked up, startled to see Samantha walking into the kitchen. Both immediately got to their feet. She gestured over her shoulder. "I knocked, but you didn't answer, and the door was open. I heard you talking, so I figured it was safe to come in. Sorry if I'm bothering you."

"No, come on in. Sam, this is my dad, Nelson Tanner. Dad, this is Sam Baker."

"You really are Duff Baker's daughter? He was a hell of a ballplayer, that man. I loved watching him play."

Sam shook hands and smiled. "Yes, he was. Your son's not so bad himself."

"Can't take any credit for that. I signed him up for football. Don't know what the hell I was thinking, other than that was my favorite game growing up."

"Well, baseball is happy he finally found his true calling."

"You haven't called me. It's been two days." Two days and five hours, but who was counting, Evan thought.

"You said you wanted time to think. I wanted to give you that time without any pressure."

He thought of the news report he'd just heard. "You know it's already out there. The story, I mean."

She stiffened, almost imperceptibly, but Evan still noticed. "Yes, I've heard. I've gotten a number of requests for interviews."

"That's perfect!" Nelson said, banging his hand against the table. "Let him tell everyone it's nothing but a bunch of lies. No one who has met Evan would doubt his sincerity. There is not a lying bone in his body."

"I'm not sure we can do that just yet," Sam said. "I was able to confirm Connor Lawson was born on January thirteenth, which is nine months after you said you had last been with her. She had him in Florida, and there was no father listed on the birth certificate. She moved to Oklahoma where her mother lived and found a job waitressing for nearly five years, until ultimately she moved to Tucson, where she currently lives. My guess, as a result of Connor's condition. The dry air is better for his lungs. I've got an investigator checking into her background, but really, the simplest way out of this would be a paternity test."

"You're good," Nelson muttered. "You got all that in just two days?"

"I got all that in two hours," Sam said. "It's not like she's trying to hide her tracks, but we are going to need her permission for the paternity test."

"Well, that will say it all, won't it?" Nelson stated. "If she agrees, we have something to worry about. If she refuses, we know she's a liar."

Evan looked at his father and wondered how he would be able to go from considering the boy a stranger and his mother a blackmailing liar, to seeing him as his grandson and Kelly as the mother of his grandson. If it was true. If he did in fact have a son.

A son.

It certainly wasn't how he'd planned to

make his father a grandfather. He always imagined it as a happier occasion.

He couldn't really move forward until he had answers.

Evan nodded his agreement. "Kelly and Connor are coming to the game tonight. I'll talk to her after and let her know I'm going to need the paternity test."

Both Nelson and Sam let out sighs of relief.

"It makes sense," Evan said. "I get that. It's just not… I mean, I get Kelly is doing this for a reason. I haven't lost sight of that. I know it's about the money. But to put her in that spot and basically call her out for lying… Whatever she is, she obviously loves her son."

"Let me do it," Sam said. "Let me talk to her. It's the best approach. It will be less personal, more businesslike, and you don't have to get involved."

"It will be colder, too."

Sam didn't wince, but he thought he noticed her mouth tighten.

"I didn't mean that as a knock against you," Evan clarified. "You know that, right?"

She smiled, but it wasn't her usual smile. "Of course. But cold and businesslike is what I do, so it's best that I get to it."

She turned and started to walk back through the living room to the front door, and he felt compelled to follow her. He'd hurt her again. He hadn't meant to, but it was obviously a sore spot with her. Being called cold.

"Sam, hold up," he said just as she was opening the door.

"I really didn't mean to imply anything back there. When I think of you, and I think of you often despite all this craziness, I never think of you as cold."

"Really? Before you said I was cool."

Evan looked into her eyes. "Cool isn't cold, honey. It's not even close."

Sam looked away. "Let's face it, Evan. Most people wouldn't consider me the warmest person. I'm not going to lie. The icy treatment. It's deliberate. It helps me to keep a little emotional distance when I want it."

"I'm not most people. I also think, for whatever reason, you've let me slip past the guards. That emotional distance you want— I don't think you want that with me. I'm glad. I credit my natural charm and good looks, of course."

He made her smile. Really smile. And it was the best he'd felt all day.

She looked at him, and he thought he would have paid any amount of money to know what she was thinking. Finally she patted him on the chest.

"Play well tonight. It's important nobody thinks this incident is going to mess with your mind in any way. We don't want the Rebels to have any cause for concern."

Evan smiled. "The first home run will have your name on it."

"I'm counting on it."

Evan watched her leave and waited in the doorway until she drove away before he turned around.

"I know that look," his father said as he came into the living room with a fresh cup of coffee. He had a copy of the morning paper and looked like he was settling in for an easygoing afternoon. After all, there wasn't a whole lot to do until they had to leave for the stadium.

"Dad, I don't have a look," Evan said. At least not some moony, gooey-eyed look.

First tears, then wine, then gooey eyes. If he kept at it, he was going to have to reapply for his man card.

"Oh, you've got the look. Your eyes practically bounced out of their sockets when you first saw her. Not that I blame you. She's quite a stunner. But is it wise to be fraternizing with your agent?"

No, it wasn't. It wasn't wise to flirt with her or to kiss her on the cheek. It wasn't wise to go to dinner with her because he enjoyed her company too much. It wasn't wise to want her. It certainly wasn't wise to do all that during what could become the two most defining moments of his life: his trip to the majors and fatherhood.

"Dad, no one says fraternizing anymore."

"Call it whatever you want. The look is still the look. Same look I used to give your mother all those years ago. It's a look that says 'mine.'"

Evan didn't see any point in arguing, since mostly his father was right. "I've got to start getting ready for my game in a little bit. I assume you're coming?"

"You assume correctly."

"I'm serious about you not talking to Kelly. Besides what I said earlier about backing her into a corner, I think Sam's approach makes more sense. Let's let her handle it. Professionally. Okay?"

His father grumbled, but ultimately he

nodded, and Evan knew he would keep his word.

"So, how long are you staying?"

"It's the beauty of early retirement. I can go wherever, whenever and for as long as I want. But I don't see me leaving anytime soon. Certainly until this matter is resolved."

"Dad, you know the resolution may be that I have a son. That you have a grandson. Are you going to be able to accept it if that's the case? Because if he's mine, then he's going to be mine all the way."

His father didn't look up from the paper. "We'll burn that bridge when we get to it."

Evan knew his father was being facetious, but it still made him nervous to think that if it was true and Connor was his son, that his own father might never come to embrace him.

Hell, for that matter, Evan didn't know how he would handle it. Did you just fall in love with some seven-year-old kid who you hadn't known existed a week before but now suddenly was family?

What did that mean in terms of his and Connor's relationship? Evan had no doubt Kelly didn't think about any of this. That he might want to develop something with

Connor. That he might seek partial custody. None of it. He was just a checkbook as far as she was concerned.

Which might be for the best. After all, what the hell did he know about being a parent? Yeah, sure, someday he figured he would get there, but then you have a baby who doesn't know any better and you get all that time to practice.

There would be no practicing with Connor.

"Evan, if the worst is true…"

Evan hated to think of a sick little boy as being the *worst* anything.

"You'll make an excellent father. So, stop worrying about that."

Evan looked at his dad and wondered if his son would ever love him the way he loved his father. "Well, if that's true, it will be because of you."

"Of course it will," Nelson said, just lowering the paper enough so Evan could see the sparkle in his eyes. "I was also an excellent father. Now you have to start getting ready. Something about a baseball game to play."

Right, Evan thought. At the very least he could swing a bat and hit something hard.

CHAPTER EIGHT

SAM LOOKED DOWN at the rows of seats in front of her. She knew Kelly would be in the first row in the last two seats. She also knew there were two seats empty directly behind where she'd be sitting. She knew that, because Jocelyn had called the owner of those seats and offered him a night in her private club box in exchange for them this evening.

The man and his son had jumped at the chance.

Sam would have loved to believe the gesture came solely from the goodness of Jocelyn's heart, as she'd been there the night of the great reveal, but it might have had more to do with protecting her star player's reputation.

Jocelyn agreed a paternity test made sense.

After all, she hadn't wanted to sully him with Sam attending a press conference with him. This was decidedly worse than that.

Sam had worn a simple pair of jeans and

a Minotaurs T-shirt in blue and red. She thought she looked very much like everyone else in the stands except for one thing in particular.

Everyone else seemed to be with someone. Teenage boys in groups. Sometimes a boy and girl sitting together. Men and women. Children. Lots and lots of children, with their arms full of buckets of popcorn and bags of peanuts. Sam could smell the scent of freshly mown grass on the field laid out before her combined strangely with that of hot dogs, and it made her mouth water like it always did.

"Smells like home," she muttered.

Nothing like the smell of the ballpark.

Sam smiled as if Duff were standing right there. Something he must have said a hundred or a thousand times. Maybe every time they ever came to the ballpark together.

She swallowed past the lump in her throat and tried to stay focused. She wasn't here to linger over fond memories of her father. She wasn't even here to see her favorite player play baseball.

She was here to do business on behalf of her client. Steeling herself against any tenderness that lingered in her heart for this place, Sam took the steps down to the second row of seats. She recognized Kelly's long, dark hair immediately from the other night.

She couldn't help but wonder if long, dark hair was Evan's preference.

Which was a ridiculous thought to have. Who cared what your agent's hair color was? So what if it was blond and barely hit her chin?

Sam sat down, and immediately her eyes went to the little boy next to Kelly. He was leaning forward in his seat, taking in all the action, with a half-eaten hot dog in his hand, poised in the air as if he'd forgotten he was holding it.

Sam touched Kelly's shoulder, and when the woman turned around to look at her, she frowned.

"I wondered when you would show up."

That surprised Sam. "You were expecting me?"

"Sure. You're not just his agent, are you? You're his girlfriend, too, right? I remember seeing you together in the restaurant. It didn't look like a business dinner when I interrupted. As his girlfriend, you're worried, now that he has a son with me, how will that impact your relationship. You're going to have to trust me on that score. I don't want anything from Evan that isn't child support."

"First, I'm not Evan's girlfriend. I'm just his agent." It sounded weird to say the words. Especially when she knew they weren't true. Maybe she wasn't his girlfriend, but she wasn't *just* his agent. At the very least, having been there for him as support on what might have been the most shocking night of his life, she was at least his friend.

"If you say so," Kelly said. Like it really didn't matter to her either way.

"I do. As his agent, I'm actually here on business."

She watched the woman stiffen, then look to her son. He seemed entirely oblivious to the conversation happening between his mom and the woman in the row behind them.

"What kind of business?"

"I've spoken with Evan, and he's heard your claim. He would like to have a paternity test done. To prove definitively that Connor is who you say he is. It's a very easy process for both you and Connor—"

"No."

Sam leaned down so she was speaking quietly into Kelly's ear. So that only Kelly would hear. "You understand that, by refusing to confirm through DNA that Connor is Evan's son, you very much weaken your case against any claim you have to child support. In fact, it all but negates it."

"I'm not going to be told I need some damn test to prove that what I'm saying is true. Evan knows me. He knows we were together, and he's going to do the right thing by his son."

Sam tried again. "Kelly, there is no court or judge or any legal action you can take to force Evan's hand without a conclusive paternity test. If what you are saying is true, then the test results will bear that out, and Evan can move forward from there and decide what to do."

"Exactly," Kelly said, looking over her shoulder again with a strange smug expression. "I take a paternity test and that opens the doors for just about anything, doesn't it? Visitation? Custody? Oh, no. Connor's my son. I had him, I'm raising him. We're not rich, but he's all mine. All I want from Evan is money, so that I can get my son in front a serious doctor who might actually be able to help him."

Sam shook her head. "He'll never agree to that. Not without proof."

Kelly threw her dark hair over her shoulder and laughed. "You know I believe you now. You must not be his girlfriend. Because you clearly don't know Evan Tanner. He'll give me what I want. He won't be able to help himself. So you go out there and get him the biggest payday you can. Because serious doctors cost money."

"Kelly..."

"Look, Connor," Kelly said, turning back to her son. "Look who's up at the plate. Number twenty-three."

"H-hey. It's Ev-han," the boy wheezed as he jumped up in his seat. The half-eaten hot dog fell out of his hand, and the crestfallen expression on his face as the dog hit the cement was priceless.

"Don't worry, we'll get you another one. That's the best part about dollar dog day. We can have as many as we want. Now, pay attention. You want to learn to swing a bat just like him."

"Yeah." The boy smiled and focused that much harder on what Evan was doing at the plate.

Sam watched the pitcher wind up and saw the fast ball as soon as it left his hand. Evan swung and hit. Hard. Deep into the left out-field and into the seats. A home run.

Sam thought it had her name written all over it.

The crowd around them erupted.

Connor was jumping and cheering until ultimately his mother had to force him to calm down and settle his breathing.

When that didn't work, she gave him his inhaler. After a couple of deep hits, he seemed to breathe easier. Kelly rubbed his back and then put the inhaler back in her purse.

Something as simple as watching a home run had been too much for him. Sam's heart clenched.

"You'll let Evan know my decision," Kelly finally said.

"I will," Sam said to the woman's back.

"Good. Then you can also tell him I'm getting a lot of requests for interviews now the story has leaked. I'm trying to keep this private between us, but if I have to tell my story to some people in order to force his hand, I will."

Wow, Sam thought. It was Kelly's first mistake. She actually thought the woman quite clever in coming up with a reason not to take a paternity test, but this let Sam know the woman wasn't as sophisticated at blackmail as she thought.

Again Sam leaned down so that only Kelly could hear her. "That's a really hard thing to do without proof, Kelly. All you'll accomplish is speculation and possibly cast doubt on Evan. Unfortunately, that will make Evan Tanner the brand less appealing to sponsors, which ultimately will impact his earnings. That works against your cause of taking him for all you can, and it sends a lot of different reporters on the trail looking for some kind of physical evidence. So, yes, I think you are well served by keeping this private. If anyone asks you anything, your answer is no comment. Do you understand?"

The woman nodded tightly.

"What you're doing isn't right. If Connor isn't his son, then telling Evan he is… it isn't right."

"Do you have a kid, Ms. Agent?"

Sam swallowed around the sudden lump in her throat. No, she didn't have kids. It was something she had given up on when her relationship with Donald had ended. There was never going to be another man she trusted, so there was never going to be a husband.

So there was never going to be a child.

Only recently she'd started to think that maybe it was something she could do on her own. Sam wanted to tell the woman she had actually looked into adoption and artificial insemination just to prove she wasn't completely without maternal instinct, but it really wasn't the time or place for sharing, and Kelly wasn't someone she would ever confide in.

Heck, she hadn't even told her sisters.

"No. I don't have a child."

"Then you don't know what you're talking about."

Maybe she didn't. Because the boy—who was now sitting calmly in his seat, not wiggling or squirming, not cheering or shouting, simply taking in and releasing each breath—was breaking her heart.

"You dating anyone, Samantha? I can call you Samantha, can't I? I mean, as you're my son's agent, I'm not sure what the protocol is here."

They were hanging outside the locker room together waiting for Evan to finish up. He'd had a decent night, hitting two out of four with the one home run, so no worries that his personal drama was impacting his game yet.

Sam looked at Evan's father. He reminded her of Evan. They didn't look very much alike per se, but it was how the two men carried themselves. The straight back, the wide shoulders. It sort of gave her an insight into how Evan would look when he got older, and for whatever reason that pleased Sam. Not that she had any reason to think she would know Evan as an older man. Professionally speaking, there would be no reason to. Still the idea of Evan's firm jaw with his father's salt-and-pepper hair…it was just a nice thought…that was all.

"Sam is fine. And, no, I'm not dating anyone. Are you?"

"Touché," he said with a wink. "I suppose it was a bit of an inappropriate question. I only ask, because when I see a lovely young woman in front of me who is single, I wonder how that can be."

"Mr. Tanner, are you flirting with me?"

He smiled. "If I didn't think my son wouldn't like it very much, I might try it. And, please, call me Nelson."

"Evan said he lost his mother a long time ago."

"Nineteen years and five months. I still miss her every day."

"You were never tempted to get married again?" Sam asked. "Evan was so young."

Nelson shook his head. "When you find that thing, that once-in-a-lifetime thing, you don't risk muddying up the memory of marriage with another marriage. Now, don't get me wrong... I'm a hit with the ladies. I've had a few long-term relationships once Evan left home. I just don't ever want someone else to be Mrs. Tanner. That's who my wife was. I gave everything I could to Evan, and, while I'm sure he missed his mother growing up, we made for a pretty good team." He paused. "Now it's your turn to tell me why you're not married."

Sam frowned. "Long boring story. Besides, for me to be the shark you need me to be for your son, it's best that the job gets all my attention."

"Oh, I don't think my son would mind more attention from you."

Sam let the innuendo roll off her shoulders. She was barely able to consider her conflicting feelings, let alone share them with Evan. Certainly not with his father.

As luck would have it, Evan was leaving the locker room at that moment, so they didn't have to talk about it anymore.

His face was wary and cautious as he approached them, and Sam didn't wait to lay it out there for both of them.

"She won't agree to a paternity test."

"I knew it," Nelson said with a sense of certainty. "She's lying."

Evan looked at Sam. "She had to have a reason."

"She said she doesn't want to give you any legal recourse to sue for visitation, maybe even custody. She's very clear the role she wants you to play, and that is not as an actual father."

Evan shook his head. "It's funny. I was thinking about how she hadn't even considered I might want to see my son going forward. Apparently she had."

"So, what's he supposed to do, just hand this woman money with no proof?"

"Dad, calm down."

"I will not calm down. This woman is messing with your life. How are you ever going to know for certain if that boy is your son without a paternity test? Forget the money…there's more to consider here."

"What money, Dad? Right now there is no money. There's a minor league deal for a couple hundred thousand, and that's it. Maybe the real answer is to find out how much money she needs. Because if it's millions, she might want to find another father who plays baseball. All of this is so much speculation at this point, it's ridiculous."

Sam could feel his frustration, and she wasn't certain what to say or do about it. She also knew that Kelly had picked the exact right candidate. Only someone like Evan would even consider believing a woman without proof.

"The good news is she recognizes that talking to media will not help. I've told her if anyone asks her anything she's to say 'no comment.' Same with you. Just don't talk about it. You aren't the first athlete to have a baby mamma, and you won't be the last, so the less footage and talking about it, the more it's likely not to be newsworthy."

"Baby mamma." Nelson snorted. "That is not who that woman is. She's a liar and a blackmailer."

"Nelson, I understand your feelings. I'm just trying to lay out the facts."

"Where do we go from here?" Evan wanted to know. "Does she just slip a folded piece of paper across a table, and I write a check for that amount, or what? And shit, I mean, what if he is my son? Don't I have some kind of right to… I don't know. He's a kid. He's entitled to a father if that father is willing to be in his life. I mean, what she's doing…to both of us—"

"It's despicable," Nelson said.

"It's desperation," Sam corrected him. "I saw him at the game today. Connor. He couldn't even cheer your home run without running out of air."

"See, that's what I'm saying!" Nelson shouted. "We can't do this. We can't let Evan's life be destroyed because of a sick kid we all feel sorry for."

"A sick kid who could be my kid, Dad. I have to take responsibility."

"Not without proof."

Sam's cell phone buzzed, and she reached into her purse to pull it out. "I'll let you two fight without me."

She took a few steps away. There were only a few reasons why the general manager of the New England Rebels would be calling her. One of them might be to voice his displeasure over Evan's recent circumstances making the news on ESPN. The other could be because they were about to start negotiations.

"Reuben, hello," Sam said coolly.

"Samantha Baker, so good to hear your voice."

"Is it, Reuben?"

"Actually, no. Yours is not one of my favorites. Especially when you're asking for more money for one of your clients."

They both laughed insincerely at the joke.

"What can I help you with today?"

"I understand you're representing our young man, or should I say old man, Evan Tanner."

"I am. As I'm sure you're aware, his contract is coming up for renewal."

"I am. I think it's about time we sit down and start talking, don't you?"

Sam waited a beat. "They're calling him up. When?"

"Soon. Most likely after the All-Star break. The team has actually started to turn it around, and if we have a shot in the playoffs, we're going to need a hot bat off the bench. My people are telling me he's the real deal, but we'll see, won't we?"

"We will."

"I want to meet him. Why don't you plan to bring him out to Boston? His off day next week should work."

Sam frowned. "I don't know that you've ever requested a sit-down with my client before negotiations start. What makes Evan different?"

"Exactly. He's different. Coming to baseball so late. Now I hear he's got lady drama, but everyone else swears he's an upstanding guy. If I'm going to hand over the owner's precious dollars, I want to take the measure of this man first. Do you have a problem with that?"

"Not even a little bit. Evan Tanner is exactly what you said, an upstanding individual who I'm proud to represent."

"Certainly a better sort than that last character you stuck up for. I hope."

The comment was pointless. It was just a dig to get under her skin. Agents thinking about their own problems were less focused on those of their clients and maybe not as aggressive as they needed to be.

"Definitely. We'll be there. Shall we say noon? We can lunch together."

"Noon, it is. I'll have my receptionist email the arrangements."

"Perfect." Sam ended the call and turned around to see Evan still in a heated exchange with his father.

"How much do you think she wants?" Nelson was asking his son.

"I don't know, Dad. How much do top asthma doctors cost?"

"Gentlemen, at least we know one thing. The money is going to be real. That was Reuben. He wants to start negotiations for your next contract."

Evan stared at her. "I'm being called up?"

Sam shook her head. "Not yet. In a couple of weeks."

"I've never been so proud and so pissed at you at the same time," Nelson said.

"Hey, this thing with Kelly isn't my fault."

"You dated her," Nelson accused him. "How many times did I tell you I didn't like her? She was manipulative then, and she's manipulative now."

Sam stepped in between the two. "I think we're a little bit beyond that now, guys. Also, here's the thing. Reuben wants to meet you first. We're going to Boston next week for lunch."

"Is that normal?"

"Has there really been anything normal about your journey?" Sam countered. "This feels like par for the course. I don't think we should be worried about it. He wants to get a sense of who you are. I think it's a good idea. He's going to see that with age also comes maturity. Something that can benefit a team in the locker room."

Evan nodded. "What do I do about Kelly in the meantime?"

"Nothing. We wait. I'm sure she's just as anxious over this contract as you. My guess is she'll head back to Arizona eventually. There's really no reason to stay in Minotaur Falls now. She's made her point. But it might not be a bad idea to start doing some research on Connor's condition. I can reach out to the top hospitals across the country specializing in children's asthma. That way, if she hits us with a number we'll know if it's in the ballpark."

"That's fine, but, just so you both know, this isn't just about the money for me. I'm not going to hand over a check and walk away. Not if that kid needs me."

Evan stormed off, probably because he didn't want to hear what his father was going to say, which left Sam and Nelson standing together watching him head to his truck.

"Your son's a good man, Nelson."

"No, Sam, my son is the best man. Which is why I'm counting on you to fix this."

Tanner walked away, clearly upset, too, and Sam really hoped she wasn't about to disappoint both of them.

CHAPTER NINE

"It's good to see you again, Samantha," Reuben said smoothly. "We tease a lot, but I mean that sincerely. I was afraid you might not have come back from that Stanson incident. Reputations can be difficult things to repair."

The three of them were seated in a corner booth in one of the nicer restaurants in the downtown area of Boston away from all the construction. It was always Sam's impression when she visited that the city seemed to be in a constant state of upheaval.

"Surely I'm not the only agent in history to get caught with a jerk for a client," Sam said in defense of herself.

"This's true. However, the public, and it would seem your clients, had more of an issue with you and the stand you took by backing him up."

"Because she's a woman," Evan said as he sipped his sparkling water. She couldn't say why, but for some reason she found it funny that he preferred sparkling to still. Or maybe he just figured it was going to cost more, and he wanted to run up the lunch tab as high as he could. Obviously Reuben was treating. But, no, Evan wouldn't think like that. He must happen to be a man who preferred sparkling water.

She made a mental note to buy some when they got back home.

"I'm sorry?" Reuben asked.

Evan shrugged. "A man stands up in front of the cameras and says his client didn't do it, then it turns out he's wrong, people don't think anything of that. I mean he's the agent, that's what he's supposed to do. Stick up for his client at all costs. Sam does it, though, and it looks like she's betraying her sex. Like she's saying it's okay for a woman to get hit by a man. Both men and women will take issue with that."

Sam smiled and shook her head. "You really are Captain America, aren't you?"

Evan smiled at her. "Just stating facts. You got hosed more than any other agent would have in the same circumstance because you're a woman. That sucks."

"Yes, it does. But we're not really here

to talk about me or my past. Reuben, you called this little powwow. I got the feeling it was because you wanted to know more about Evan. That's understandable because you're going to be paying him a significant amount of money in the very near feature. Did I mention his batting average was up to 3.66 and that he's the leading home run hitter in Triple A right now?"

Reuben chuckled good-naturedly. "No, somehow you missed those facts previously. You seem to be a fine man, Tanner. If a little long in the tooth for your average baseball player."

"Sometimes it's not the quantity of years, but the quality," Sam quipped. It would be their biggest hurdle in the contract negotiations. How many years of guaranteed money do you give to someone who was twenty-nine? Sam wanted five; she figured Rueben would offer three.

But that negotiation wasn't going to start now. Sam and Reuben would do their battle by email and phone. Evan wouldn't be party to any of it. Just the outcome.

"True, true. Also, I understand you're new to the game. Seems a pretty amazing thing that you could learn the nuances at such a high level in such a short time."

"That's not amazing," Evan said. "That's just hard work."

Sam beamed. She couldn't have said it better herself.

"Okay, then we're on to the nasty stuff. The stuff that makes the headlines on ESPN, which I really hate because the stuff that used to make the headlines always revolved around sports and teams and games. Did you get that girl pregnant and desert her?"

Sam was about to chime in when Evan held up his hand. The question was directed at him, and he would answer it.

Sam backed down immediately.

"I did not desert her. I can't say for sure if the child is mine. The timing could be right. But I never would have knowingly left a woman who was pregnant with my child. I would have married her. Without question. Kelly Lawson didn't give me that choice."

"Yes, but now you're a professional athlete about to hit it big. Makes you look much more like marriage material, doesn't it?"

Sam thought about that. If it was true and Connor was his son, would Evan go so far as to marry Kelly now? Why that made her agitated and suddenly sick to her stomach she wasn't willing to address head-on, but if he attempted to do that, she would fight him. Or fight for him, she supposed.

He didn't deserve to spend his life with a woman who didn't love him enough to choose him no matter what his career. He didn't deserve a woman who would keep his child away from him, for that matter, either.

He deserved the best kind of woman. A woman with an open heart and no shadows. Who would believe and trust him always. Because he was that kind of good.

Not someone like Kelly.

Sadly, not someone like her, either.

Sam frowned. When had she become undeserving of the love of a good man because of her untrusting and frosty nature? When had she let her skepticism and bitterness turn her into someone whom a man like Evan was too good for?

Suddenly she was angry at herself. She hadn't done a thing to make her less worthy. Someone had done that to her. Only now she could see she was letting it affect everything.

To the point where she didn't consider herself worthy of Evan's attention.

Attraction.

Affection.

"Kelly has her reason, sir. I would ask that you not speak against her."

Right, Sam thought, because Evan was the type of man who would protect the mother of his child. Regardless of what she had done to him.

Any woman on this planet would kill for someone like him. But not her. And not because she was his agent, but because she thought she wasn't good enough.

The anger inside her continued to fester as Reuben asked Evan more pointed questions about how they were dealing with the situation.

Evan followed Sam's direction of not commenting, and Sam had this crazy desire to stand up in the middle of the restaurant and tell everyone that she was a good person. Hardworking and loyal. A good daughter, a good sister. For that matter, she'd been a hell of a good fiancée, too.

She wasn't the problem. It was the fact that someone destroyed her faith in love. That was the problem. Because that person did that, she wasn't worthy of Evan.

That wasn't fair. That was giving Donald all the power even now.

"Reuben! I heard you were going to be here."

Sam heard the voice and shook her head. This couldn't be happening. She couldn't be having this epiphany now and have *him* show up in the exact moment. As if to show her exactly what he'd cost her. Or maybe this was her fate, to finally confront the person who had so radically altered her life, so that she could move on.

"Oh, hey, Donald. Didn't expect to see you here." Reuben was standing and offering Donald his hand. The way the booth was shaped with Sam on the other side of Evan, it was clear Donald hadn't seen her yet.

No doubt this wasn't going to be a happy reunion.

"In town dealing with the Pats on some issues with one of my guys. And, hello, two birds with one stone," Donald announced as he turned to the opposite end of the booth. "Evan Tanner. You said you wanted to meet in person. This is perfect. We can all grab lunch together and talk."

"Sorry, Donald. I already have an agent.

I figured you would have heard about it by now."

"I've been out of the country...a vacation...with a..." He faltered to a stop when his eyes fell on Sam. His whole body froze.

"A new girlfriend?" Sam asked. "I heard your last engagement ended. Through the grapevine, of course."

"You bitch," Donald growled.

"Whoa," Evan said, and then Donald had the misfortune of leaning in across the table aggressively toward Sam.

"You think I don't know who sent her that note?" Donald raged, spit coming out of his mouth so that Sam was forced to look away. "You don't think I know who sent the note before that one? Where do you get off, messing with my life like that?"

Evan was up and in seconds had Donald's arm up behind his back high and tight so that he couldn't move without inflicting pain.

"Now, I don't know what this is about," Evan said calmly in his ear. "But you're going to apologize to the lady and then leave without another word."

"I'm not apologizing to that jealous bitch. She's ruining my life."

"Oh, please, Donald. You and I both know what I do is not done out of jealousy."

"It was one time!"

"That's what's sad. You think it's the number that counts."

"You leave now," Evan said, "or I break your arm."

"You break my arm, I have you arrested for aggravated assault," Donald fired back. "How would that look to a potential employer?"

"Not good," Reuben said calmly. "Not good at all. Evan, we need you on the team, so I suggest you let him go. Donald, I have to say your lack of…control…not to mention social graces, is a bit shocking in these circumstances. It would be best for all parties if you left now."

Evan released the man's arm, and Donald instantly did a whole body shrug as if he'd been able to free himself instead of having to be let go. He looked directly at her when he said, "This isn't over."

"Oh, no," Evan said calmly, sitting himself down next to Sam, so that Donald was no longer in her line of sight. "I don't know what *this* is. But I can tell you it's definitively over. You got me? Donald?"

Donald said nothing but instead righted his jacket, turned and left them.

Reuben clapped his hands. "Now, this is an exciting lunch. Tell us, Sam, what awful thing are you doing to ruin his life? Is this some bitter rivalry between agents? You used to work at his agency, didn't you? I know you're stealing his clients."

"Nothing so dramatic. Just telling the truth. It doesn't put Donald in a favorable light."

"Ooh, cryptic. I like it. Well, I'll leave you to your secrets. Shall we enjoy the rest of our lunch, then?"

Sam smiled, and Evan looked at her as if to say, eventually she would have to tell him the story. Instead, Sam and Reuben gossiped about baseball players they knew, and Evan did everything he could to impress Reuben, which was mostly just being himself.

When it was over and they found themselves on the street again, Reuben shook Evan's hand. "It was good to meet you, Evan. I'm glad we did this. Sam, I'll be in touch."

Sam shook his hand, as well. "Looking forward to it, Reuben."

Reuben just shook his head. "You're not going to make this easy, are you?"

Sam smiled politely. "When have I ever?"

"Good point. You two headed back to New York now?"

"Not until tomorrow morning. Evan has a home game, but it's in the evening and it was hard to find commuter flights to Albany later in the evening."

"Ah, then a night in Boston. Enjoy."

With a final wave he left them, and Sam thought about what they were going to do with themselves. If Evan even wanted to spend the rest of the day with her. Technically, they could go back to their hotel and do their own thing before meeting up tomorrow morning to catch their flight. It was most likely what she would have done with any of her other clients. Maybe take them out to dinner later, but beyond that it wasn't like she would have spent the day sightseeing.

What was upsetting to her was that that was exactly what she wanted to do with Evan. She wanted to spend the day showing him around Boston, talking, enjoying his company.

She wanted it so much Sam was about to suggest they head back to the hotel instead when Evan turned on her, his expression angry like she'd never seen before. Only she knew it wasn't directed at her.

"Okay, the dog and pony show is over. Now, tell me what the hell happened with that guy."

Or instead of going their separate ways, she could tell him her darkest secret.

Decisions. Decisions.

Evan took it out of her hands. "I need to know, Sam. I need to know, so I don't think of any number of awful things that might lead me to find him and do more than just break his arm."

"You don't need to defend me."

"Yes," Evan said tightly, "I do. Damn it, Sam, you can dodge this thing that's happening between us all you want, but the bottom line is when I needed someone, you were there, and when you need me, I'm going to be there, too. That's how this works. It's time you realize that."

Sam opened her mouth to point out that's not really how an agent/client relationship worked, when right there in the middle of a busy street, he pulled her to him with an arm wrapped around her waist and kissed her.

Kissed her like she didn't imagine she'd

ever been kissed before. With so much raw passion and frustration.

That shouldn't have been as arousing as it was.

She felt consumed by him. So much so, the people and the city and the cars and traffic, all of it was gone. There was just Evan and his mouth and his taste and his arms wrapped around her. She felt weightless and wondered if he'd actually lifted her off her feet.

Then suddenly it was over, and she felt as if she'd been dropped out of a plane, the sense of falling was so acute.

"I'm sorry," he said, taking a step back and running his hand through his hair. "I didn't mean to do that."

"You didn't?" Damn.

"Not in the middle of the street. Don't get me wrong. I totally meant to kiss you. I just imagined it would be somewhere more private." A group of older women walking by them were smiling and, it would seem, ogling Evan. With good reason, Sam thought. He was one hell of a kisser.

Sam closed her eyes. Now that she had a little bit of her bearings back, she could see the reality hadn't changed. "Evan, I'm your agent…"

"Yes. You are. You're also my friend and my lover, if you'll have me. I'm not buying into your reasons against it, Sam. Why can't we have both relationships, and why would it be so wrong?"

"Because it would complicate things, Evan…"

He ran a hand through his hair. "It's already complicated! We've already called out the elephant in the room, so there's no going back. Only forward. I'm tired of trying to dodge this. Denying my feelings for you is just another thing I don't want to waste any energy on doing."

Sam scowled. "Oh, so you've decided we're doing this thing because it's what you want. What about what I want?"

He moved in on her again and dipped his head low. "What do you want, Sam? Because that kiss a few seconds ago sure as hell felt like you wanted me. Bad."

Denying it would be silly. "What I want and what is smart are two different things right now. I'm trying to remake my reputation. You heard Reuben—that's not an easy thing to do. Especially for a *female* sports agent—just as you said. If people found out I was sleeping with my clients, I'm not sure that would help."

"Client. Singular. I'm more than that, and you know it."

He was more than that. And she did know it. Evan Tanner was flat-out one of the best men she'd ever met. How could she not at the very least have a crush on him? Why did that have to scare her so much?

"I work for you. You pay me. When I say complicated, that's what I'm talking about."

"That's an excuse," he accused her. "You're looking for roadblocks so you can tell yourself why it's easier not to pursue this thing we have. But it's not going away, and I'm sure as hell not going away. Now tell me what happened between you and Donald."

It was true. Beyond her very rational reasons why they shouldn't pursue a relationship, she was also looking for excuses to keep Evan at arm's length. Which apparently wasn't far enough away to keep her from wanting him. She wanted his mouth back on hers certainly, busy street or not.

Maybe talking about her ex was a good thing. Maybe that would be the cure for the desire coursing through her veins right now.

At the very least it would remind her why she was putting up all those roadblocks. Why she lived her life behind her very safe wall.

"Let's walk," Sam said. They ended up walking through the Boston Common park off Beacon Street where it was less crowded. The sun was bright, a light breeze teased her hair. It was a beautiful day that was about to get ugly.

"Donald and I worked at the same sports agency in Chicago," Sam began. "We started dating and fell in love. We got engaged, and everything seemed wonderful. Happy ever after, the end."

"What happened?"

Sam could hear the growl behind his question. "Donald was…is…very arrogant. Very much in command of things. At first I thought it was such an attractive quality, the way he took charge of everything. After we were engaged, though, things started to get worse. He was super jealous of any man I came into contact with, and as you can imagine, being a sports agent, that was a lot. We started to fight about it constantly. He alluded to me finding another way to use my law degree."

"Sounds like an insecure jerk," Evan muttered. "Why would you put up with that?"

It was a question she had asked herself over and over again since she'd left him. How could she not have seen the signs? Why hadn't she realized that all his subtle hints about finding a different job, staying with him instead of going out with her girlfriends, making sure he always knew where she was at any given point in the day were all symptoms of a larger disease.

Control. Donald had wanted total control over her, and she had been stupid enough or naïve enough, or maybe in love enough, to not have seen it until it was too late. In some ways maybe the best thing that could have happened to her was the fight that night. If it hadn't happened, she might have married him. All those tiny signs would have turned neon, and Sam knew, just like her sister Lane, she would have been too stubborn to give up easily.

Sam shrugged. "I don't know. I thought I had something. A future. A family. Something that was worth more than a few fights or a sense of being controlled."

"What happened to make you change your mind?"

Taking a deep breath, she told her story. "I had an old friend from law school come into town for a visit, and it enraged Donald until I finally convinced him there was no reason to worry. I would never ever cheat on him. Eventually, he believed me, but even after that fight I knew something was wrong. Then one night I came home, and he was drunk and furious. I had invited my law school friend to our wedding. We argued, and he hit me."

Evan stopped walking. "He hit you."

"Yes," Sam said tightly. The echo of the sound of it was still in the forefront of her mind. "Just once. Across the face with his backhand. It hurt really badly. You know, like that scene in *Pretty Woman* where she gets popped by Stuckey. Anyway, I got up and left the apartment. I went to a hotel because I was too embarrassed to tell my friends what had happened. I waited until I knew he would be gone the next day, packed up all my stuff and left."

"You didn't press charges."

"No. Again more for the embarrassment factor than anything else. I didn't want to tell people how badly I messed up. That my judge of character was so completely flawed.

I dated him. I got engaged to him. I was going to commit my life to him. I figured it was victory enough to walk out after only having it happen once rather than going back after an apology."

"Did he try to get you back?"

"Many times. Emails, calls. In the end it was all so predictable. It was because he loved me so much. It was because he couldn't handle the thought of me being with another man. It only happened that one time. He said it like it was his mantra. He only hit me once. He doesn't understand that it's in him, the inclination to strike another person he loves out of anger will always be there. I suppose there's therapy, but I can't see Donald ever admitting he has a problem."

"And the notes?"

Sam bowed her head. "He's been engaged twice since we ended our engagement. When I hear about it through channels, I write a note to his fiancée letting her know what happened to me. Then, of course, it's up to her to decide what she wants to do with that information. He can be as angry as he likes with me, but I doubt those women broke their engagements over what I wrote to them. No doubt, whatever I said was just reinforcement of something they probably already suspected. If not experienced. Like I said, Donald is someone who wants control, and I don't see that changing, no matter who he's with."

Even clenched his fists. "I'm going to hurt him so bad."

"You are not," Sam said sternly. "Donald was right. He'll press charges, and that will not help your professional career."

"It's baseball," Evan said. "I've learned they expect characters in baseball."

"Characters, not criminals. You don't need to be everyone's knight in shining armor. I handled it the way I handled it. It's done now. A part of my past."

Even took her two hands. The sun was still shining down on them, the day was actually getting hotter, but still she felt chilled from the inside out.

Icy.

Like her nature, she thought. Always cold. Never warm.

Except her hands where he tucked them into his. They were warm. Her fingers and her thumb where he rubbed it over hers.

"Is it, Sam?" Evan asked her gently. "Is

it part of your past? Or is it the real reason you're afraid of this?"

Sam didn't have to ask what *this* was. In the end, maybe the truth was her best option.

She pulled her hands back and crossed them over her chest.

"Yes. Yes, it is the real reason. Now you get why there can't be anything between us. I'm too cold inside to let it happen. Donald broke my ability to trust. Without that, how could I ever have any kind of real relationship? I would always be waiting for it, some event that would showcase what a mistake I made. It's better that I don't try. It's better for you to walk away. You deserve someone who isn't an ice queen."

Evan took the news with a wolfish smile Sam didn't expect. After all, she was denying him what he wanted. At the very least he should have looked disappointed.

"Sam, if you're cold, then my most favorite thing is going to be warming you up. Now, let's talk about what we're doing for dinner tonight. I'm thinking a nice steak place."

Steak? She'd just told him why she couldn't be with him, and the man wanted steak.

"Evan—"

"Nope. I'm not hearing any more about how cold you are, Sam. Or what was that about me deserving better? You think there's someone out there who's better than you? They can't be smarter. They sure as hell can't be prettier. They can't be as tough or as… and, yes, I'll say it again…as cool as you are. You've got a guy cursing at you, directly in your face, and you didn't bat an eyelash. No, Sam. I'm not buying that you're broken. Or that, if you are, I can't help you fix it. Let's start with something simple. Like a date."

"A date? You and me. Steak and some nice wine."

"It's been a while for me, but I recall that's about right."

A date, she thought. With Evan Tanner. Sam wanted that. She wanted that so much, she didn't care about doing the smart thing. Not this time.

I'm not buying that you're broken. Or that if you are, I can't help you fix it.

Sam looked him in the eyes. Was it possible? Could a man as good as Evan have the ability to help fix her? And did she want that?

Yes. Yes, she thought, that was exactly what she wanted.

CHAPTER TEN

"I'VE GOT TO let you go, Dad. I'm taking Sam out for dinner."

Evan had just called to check in, something he felt compelled to do because his father was staying at his house. Evan also wanted to make sure he had no plans to confront Kelly in Evan's absence. He'd gotten his father's promise before he left, he wouldn't cause trouble, but he knew how protective his father was.

Nelson would have a very loose definition of what *trouble* was.

The old man said he'd been good, so Evan had to believe him.

"Taking her out to dinner, huh? If she's the agent, shouldn't that be the other way around?"

"Not sure where you're going with that, Dad." Evan couldn't say why he was reluctant to talk about his feelings for Sam with his dad. Maybe he was afraid of hearing what he'd heard about Kelly all those years ago. That he didn't like her. Evan would hate that. He would hate the idea of Nelson not liking Sam.

It's how he knew this thing with Sam was a big deal. His feelings were already engaged, despite this technically only being their first date. He hadn't stopped thinking about her, not really, since meeting her all those months ago. Should have told him everything he needed to know about his feelings.

"All I'm saying is, I saw the look. Now *you're* taking *her* out to dinner. I'm not blind. I see what's going on. I'll say this, too—I'm not sure it's the right time for this, son. You've got a lot going on back here, not to mention you're about to be called up to the Bigs shortly. Is this really something you want to take on at this point? A new relationship. A new relationship that comes with a host of challenges."

Evan heard what his father was telling him, and he was probably right. This was probably the worst time to think of starting something up. Sam, being his agent, might be the worst person to take it up with, too.

All of that made perfect sense. Except Evan didn't care.

"Dad, relax. It's a date. It's not like I'm suddenly not going to be able to hit a ball because I'm getting to know a woman a little more... You're not kidding me—I know that's what you're really worried about. You watch too many baseball movies."

His father chuckled. "Okay, there might be a little of that. But it's not just your game I'm worried about. There's no easy way to say this, but, Evan, you're...vulnerable right now. I don't want to see you get hurt."

Vulnerable. It was a word no man wanted affiliated with himself. However, he couldn't disagree. The shell shock of finding out he might have a son, it broke something open inside of him. He was trying to keep his feelings for Sam and his feelings about Connor separate in his mind. Which was probably pretty foolish. Still, he was stubborn enough that he was unwilling to back off.

"I get that, too, Dad. But I'm telling you... there's something about her. I met her when Scout recruited me, and the truth is I haven't stopped thinking about her since. You're against it. She's against it. Common sense is against it. I've got to go with my gut on this."

"Your gut or your dick?"

"Dad," Evan groaned. "Don't say dick. It's too much like sex, and I don't want you anywhere near my sex life."

The old man chuckled again, a good thing. It meant his warning to stay away from Sam was just that: a warning.

"Since I saw you give her that look, I've been doing some reading about Samantha Baker. Interviews, articles that featured her and her agency. Apparently, she's smart, she's beautiful, and she has a reputation for being ruthless. You think you can handle all that?"

Ruthless. The idea was almost laughable. Then again, the people who wrote those articles never saw the vulnerable side of her the way he did. They didn't see the way she would look down at her hand, joined with his, and smile like he'd given her some kind of a gift.

No, they only saw the icy walls. Walls she felt like she needed because some asshole she'd believed in hit her.

Broke her.

"You know, Dad, I have no idea but I sure as hell want to give it a try."

"Then, go for it. Take her some place nice.

If she does her job right, you can afford any place in the city."

Evan smiled. "Will do. I'll talk to you tomorrow. We should be back around noon."

"Have fun, son."

Evan disconnected the phone and checked in the mirror. He'd thought ahead to this night and brought a suit. His plan all along was to take Sam out and woo her with good food, good wine and maybe some dessert. He hadn't thought to come out and ask her like he had. His idea was more to steer her in the right direction.

Now, he was glad he had. This night had a label to it. It was a date.

Then, maybe after their evening, they could enjoy a different sort of dessert altogether.

For a moment he thought of Connor stuck in a motel room in Minotaur Falls, and he felt a fistful of guilt. He should be taking the kid out for hot dogs or something, but instead he was with Sam, thinking about tonight.

It made no sense, especially if the kid was not his son.

He was going to have to talk to Kelly when he got back. He needed answers, and she was the only one who could give them to him.

Evan checked his watch. They were meeting in the hotel lobby in five minutes. Pushing aside thoughts of Connor for now, he decided this night was for him. He hadn't done anything wrong, and if he was going to have a chance of thawing Sam's icy exterior, it was going to require all his focus.

It was the one thing baseball had taught him. It didn't matter if there was no action coming his way in the outfield. He still needed to focus, because at any given moment, that could change with the crack of the bat.

He was the first one down in the lobby. It gave him an opportunity to pick a spot where he would be able to see her before she could see him. This way he could look his fill without making her aware of how beautiful he thought she was because he knew it made her slightly uncomfortable. As if he were seeing her too closely.

Sam had walls, there was no doubt. Now he knew where those walls came from.

Donald.

Evan thought about how it would feel to hit that asshole just once. He cringed at the idea that he could've ended up signing with that guy. Where the hell was his bad press? Why didn't everyone know what kind of human being he was? Evan wondered if he'd ever been hit in his life. If he knew what it felt like to take that from someone else.

Sam was worried about charges, but Evan thought it might be worth it for one good pop to the guy's face. Maybe once he felt that pain, he would understand what he'd done, what he'd broken inside a beautiful woman.

The elevator doors opened, and out she came, perfectly on time. She was wearing a yellow halter dress, which worked so well with her natural blond looks, and white high-heeled sandals that made her legs seem endless. She was a glass of frosty lemonade on a sweltering summer day, and his tongue nearly fell out of his mouth.

Ruthless.

Not this woman. Not his Sam.

"Sam," he finally managed after a second of her looking around for him.

She seemed to pause when she spotted him.

As she approached, she nodded. "Nice suit."

"Nice dress," he countered.

Sam's lips twitched. "We don't necessarily look like an agent and her client going out to have a professional dinner."

"Excellent, because that's not the look I was going for." Evan pulled on the lapels of his suit jacket. "This is what it's going to be like once you land our big payday. Suits, champagne, fancy cars. I wanted to give you a preview."

Sam shook her head. "Why do I have the impression that is totally not going to be you?"

"Maybe because this is the only suit I own. Not sure why I might need more, and I have no intention of getting rid of my truck, because it's badass."

"You don't like champagne?"

"Don't know. Never tried it. But it can't be worse than the sour water you drink."

"It's cold sour water with bubbles."

"Yep, not interested." He moved so his elbow was out from his body as an offering.

Sam hesitated for only a second before she took his arm. The concierge found them a taxi. They had reservations for one of the best steak houses in the city.

Arriving promptly, they were seated and handed menus. Evan tried not to let his eyes widen at the prices. The least expensive steak on the menu was fifty dollars.

He could afford this. It was crazy that sometimes he had to remind himself of that.

"So, I was doing some research related to the medical costs for asthma…"

"No," Evan said firmly. He didn't want to bring Kelly and, for that matter, Connor with them here on this date. "I don't want to talk about that. Not tonight."

"Evan." Sam sighed. "I get that you want this to be a date."

"A romantic date. One in which we look into each other's eyes and think about all the dirty stuff we want to do to each other in bed. That doesn't involve talking about a sick kid. I feel guilty enough already."

Sam blinked. "Why guilty?"

Evan shifted in his chair. "I don't know. I just picture him stuck in some motel room back in Minotaur Falls. Probably wondering what the hell he's doing here. I mean, I have no idea what Kelly has told him about any of this. He's got to be confused."

"My guess is she's told him nothing. If she had no thoughts of allowing you any type of custody, it's unlikely she would tell the boy who you were. However, if she's lying, then she would also be unlikely to tell the boy anything. It's one thing to lie to you and tell you he's your son. I think it's a much greater sin to lie to her son and tell him you're his daddy if it's not true."

"Either way, it sucks for the kid."

"I know you don't want to talk about it, but what is your plan? I mean, Kelly has a job waiting for her back in Arizona. It's a waitressing job and maybe she thinks she can find another one easily, but I can't imagine she can stick around in Minotaur Falls much longer."

Evan nodded. "Well, I guess I have no choice, right? I guess I need to…what…draw up some papers? Arrange for some kind of settlement?"

"If you do this once, without proof of parentage, then you're opening yourself up for any future demands she might have. By giving into her, you're conceding that Connor is your son, which could open a bunch of other doors. Not just related to his medical condition, either. She could want monthly support, a college trust fund…"

Evan got that. He just didn't know what to do about it.

"You could be paying for any number of

things indefinitely without Kelly having to offer you anything in return. Like allowing you to see him or establish a relationship with him. He would be your son in name only, and you would be nothing more than a checkbook. Is that really what you want?"

Evan sighed. "Yes, this is just as romantic as I hoped it would be."

Sam smiled sadly and reached across the table to put her hand on top of his. He liked the way it felt. Reassuring. Warm.

"I like you, Evan. Forgetting all the other stuff, I just like you. I don't know how anyone couldn't. You're too good a guy to be taken advantage of like this. Someone has to tell you what the consequences of your choices might be. If that has to be me, then so be it. I'm telling you all of this not just as your agent. Your friend, too. If I didn't represent you, I would tell you the same thing."

Evan turned his hand over, and Sam didn't pull hers away. Instead they locked fingers, and she was looking at those locked fingers. She clearly liked seeing them connected. If he slid deep inside her, connected her to him, would she want to see that, too?

"Come back to my hotel room with me tonight. Let me make love to you."

Sam looked up at him. He could see the flare of desire before she threw her own internal ice bucket on it. He wasn't even sure why he had asked her like that. It was hardly his typical behavior on a first date. Normally, he wasn't the type to rush into sex. He liked to let the tension and the foreplay build before jumping into bed.

He also wasn't the type to kiss someone on a busy street in the middle of the day.

All that went out the window with Sam. It was like they had started this thing two years ago, and the tension had been there ever since. Just waiting to be back in the same space again.

"Evan…"

"I know. It's wrong for so many different reasons. Hell, this is just our first date. It's not even going well because we're talking about something that is in no way indicative of who I am as a man. But say yes, Sam. Say yes because you want to."

She was about to say something, but then Evan felt his phone vibrate. He might have ignored it except he was waiting every day now for the call that would bring him up to the majors. He pulled his phone out of his pocket and checked the screen.

It was his father.

"Hold on a sec, Sam. Dad wouldn't be calling if it wasn't important. He knows I'm out with you." Evan turned a bit from the table and answered. "Yeah, Dad?"

"Son, it's Connor. He's having a severe asthma attack. Kelly just called the house. She's taking him to the hospital. I… I didn't know what to do but… Oh, hell, I had to call."

"No, yeah. Thanks."

Evan disconnected the call and tried to get a handle on his emotions. This kid might not be his. He didn't know him except for a quick introduction. Yet suddenly he felt this paralyzing fear. What if Connor was his kid, and now he was sick? In the hospital sick. Without him.

"I have to go," Evan said, standing without even realizing it. He looked around and got the attention of their waiter, making the universal sign for check. They had only ordered drinks, a soda for him and wine for Sam. Evan threw down forty bucks on the table, figuring that should more than cover it. How much could a glass of wine be, after all?

Severe attack.

What the hell did that even mean?

"Evan, talk to me."

"It's Connor. He's had a…severe attack. I'm not sure what that means, but I believe it's bad. He's in the hospital. I need to get there. How the hell do I get there? Shit, there weren't any flights out tonight. I'll need to rent a car."

Sam stood and put her hand on his arm. "First, take a deep breath."

Evan tried. "I can't. I can't breathe. This is so freaking scary. What if he is my kid? He's in trouble. I have to get there. What if…"

They were walking out of the restaurant, and Sam was already hailing a cab. Once the car pulled over they got in the back, and Sam gave the hotel name to the driver.

"If you rent a car, that will take at least an hour and then you have a six- to seven-hour drive to the Falls. By that time our morning flight would get you there only forty minutes later," she said reasonably.

Evan wasn't feeling in any way rational. "I can't stay here all night. Waiting and not knowing."

"Agreed. Which is why it's good to know people."

He watched as Sam pulled her phone out of her purse and scrolled through her contact list as if deciding which one was best. She tapped, and then a few seconds later, she was talking. "Jocelyn, yes, it's Sam. It went well with Reuben, yes. No, I don't know when you're losing your star player, but listen. I called because I need a favor. You used to be a billionaire…any chance you know someone with a private jet? Evan needs to get back to Minotaur Falls tonight. It's Connor. He's in the hospital."

Evan wanted to put his head down in her lap and weep, he was so grateful. He wouldn't have even considered such an option. A private jet. Yes, that was exactly what he needed.

"Right. Thanks."

Sam disconnected the phone. "She's going to make some calls, and, if that doesn't pan out, I have a few former clients who'll come through for me. They might not let me represent them anymore, but they wouldn't say no to a favor. We'll get you back there tonight. I promise."

Evan nodded. "This is crazy. This is flipping crazy. Two days ago I don't even know this kid existed, and now… I can't think straight."

"Stop worrying about how you're feeling,

just go with it. We'll go to the hotel, pack up our things and check out. Jocelyn will have hopefully gotten back to me by then."

Evan took her hand again. His fingers through hers, squeezing tight. "This is not what I wanted for us tonight, Sam."

"I know." She smiled. "Clearly you think I'm the type of girl who puts out on the first date."

He could kiss her for that, but his mouth was bone dry from fear. "Admit it. You were going to say yes."

"I admit nothing," she said coolly.

But she let him hold her hand the entire drive back to the hotel.

When Jocelyn found them a private jet and pilot who would take them to Minotaur Falls within the hour, she let him hold her hand through the entire fifty-minute flight, too.

He was pretty sure if she hadn't, he might have shaken apart.

CHAPTER ELEVEN

"I'M GOING TO get another cup of coffee," Evan announced.

They were all in the waiting room. Evan's father had picked up Sam and Evan from the private airport about forty minutes away from the hospital. Sam was still in her yellow dress, Evan in his suit, although he'd taken off his jacket.

Kelly hadn't said much when they arrived. Only that Connor was in with the doctors and a nurse had come out once to report they had put him on a ventilator to stabilize his oxygen intake. Once they felt his lungs were strong enough to breath on their own, they would remove it, she told them. It was only a temporary measure.

Kelly knew this from the last time he'd been in the hospital, apparently.

"I'll go with you," Nelson said, standing up. "I need to do something."

"Sam and Kelly, can we bring you back something?"

Kelly nodded slowly. "Coffee, please. Yes, that would be...very nice."

"I'm good," Sam told them.

As they walked away, Kelly fell back into the chair, her head against the wall. "Wow, I've never had this before."

"What?" Sam asked.

"Support. Every time this has happened before, it was always just me and Connor. Him in there doing his part to breathe, and me out here wondering if this time was going to be it. If this was going to be the time I lost him."

Sam reached for the woman's arm and squeezed. "You can't think like that. He's in good hands. It's a small hospital, but it's got an excellent reputation."

Kelly lifted her head as if trying to marshal some inner strength. "I know, but it's how I think. I tell myself to expect the worst. Then if it happens I might be prepared. Which is ridiculous, of course. If the worst happened, I would completely lose my shit. Connor is my life."

"It's not going to happen," Sam said adamantly. "And we're here now, so you don't lose your shit."

Kelly looked at Sam. "Evan doesn't even know him. Not really. Yet you two got a private plane out of Boston to be here. Times like these I really do call myself a fool for breaking up with him."

Sam bit her lip, but in the end she couldn't help herself. "So why did you? I mean, Evan told me you wanted him to try and play football…but I just can't imagine…"

"That I was that shallow?" Kelly asked with a small huff of a laugh. "I was twenty-two and stupid. Maybe I was that shallow, too, but it wasn't just about the money. Evan was too big not to be a star. Seriously, look at him now." She hesitated. "That wasn't the only reason I knew it wouldn't work between us. Evan was…is…brighter than anyone else in the room. You know what I mean? He's this legitimately good guy, and there were times I felt like I wasn't…enough. In the end, I resented him…all that goodness. Which now I can see was just stupid and immature. I should have been wallowing in it. I should have been honored that he wanted to be with me. Instead I threw it all away."

Sam wanted to say that, yes, Kelly was

stupid. But if the woman hadn't thrown away her relationship with Evan, he'd have been married with a child the first time she'd met him.

If Kelly was telling the truth.

"I know you refused the paternity test. I even understand your reasons. But you have to see now, more than ever, how important this is for Evan. He has to know if Connor is his son. If for no other reason than to know if he should be here with you. If he should be at Connor's side. You can't play this game with a man like him. I saw his face when his father called him with the news. He's already genuinely invested in this boy."

"Then why does he need a paternity test?" Kelly said tiredly.

"He's not just going to hand over money, Kelly. He's going to want a relationship with Connor, as well. You have to know that."

Kelly let her head fall into her hands, and Sam could see the exhaustion in her body. They'd been up all night, but Kelly had the extra burden of being the child's mother, with all the fear and anxiety that came with it.

"Maybe that's not such a bad thing, huh? Maybe Connor could use a good man in his life, and maybe…well…maybe I could use someone else out there who will worry about my son like I do. Who will be here with me the next time this happens."

"Kelly, if you let Connor take that test and prove he's Evan's son, you'll have an ally for life, and Connor will have an amazing father."

"Not something you would be real keen about, would you?"

Sam blinked. "I don't know what you mean. I'm trying to help you."

Kelly let out a harsh laugh. "Right. You can tell me you're his agent and only his agent all you want. I see the way he looks at you. The way you look at him when you think he can't see you. There's way more going on between you two than you're admitting to."

Sam wasn't going to acknowledge anything. Certainly not to Kelly. "How does this have anything to do with Connor?"

"I'm just saying that, if I do let Evan into Connor's life, I come with it. Not a lot of new girlfriends would like knowing their boyfriend has a responsibility to another woman and her child. Let's face it, you would love to see me go away."

Sam considered where Kelly was going with that line of logic.

"Interesting. You think I want you to take the test, so I can prove Connor isn't Evan's son, which will mean Evan comes with less baggage. One, you don't know me very well. I would never consider a little boy baggage. In fact, nothing would make me happier. And two, it means you think I believe the test will be negative. Why is that?"

"Isn't it the truth?" Kelly charged. "Don't you all think I'm lying? You and Evan's dad. Evan, too, probably. He's just too nice to come out and say it. All of you are judging me for either what I'm doing now, or the decisions I made back then. But none of you understand… How do you feel right now?"

"What do you mean?"

"Sitting in this waiting room. Here in this hospital. Knowing there's a little boy with a bunch of strangers standing over him while he struggles to breathe. How do you feel?"

She knew how she felt. Knew the fear Evan felt. She truly couldn't imagine what Kelly must be going through. If that were Sam's son, her little boy going through all this, she would be beside herself.

"It's awful," Sam whispered.

"This is your first time," Kelly said flatly. "This is my eleventh time in five years. You'll excuse me if I don't care much about what you think."

Sam nodded. "Kelly, I get that. I really do. Maybe you'll say I couldn't possibly know what you're going through because I'm not a mother. That's a fact, too, but I recently lost someone I loved dearly to a sickness I couldn't do anything about. I think if I could have done something, if there had been some path to saving him, then I might have done anything to make that happen, too. Anything."

Kelly said nothing.

"However, here's the thing. If you go down this path with Evan and Connor, and it's not true, consider the damage you would be doing to both Evan and your son. What if they do form a relationship, a bond? Then down the road the truth is revealed. The secret you hoped to keep forever is suddenly out there. For both of their sakes, tell the truth now. Only you know what that is."

Kelly's face hardened. She turned to Sam and practically spat the words, "Connor is Evan's son."

"Then you're a very lucky woman."

Sam stood and walked away. She wasn't helping Kelly, and right now the woman didn't need any extra pressure on her. Whether she was telling the truth or not, it didn't matter. The woman was in a world of pain, and Sam planned to respect that.

In the end there was no change. The treatments they were trying weren't as effective as they had been previously, and the doctors felt that, to be safe, they would keep Connor on the ventilator and in ICU for the next few days.

They were all running on fumes, so it was decided they could do nothing more than go home and get some sleep. Kelly included. Having been through this before, she knew she needed solid sleep to have the energy for the long haul. She refused the offer of a ride and instead called a cab.

Evan and Sam got into Nelson's car to drive back to the airport to get Evan's truck.

"Look, son…"

"Dad, seriously, I don't want to hear it. I know what you think of Kelly, but I can't change who I am. I need to be there for that kid. Whether he's mine or not."

Nelson met Sam's eyes in the rearview

mirror. They were both thinking the same thing. That Evan had already taken an emotional step forward.

If Kelly was lying, it would cost him dearly.

"No, I'm done lecturing. In fact, I think it might be best if I go home. You don't need the additional stress of me telling you what I already have. And truth is I don't know if I can stand by you and keep my mouth shut. That's who I am."

Sam didn't say anything, but she worried about what losing Nelson's opinion on the matter might mean for Evan. Especially now when Evan was only thinking with his heart.

"But you're going to have his back," Nelson added. "Right, Sam?"

"Of course," she promised him. "He's my number one client."

Nelson nodded, and again their eyes met in the rearview mirror in an unspoken agreement. Nelson didn't want to alienate his son by harping on the facts. That was Sam's job now. Sam gave him a small nod to acknowledge what he was trusting her with.

Once they got to the airport, Sam chose to stay with Evan. As tired as he was, it would be easier for him to make the drive back to Minotaur Falls with company.

A full hour later he was pulling up to her house.

"You didn't have to go to the hospital with me," he said.

"I know."

"You didn't have to make this drive with me, either."

Sam nodded. "I know that, too."

"Not something an agent does for her client, I would think."

Sam took a deep breath. "No. I've certainly never done it before for anyone. But I didn't do it because I'm your agent."

"I'm wooing you," Evan said with a sad smile. "And it's working. I can tell."

Sam smiled, too. "Come inside, Evan. I'm going to put you to bed."

Evan's eyes grew wide. "Darling, that sounds like the best offer I've had in years, but right now I'm so tired I doubt I could make your world shake, let alone tremble. I'm not taking a chance on messing this up out of the gate."

Sam rolled her eyes. "I said putting you to bed, not taking you to bed. You don't need to do any more driving. You're dead on your feet as it is."

"Will you sleep with me?"

Sam sucked in her breath. She knew he didn't mean sex. They were both too tired and too emotionally drained for sex. What he was asking for, in many ways, was much more intimate.

Sam hadn't slept with someone in a very long time.

"I know it's crazy, and I know I don't have any right to ask. I just… I just don't want to be alone. We'll call it a nap. There's nothing wrong in taking a nap together, is there?"

There was everything wrong with it if she didn't want to move beyond a professional relationship. Although she had pretty much compromised that when she'd agreed that their dinner out last night was a date. Yes, Sam was pretty sure she was beyond that now. She was in a personal relationship with Evan.

The worst had already happened. Their relationship was no longer purely professional.

She was tired, too, and if she could do anything to give him some semblance of comfort when he needed it, then wasn't that what a woman he was personally involved with would do?

"Okay. We can take a nap."

His look of profound relief wasn't lost on her. Together they got out of the car and made their way inside. Once upstairs they took off their shoes. Sam found a pair of yoga pants and a tank top that she changed into to be more comfortable.

Evan was looking down at his suit pants.

"You really want to take those off, don't you?" Sam said with a little smile.

He looked sheepish. "I really do. But I seriously am not trying to mess with you."

"Boxers or briefs?"

"Boxer briefs. And a T-shirt under this shirt."

Sam nodded, and within seconds he was wearing exactly what he had described. "Now for napping, there are firm rules," Sam outlined. "We use only the top quilt. No getting under the covers."

"I can do that," Evan said as he stretched out on the bed. "How many pillows do you have? There are like a hundred on this bed."

Sam watched him clear out a few while she did the same. "You can never have enough pillows. Beyond being pretty, they can be used for snuggling, and snuggling is also something you can never have enough of."

"Is there a rule against snuggling while napping?" Evan asked.

"I don't know if we're ready to take the next step into snuggling. I think we should just stick to sleeping."

Sam joined him, tossing the quilt that had been folded up at the end of the bed over them. She checked the clock and saw it was nearing eleven in the morning. "What time is your game tonight?"

"Seven-oh-five. Normally, I like to get there around four-thirty, get something to eat before I change and warm up. I think pushing it to five today will be fine."

Sam nodded and reached for the alarm clock on the nightstand. "Not that I think we'll sleep that long, but I'll set the alarm for three. That should give you enough time to get back to your place and then to the stadium."

Evan sighed and put an arm over his head. "How the hell am I supposed to think about baseball when that little kid is still in the hospital?"

"I don't know," Sam said gently. "I just

know you have no control over what happens to that little boy. So maybe putting him out of your mind for a while will help. Yes, baseball is a game, but it's your work, too. Focus on that."

They settled on their backs, which Sam knew wouldn't work for her, but she just needed to wait until Evan was asleep, and then she could find a more comfortable position.

Then Evan turned on his side toward her, and for some reason she felt compelled to turn toward him, as well. They both had their hands tucked under their cheeks. It's how Sam slept best.

"When you found out Bob was your dad, your biological father, how did you feel?"

Sam sighed softly. "Oh, Evan, it's not the same thing."

"I know… I just…how did you feel?"

Sam thought about that day. It had been the summer before starting college. Sam had worked at a local diner, afternoon shifts. Normally she walked home, but that day Alice had come around to pick her up. They went to a park that was just outside of town, her mother only telling her ominously, *We need to talk.*

Sam had been convinced her mother was going to tell her she and Duff were getting a divorce. Sam could see that writing on the wall. It hadn't just been all the arguments; it was the lack of synchronicity. They weren't clicking together as a couple should. While they were good to keep their fights out of earshot of Lane and Scout, Sam could feel the tension anytime she was around them.

It had gotten especially bad that summer.

Instead, though, her mother had told her the story of an old boyfriend named Bob Sullivan. How they had been together before she met Duff. How much they had been in love. Why they had separated. When they had separated. That's when she said it.

"I didn't know at the time I was pregnant."

It had taken a few minutes for it to sink in, and her first thought had been to ask about what happened to the baby. Until she did the math in her head and realized she was that baby.

"I was stunned," Sam told Evan, reliving those first moments. "Maybe even a little angry. I mean, as much as I would never admit that Duff wasn't my father, my true father, there was definitely something broken in that moment. Like she'd taken something away from me. A piece of my father, my sisters. I was no longer like them. Fully connected to each other through the same blood. It was jarring."

"And Bob? Were you angry he'd abandoned you and your mom?"

"I don't know that it was his fault. He didn't know she was pregnant, either. Knowing the kind of man he is, I'm sure he would have married her immediately if he had known. He was just being a stubborn jackass in thinking by breaking up with her he was saving her pain in case anything happened to him on his mission. Stupid, when you think about it. As if just by that act of breaking up it would prevent her from suffering if he had gotten hurt or worse. Because of that, he missed out on what he really wanted. For eighteen years."

"But you got Duff."

"Right. I got Duff. How lucky was I, really? Because here's the thing, Evan. While it did feel like my mom had taken a piece of something away from me, I realized when I met Bob, I was getting this whole other piece instead. Bob is amazing. We've become very close."

"I can't imagine Connor being anything but angry with me when we decide to tell him. A kid wants a dad, and he didn't have one for seven years."

"That's on Kelly. She could have given that to her son. She chose not to."

"You think he'll understand that? He's a kid. He'll know he wanted me, but I wasn't there. I hate that. I hate knowing that his first emotions toward me are going to be anger."

Sam wished she could tell him that wouldn't be the case. She also wished she could tell him that conversation couldn't be had until there was written proof this boy was his son. The consequences of not having that, in Sam's opinion, were too severe if Kelly wasn't telling the truth.

"Don't worry about that now. Just sleep. That's what you came here to do."

His eyes drifted shut, and watching felt so intimate. Here he was at his most vulnerable as he gave himself up to exhaustion, and Sam had a front-row seat. She wanted to reach out and run her hand along his cheek and his chin. Over his lips. Down his nose. Memorizing the sight of Evan Tanner in her bed sleeping next to her.

Of course she didn't. That was another

Because now it felt like everything had changed. He no longer felt like who he'd been yesterday: a single, unattached man interested in a woman he wanted to sleep with.

Today he was possibly a father. A father of a sick child.

Suddenly it all came back to him. Why he was asleep in the middle of the day, why Sam was in his arms. Why they had left Boston and their date to come back to Minotaur Falls.

Connor was sick. Whether he was Evan's son or not, he felt a connection. A responsibility for the boy.

Any hope of starting a relationship was pretty hopeless. None of this was fair to Sam. His burden didn't also need to be hers.

But he was hard, and the thought of kissing Sam's neck and having her roll toward him and sinking himself deep inside her was making it more difficult to think about the reasons why he shouldn't be doing just that.

He needed to get out of bed. Get away from her.

He needed to put his mouth just right there under her earlobe where her hair had fallen away and the skin looked so soft. He could only see that spot because she was lying in his arms.

One kiss. Just that spot. He was going to get out of the bed after that.

Promising himself he could be that disciplined, he leaned down toward her. A soft kiss on her neck. The press of his lips against her skin. The sleepy scent of her filling all his senses. It felt decadent.

She shifted, and he felt somewhat guilty for waking her up. Although the reality was the alarm was probably about to go off. Then she did what he'd fantasized about. Just rolled to him like they were two people who got up together on a regular basis. Like this was their leisurely Saturday morning ritual.

She made a humming sound in the back of her throat. Then when she opened her eyes and looked into his, he could tell the moment she realized where she was. Who she was with.

She didn't push him away. She didn't pull away, either. They just looked at each other as if waiting for the other to decide what happened next. Then she did it. She tilted her head up and wiggled her body ever so slightly, so they were at an even level. She bent her head, leaning in toward him…

"No," Evan said, mustering the last vestiges of the discipline he told himself he had. Knowing he was on pretty shaky ground he immediately rolled out of bed and then winced when he glanced down at himself, the level of his desire clearly outlined in the boxer briefs he wore.

"No?"

"No," he said again. "I want you. It's obvious I want you. But now, with Connor… I don't want to start something with you, when I don't know if I can be fully committed to making this work."

Sam sat up on her elbows, one eyebrow raised as she gave his still throbbing erection a quick glance.

"Oh, I'm pretty sure it works."

"I don't mean that."

Her smiled faded. "I know. But maybe it could be just sex…for now. Why does it have to be more?"

It figured. Any other time a guy might jump at the chance of a sex-with-no-strings-attached relationship. Except the one woman to offer it to him was the one woman he wanted lots of strings with.

All the strings.

"Lady, are you sitting in that bed, scantily clad—"

"Scantily clad? I'm in a tank top and yoga pants. Also, did you just time-warp back a hundred years?"

"Scantily clad enough and tell me you just want sex and that's all."

Sam fell back on the bed and pulled the cover over her head. She squeaked out a mouse-like yes. Then the cover came off her face. "Is that wrong?"

"Not wrong in the sense of knowing what you want and asking for it."

"Good. Because I'm not ashamed of that."

"And you shouldn't be," Evan said, deciding it was safe now to sit on the bed and reach for her hand without fear he'd fall victim to her sex-only plan. "It's not wrong to want sex, Sam. It sure as hell isn't wrong to want sex with me. I want more than that with you."

"Even though we both know that makes no sense right now. Really, for either of us."

Evan hated logic. But he knew what he wanted. "I don't want us to do this lightly."

"I don't think there would be anything light about it," Sam said. But then she pulled her hand from his and rolled off the other side of the bed.

Evan stood and looked at her, and he wanted her all over again. Her messy hair, her trim little body. Her eyes, which were the opposite of cold right now.

"I…" He didn't know what to say. He didn't know how to say it. He only knew how he felt. "Just don't leave me, okay? Give me time to sort this out somehow."

He waited for her to say of course she wouldn't leave him, because, after all, she was his agent. It would have been so like her to put that wall back up between them. Especially given he'd rejected her offer of sex.

Had he really done that? Had he actually decided not having sex with her made more sense right now? Because his body sure as hell didn't agree.

"Okay."

That one simple word gave him all the hope he needed.

"Sam, you have to know I think I'm falling—"

The alarm clock went off, and the two of them jumped.

The moment was broken, and somehow Evan knew she wasn't even close to hearing the truth. Apparently they needed to wait for that, too.

Sam smiled at him a little sadly. "Time to play ball."

Time to play ball, indeed.

Two weeks later.

"SAM, WHAT'S HAPPENING to my boy?"

"He's not your boy yet, Reuben. We're still negotiating, remember?" Sam held her cell to ear and watched as Evan swung and missed. Another strikeout. That was not going to help his batting average. She sat high up in the stands with no one around her. It was a Monday evening game, and while the place seemed slightly more crowded than average, there were pockets of empty seats around the stadium. A perfect summer night as twilight was falling. It was a night for baseball.

"He keeps playing like he is, and those negotiations might come to an outright stop."

"It's a slump, Reuben. Baseball players have them. In the next few weeks he'll bat his way out of it."

"You better hope so. I find out a player lets real life get in the way of his game, that's going to impact what I'm willing to pay for that player. News flash, tough shit in life happens all the time."

Sam winced. Reuben wasn't wrong. Despite the fact that baseball was just a game, there was an expectation real life shouldn't ever interfere with it. Heck, players only got three days off if they wanted to be there for the birth of their child, and some managers frowned on that. They would like all players to plan births of their offspring for the off-season.

"It's two weeks. It's a slump. He'll come out of it. When he does, you're going to be reminded you have the opportunity to have on your roster for an extended period of time one of the best hitters in the game right now."

"I hope so, Sam. I truly hope so. I'll be in touch."

Sam disconnected the call and stared at her phone. "He'll come out of it," she muttered.

He had to.

Connor had been sent home after two days in the hospital only to suffer another attack six days after that. That put him back in the hospital again, and now the doctors were reluctant to release him until they could assure themselves he was stable. When Evan wasn't on the field playing baseball, he'd been by Connor's side in the hospital. Sleeping only when he absolutely had to, which of course meant minimally.

No wonder his game was taking a hit. Forget the mental distraction, the physical toll was clearly showing on the field.

She needed to talk to him, but what could she say?

Evan, it's possible you're destroying your chances for the majors by worrying about a sick boy who may or may not be your son. Oh, and I'm not saying this because I may or may not have feelings for you. Feelings you've decided we can't move forward with because of your situation. Because that might make me a heartless bitch, which I am not. I'm just worried for you.

Sam ran back those words in her head and grimaced.

She needed to talk to Kelly again. She needed the woman to agree to the paternity test. It wasn't right keeping them in this limbo with Evan's concern for the boy growing every day. Not to mention if the distraction of Connor ended up costing Evan his big contract, then Kelly's plan to use his money to get Connor the best doctor was moot.

Her phone rang in her hand, and she considered turning it off, not really in the mood right now. But when she saw Scout's name pop up, she suddenly had this need to talk to someone who would understand.

"Scout, hi."

"What's happening to Evan's batting average?"

"It's falling," Sam said as if Scout didn't already know that.

"Are you two sleeping together?"

"What! Where the hell is that coming from?" She hadn't said a word to her family about her feelings for Evan. She barely wanted to acknowledge them herself. However, Scout had suspected an interest on Sam's part when she first met Evan.

"I don't know. I always thought you were more the Kim Basinger type rather than the Glenn Close type. Beautiful, but cool— where Glenn was homey and warm. Me, I stand up in a crowd of fans, my guy is taking the cover off the ball. You… I worry he starts to swing and miss."

Sam closed her eyes and summoned her patience. To understand Scout, one had to recognize that her mind revolved around baseball at all times. That included anything related to baseball, which meant baseball movies. *The Natural* seemed to be a perfect fit for Evan. So of course, Scout had cast Sam as the slightly evil girlfriend.

"This is not a movie," Sam said between gritted teeth. "This is my life. And, no, we're not sleeping with each other."

Yet.

"Okay. It's not you causing his slump. That's a good start. Then what's happening? They won't call him up if he's slumping. It's going to be hard enough to face major league pitching as it is. They won't want his confidence shaken."

"You must have heard the stories. It would have made the MLB Channel, which, let's face it, is the only TV you watch."

"I also like *The Bachelor*. I don't know why. All those catty women, so much fun. It's the kid, then?"

"It's the sick kid," Sam said, her heart breaking for both Kelly and Connor. None of this should be happening to a little boy. "He's got asthma really bad. He's in the hospital now after a second attack. Evan's with him as much as he can be. Obviously, it's impacting his routine, and you know how players are with their routine."

"OCD, the lot of them. You should see Jayson load a dishwasher. I've never seen anything like it."

"Yeah, well, it's definitely messing with Evan's head, and the worst part, the really horrible part, is that he might not even be his son. It's very possible Kelly is lying."

Although even that made Sam cringe. The boy was sick. Having Evan there had given him a bright spot in his day. She couldn't fault Evan for wanting to do what he could to make a sick child's day better, son or not.

"The mother won't agree to the paternity test?"

"No. She's afraid Evan might use that against her for visitation or custody. She wants the money and nothing else. That's ridiculous, of course, because she knows Evan and knows he would never walk away from his responsibility like that. Evan isn't like any other man I've ever met. Beyond kind and caring and being completely sweet with this little boy. He's always going to be there, no matter what."

There was a pause on the other end of

the line. "Are you sure you're not sleeping with him?"

"Scout! I said I wasn't."

"But you want to."

Sam winced. Sisters. Sometimes they could be so annoying. Scout more than most. Lane, at least, would have kept her suspicions to herself, recognizing this was a private matter. Lane would have used subtlety and tact.

Two words Scout wasn't familiar with.

"Why do you think that?" Sam asked, wanting to know exactly what gave her away, so she could control it going forward.

"There's something in your voice when you talk about him. Or maybe it's the absence of something."

"What?"

"Cynicism," Scout said plainly. "When you talk about Evan, there's hope and sincerity and faith in your voice. You believe in him."

She did. She couldn't believe it herself, but she did.

"He doesn't want me," Sam said sadly.

That wasn't really fair.

"I mean, he doesn't want to get involved right now. He's got too much going on."

"Too much going on for sex? Wow, that is weird for a guy."

"He doesn't want it only to be about sex. He wants more from me."

"And that's scaring you shitless," Scout concluded.

"Nice mouth, sis." Except it was true. All of it. Sam had just gotten her mind wrapped around the idea that she could sleep with the man, despite the fact he was a client. Except Evan wanted more.

Believing in him was one thing. Acting on that belief and trusting herself to him was something totally different. She didn't think she was ready for that. Which made her angry with herself for not being able to move on with her life, but she had to face her reality.

Evan wanting more scared her and conversely thrilled her.

"Don't overthink this, Sam. You need this guy to restore your faith in men."

"I don't know what to do." She sighed.

"Well," Scout told her, "I suggest you stand up the next time he comes to the plate. If he hits one out of the park, you'll know that's for you. It will be the baseball gods telling you it's meant to be."

"You're ridiculous," Sam said.

"Okay, then if you want to take the non-movie approach...seduce him."

"What?"

"He's a guy. And he might be a guy trying to do the right thing by you right now, but ultimately he's still a guy. If you're right and he wants you, he's not going to be able to resist you for long. Seduce him."

Sam mulled that over. Did she even have that in her? The ability to seduce a man out of his good sense? "How?"

"Are you kidding me?" Scout snorted. "Get naked. They are helpless against breasts."

"You're saying just show up at his place naked?"

"No, show up at his place with a trench coat on. It's Minotaur Falls, for heaven's sake. You don't want to shock people. Then when he lets you in the house, you take the coat off. Trust me. He won't be able to resist you, and then at least you can see if he's everything you think he is. Let's face it, Sam. You wanted him two years ago when you met him. You just weren't ready back then. You miss your chance now, and it might not come back around."

Sam couldn't argue with Scout's logic.

Yes, Evan wanted her. Wanted her beyond just being a sex buddy, but if things dragged out with him and Kelly and Connor, then what they had might fizzle out. Drowned underneath real life and hard choices.

"I'll think about it."

"Okay. Oh and, hey, why I called—"

"I thought you called about Evan's batting average."

"Well, that was important but not as important as this. I'm knocked up. For real. Preggers!"

A swell of joy caught Sam off guard, and she could feel tears well up. Although she knew better than to even sniffle while she was on the phone with Scout.

Not after the last time Scout made her cry.

"Oh, Scout. I'm so happy for you."

"Yeah, Jayson and I are excited. We're hoping for a girl who can pitch like Mo'ne Davis and ends up becoming the first female major leaguer ever. Wouldn't that be awesome?"

Sam smiled. She knew of Mo'ne Davis from her success during the Little League World Series tournament. A girl with a rocket for an arm who went toe to toe with any boy her age.

"I'm going to hope for a healthy boy or girl."

"Oh, sure. That, too. But Jayson and I are going to start explaining things while the kid is baking. You know, easy stuff to start, like when a batter should hit and run."

A thought occurred to Sam. "Does this mean you're not going to make it to the unveiling? Pregnant women aren't supposed to fly."

"Only after seven months," Scout assured her. "I checked. Besides, I wouldn't miss this for the world. We're talking Duff here. Even if it meant Jayson and I had to drive from California, we'll be there."

"Okay. Well, then, I guess I'll see you soon. Give Jayson my love and tell him how happy I am for both of you."

"Will do. And, Sam, you do what's best for you, too. I mean that."

"I know you do."

Sam disconnected the call and imagined holding a little baby in her arms. For so many years she'd never had these kind of thoughts. Never felt the pangs other women did at her age to want a baby before the biological clock alarm went off.

Except now, suddenly, she was feeling it

all the time. Pangs. Little baby pangs. Or maybe family pangs. She thought it was because she was starting to realize there was never going to be a man in her life to make a baby with, so maybe she should do it by herself.

Now there was a man who wanted more with her.

How much more?

The thought of Evan holding a little baby girl…her baby girl…

"You're being sentimental," she whispered to herself.

Shaking off those thoughts she turned her attention back to the game. During her conversation with Scout, she hadn't realized the Minotaurs were lighting the opposing pitcher up. They had batted a round, and Evan was up again. He swung at the first pitch and missed. She could see it in him, too. A sense he wasn't comfortable in the box.

As foolish as it was, Sam found herself standing up. There was no one behind her. No one to wonder what she was doing. She was simply a woman in the stands. Nothing else. Just standing still and watching him.

Believing in him.

The next pitch was a dipping curve ball. Another swing. Another miss.

"Come on, Evan, give me a sign."

Third pitch, high heat. She heard the familiar sound, and she smiled as he knocked it out of the park.

Sam smiled. "Suck it, Scout. I knew I was Glenn Close."

CHAPTER THIRTEEN

KELLY LOOKED OVER at the bed next to her in the motel room. It was a Saturday, mid-morning. Connor had been out of the hospital now for a few days, his breathing much more relaxed and steady. He should have been outside playing. Maybe with friends. Maybe just riding his bike. Instead, he was quietly reading his book. Kelly wondered if he felt the fear she did. The fear that any strenuous activity might bring on another attack. Something they both didn't want.

She hated that idea. Hated that her baby lived in fear.

"How's the book?"

Connor shrugged his shoulders. "It's okay."

"Maybe we can go to the library in town. Get you a card and you can find something you like better."

Another shrug.

Kelly tried to think of something. Anything that might pique his interest, but after these last two attacks he seemed...defeated. As if he was finally coming to accept that this was going to be his life. In and out of hospitals, sometimes on the very precipice of death. Doctors, nurses, machines surrounding him...

It broke her heart.

"Mom, how long do we have to stay here? I want to go home."

Kelly studied him. Home was an apartment in Tucson. Not much bigger than the room they were staying in now. Still, he did have his own room there, even if it was the size of a closet. His own things.

She didn't know what to tell him. Leaving without something wasn't an option. She had risked everything, done too much to turn back now. Eventually Evan would get his contract, and then, once he knew how much money he was going to get, he would have to commit some of it to her and Connor.

She probably needed a lawyer to create some official-sounding document Evan needed to sign. Not that she could afford one. However, if lawyers got involved—even if they were representing her—they would probably require a paternity test.

That was not going to happen.

Kelly needed to count on Evan to do the right thing. He would. He was that kind of a guy. But would he do that if they were out of sight and out of mind?

It would be much easier for him to deny the existence of Connor if he wasn't seeing him nearly every day. Not to mention seeing his condition, firsthand. Evan sat with Connor in the hospital anytime he could. He saw how hard it was for Connor to breathe. It made an impact on Evan.

Kelly wasn't blind to that, to the emotional pain Evan experienced. The more he got to know Connor, the stronger the bond became, the better.

No, she couldn't leave town. Not until things were more certain.

The knock on the door startled her. The cleaning people only came every other day, and this was an off day.

Kelly got up, opened the door and wasn't surprised to see Evan. They hadn't seen him since Connor got out of the hospital a few days ago, so no doubt he wanted to check in. Since he believed Connor was his responsibility now.

Kelly waved a hand. "Hey."

Evan nodded, then looked behind her. "Hey, buddy, how you feeling?"

"Fine."

Fine was Connor's answer all the time these days. Whether he was having a good day or a bad day, he was always fine. At least Kelly knew today was a good day. As long as he wasn't out running around and playing but lying quietly in his bed and reading a book. Yes, today he was fine.

"Good to hear it. You up for another baseball game soon?"

Connor sat up on the bed as if to prove he truly was fine. "Sure, anytime."

"Okay, let me see what I can do—if your mom thinks it's okay."

"I'm fine," Connor said again, only this time there was a slight wheezing in his breath.

"Can I talk to you?" Evan asked her. "Outside."

"Be right back, baby,"

Kelly nodded and shut the door behind her so that they stood outside on the patio that made up the courtyard of the motel.

Evan paced in front of her, running his hand through his hair, which let her know he really didn't like what he was about to say. It had been seven years, but she still remembered what the hand in his hair meant. He was agitated.

"We can't keep going on like this," he finally managed to say.

"What do you mean?" Kelly hedged.

"This. This! What you're doing. I mean, what is your plan? You and Connor stay in this crappy motel until what? I give you a check. I mean, how much do you want? Is a hundred thousand going to be enough? A million? You understand I have no control over what I'm getting. No, that's not true. I have some control. By playing well I have control, except that isn't happening right now, because I can't stay focused on the game."

"Oh, I'm sorry," Kelly said, folding her arms over her chest. "Is my sick son making it difficult for you to play baseball?"

"Don't pull that with me, Kelly. You are only in this for money, and playing baseball is how I make money. The worse I play, the less I make. Trust me, at my age I only have one shot at a solid contract. I lose that, and you don't get anything you want."

Kelly considered how accurate that was. She hadn't considered what the distraction might do to his game. He was right. To get the most out of him, she needed him to be playing his best baseball, not his worst, especially right before a contract signing.

"What I'm telling you is that I don't have a hundred grand just sitting in the bank I can hand over to you. So, what do you want?"

Kelly pulled on her bottom lip and thought about it. The truth was she really didn't know how much money was going to be enough. She knew the doctor, but not what he charged. She'd tried to find out that information, but the bureaucracy of getting the help her son needed was almost as frustrating as not having the money to pay for it.

Until she could get the big-league doctor to take their case seriously and meet with her, she also had no way of knowing how long Connor might need treatment, or what that treatment entailed.

There was no number she could give Evan. Instead she said, "I want a guarantee."

"Really." Evan laughed harshly. "I would like that, too. A guarantee he's my son."

She shook her head. There was a moment when she considered what it might mean for Connor to have a real father in his life, but she quickly dismissed it. Connor was hers. Only hers.

"Not going to happen. I know you. You'll be all in with him, and that's not what I want. I'm not looking for a father for him only…"

"Money. I get it. Have you considered why that is? Why you don't want to give him a father if he actually has one?"

"Connor is mine," Kelly said tightly. "He always has been, and he always will be."

"Then, what do you want?" Evan asked her again, clearly exasperated.

"You get your contract, then we'll agree on a settlement."

Evan sighed. "I don't know when that's going to be. What are you going to do in the meantime? Hang out here in this dumpy motel?"

"I can't really afford the Plaza," she snapped.

Evan shook his head. "It's not right. For him to be shut up here while we all just wait and see… I can't believe I'm saying this… my dad would go nuts. But it's the right thing to do. You should move in with me."

Kelly could feel her jaw actually drop. "What?"

"I'm renting a house. It has three bedrooms. A backyard with a swing set. At least I won't be worried about him staying in this place. I'll be able to see him every day, so I'm not screwing with my normal routine. Plus, you'll have space to move around. A kitchen where you can cook instead of feeding him crap all the time."

"Crap?" Kelly charged. "I feed him what I can afford. Besides, where do you get off telling me how to raise my son?"

"I'm sorry. I didn't mean… Look, I'm giving you an option. Free room and board until we sort this out."

Kelly could feel his tension. His agitation. He wasn't doing this to normalize his routine. He was doing it for Connor.

"You're worried about him."

"He's been in the hospital. Twice! Yes, I'm worried about him. I'll be slightly less worried if I know he's in a decent place and eating something besides fast food. I've been reading about asthma, and diet can play a role in the management of—"

"I know diet can play a role!" Kelly snapped. "You've been *reading* about asthma for, what, a couple of days? A few weeks? I've been living with it since he was born. I know all there is to know, and I'm doing everything I can for my son. Including asking you for money for his care."

Evan closed his eyes. "You're right. I'm sorry. You obviously know more about this than I ever could. Come to the house. Give me that much less to worry about, and maybe I'll actually start hitting something on a more frequent basis than just one lousy home run in seven games."

Free room and board. A kitchen where she could go back to making Connor some of his favorite meals. A backyard where he could play.

She really had no choice.

Kelly nodded stiffly. She didn't know if this was a smart move or not, but it meant a better situation for Connor, and that was all that mattered.

Evan nodded, too. "Okay. Good. Go pack up your stuff. I'll check you out of here."

Kelly watched him head toward the motel manager's office.

He really was a good guy. The best guy.

And, yeah, that really sort of sucked.

SAM LOOKED AT the house from her car and told herself to drive away. Right now he didn't know she was outside. He didn't know she was wearing a belted raincoat. That all she was wearing was a belted raincoat.

Scout said she was cold. No, that wasn't a fair description. Beautiful but cool. However, definitely not hot. Then, why did she think Sam could pull this off? Because Evan was a guy, and all guys could be seduced with the right motivation?

Sam had never been the type. With Donald, he was always in control. In their relationship. In sex.

Now this was her taking the lead. Her deciding she wanted Evan for herself. Despite the fact that she really shouldn't even be considering this. That it was wrong professionally. That he had too much going on in his life. That he couldn't give her what he wanted, so he didn't want to give her anything at all.

She hadn't even seen him this past week other than to watch him play, and she realized she missed him. Missed him a lot, actually, which was what pushed her into this decision.

Take Scout's advice and seduce him.

No, there was nothing cold about this. Nothing icy about walking into a man's house practically naked. Taking a deep breath and gathering all her courage, she opened the car door and got out. She tightened the belt and looked down to double-check that the coat covered her completely to just past her knees. She'd chosen her nude Jimmy Choos stilettos.

Walking up the path to his front door, she considered what she might say. What she might do. Maybe it was best just to walk into the house and drop the coat and let him take it from there.

If he *took* it. If he didn't reject her like he had that afternoon when they woke up together.

This would be different. This time she wouldn't let him back away. He'd wanted her in Boston. Two weeks of visiting a sick boy, worrying about him, it was understandable why he didn't want to add to his load.

But Evan Tanner was the first man she'd wanted since her breakup with Donald, and the truth was she was tired of thinking this part of her life was over. Tired of being so damn frigid.

Today things were going to heat up. Significantly.

She rang the doorbell and waited. She could feel her heart pounding, and actually she was more than a little aroused. The thought of kissing him again finally, after all this time, made her dizzy with excitement.

Evan opened the door and smiled. He was happy to see her. Happy she had come.

"Hey, Sam. I've missed you this week. Come on in. I have some news."

Evan backed away to let her inside. Instinctively she tightened the belt again.

"I didn't know they were expecting rain today," he said with a smile even as he could see it was a beautiful sunny summer day just beyond the door.

This was it, Sam thought. Just do it. She reached for the belt...

...And stopped when Connor walked into the living room holding up a baseball mitt.

"Hey, Evan, is this really yours?"

Sam's heart pounded heavily in her chest, but now it was purely out of fear. She was naked under her coat, and there was a seven-year-old boy standing in front of her with a baseball glove.

This was a doomsday scenario.

"Yep. Someday soon, hopefully, that glove is going with me to the big leagues." Evan turned back to her. "Sam, take off your coat and stay a while. We were going to have lunch before heading over to the stadium later."

The *we* became obvious when Kelly walked out of the kitchen carrying two plates with sandwiches and some kind of pasta salad on them. She set them down on the dining room table.

Now Sam was standing in the room wearing nothing but a raincoat with a seven-year-old boy and Evan's ex-girlfriend.

"I'm sorry…"

She started backing away toward the door, not really knowing how to exit this scene gracefully but knowing she had to get out of the house immediately.

"I was going to tell you when I saw you. I'm having Kelly and Connor stay here while they're in town. I've got the space, and this way I think I'll be able to focus at the park."

He sounded nervous about telling her this. Maybe it occurred to him the woman he said he wanted more than just sex with wouldn't be thrilled to know he'd moved his old girlfriend and her son—potentially his son—into his house.

Sam was nowhere close to processing that information. She just knew she needed to get out of the house with some semblance of dignity intact.

"Uh…yeah…good. I'll see you later."

Sam had made it the front door, but when she reached for the door handle, Evan was behind her. He held his hand against the door to prevent her from opening it.

"Are you mad about this? Because I was going to tell you," he said in a low voice only she could here. "It's better this way. Better for Connor, better for my state of mind. You have to see that."

"Connor, put the glove down, and come eat your sandwich," Kelly called.

Connor walked over to the table.

"I really have to go," she said.

"Talk to me, Sam. You came over to see me. Have lunch with me, and then we can go outside for a while and talk." Then he actually pulled on the belt of her coat. "Take you coat off, relax—"

"I'm naked," she whispered in a rush.

His head jerked backward. "I'm sorry. What was that?"

Truly, she felt like she was in a bad episode of *Modern Family*. This simply could not be happening to her. Not to cool and sophisticated Samantha Baker. What the hell had she been thinking?

She'd listened to Scout.

Her jaw tight, she muttered again, praying Kelly wasn't trying to listen, "I'm naked. I came over… I thought…to surprise…let me go. Now."

Shock paralyzed him for a moment, and then, because he was only a man, he couldn't stop himself from looking down at the coat. "You mean under the coat? Completely…"

"Hey, so, Sam, are you staying for lunch?" Kelly asked, walking into the living room. "I can make another sandwich. There's plenty of lunch meat."

"No." Both Sam and Evan answered together.

Sam put her hand on Evan's chest and gave him a hard shove to get him off the door. She threw it open and started walking as fast as she could in her confident Jimmy Choos, which wasn't very fast because her Jimmy Choos were very high. But finally she made it to her car.

She had the keys in the ignition when Evan knocked on the window.

She couldn't face him right now. The humiliation was too devastating. It figured, the one time in her life she tried to do something like this, it would backfire. She wasn't some seductress; she was a businesswoman, for heaven's sake.

"Hey, Sam. Unlock the door."

"No! I can't talk to you right now," she told him, feeling the heat in her cheeks.

"Please."

"Stick to being a coldhearted agent," she muttered to herself. "That is what you know best. That is where you succeed."

She put her foot on the gas to let him know she was serious about not talking to him, and he backed away from the car.

As she drove away she didn't look at him. She didn't check the rearview mirror. She didn't even want to think about what he might offer as an excuse to Kelly and Connor. Although if Kelly wasn't an idiot, she might have already figured it out.

That thought brought with it a new rush of humiliation.

All she wanted to do now was get home, put on as many clothes as possible and drown herself in a gallon of cold sour water. Maybe she would have to cut him as a client. Tell Evan she no longer felt she could represent him. He might agree, given how insane her actions were.

"So much for your great comeback," she told the empty car. "Now what? Comeback again?"

No, it was fine. She would not overreact simply because she was embarrassed. Of course she could continue to be Evan's agent. She would simply only ever communicate with him by phone or email.

There. Easy. Done.

She would never have to see his face and know what a fool she'd made out of herself.

Still calling herself an idiot ten times over, she wasn't paying attention when she pulled her car up into the driveway and had to slam on the brakes to keep from hitting the truck that was already parked there.

Evan got out of the truck and walked over to her car door.

"Get out of the car, Sam."

She hit the button to roll down her window. "Wow. You drive really, really fast."

"Yes, a man will do that when he knows there's sex on the line. One last time, Sam. Get out of the car."

Maybe it was the sound of his voice or the way he was looking at her, but suddenly she didn't feel quite as embarrassed anymore. His body seemed tight and on edge, as if he was about to pounce.

"Are we going to have sex?"

"First, you're going to get out of that car. Then, I'm going to take you inside. Then, you're going to take off that coat for me, Sam. Nice and slow, too. You'll just have to see what happens after that."

Sam gulped. Then she did the scariest thing she could think of, and she got out of the car.

CHAPTER FOURTEEN

EVAN DIDN'T WAIT for Sam to get out of the car and follow him. He had already seen in her face that she'd made her decision. He turned and started walking toward the house. Climbed the few steps onto the porch and opened the outside door. He felt like he was fifteen and about to do this big thing for the first time. And he loved it.

She'd come to his house naked wearing only a coat. He knew her well enough to know that was so outside her comfort zone as to be almost comical. Almost.

Why that was the biggest turn-on for him he couldn't say, but he wasn't strong enough to fight it this time. It didn't matter that Kelly and Connor were in his life. In his house. It didn't matter that his game was still slumping and his chances of reaching his goal of getting to the majors was starting to come apart at the seams.

Sam had come to him. Naked and vulnerable.

Then she was there in her coat standing next to him by the door. She was unlocking the front door, and if he leaned down just a little he could smell her hair. Which had the faint hint of lilacs.

Once the door was opened, he followed her inside. She stopped in the living room as if she was suddenly uncertain of where to go. Of what they were going to do. He reached for her hand. Caught it. Linked her fingers in between his.

"So, what would you have done if we had been alone?"

She dipped her head but didn't try to pull her hand from his. "I don't know. I didn't know what to say or do. I only knew…"

"What?" he pressed.

"I only knew that I wanted this. That I wanted you. I didn't want to wait for someday when it might make more sense. Because none of his makes any sense."

Evan disagreed. He thought they made all the sense in the world. "I wanted you the first moment I saw you."

Sam huffed almost like she didn't believe him, but nothing was truer.

"It was here. In this house. I rang the doorbell, and you answered and you took my breath away."

"You came for Scout, if I recall."

He squeezed the hand still tucked inside his. There was no point in reminding her there had never been anything between him and Scout. She knew it. "Why did I wait almost two years to make this happen? More importantly, why did you wait, too?"

She looked at him as if he was some gigantic puzzle to solve. As if she still couldn't believe she had acknowledged wanting him. But it was more than that. More than just wanting him. She had acted on it. She had made the big, bold move for him.

Her walls, the ones that served as her guardians, her protection, he could tell they were trembling. He knew how shaky they had to be if all she wore was a raincoat. For him. All he had to do was push against them, and they would fall. For him.

He didn't need an answer. She had already told him without words what he needed to know. What was happening between them was more than just sex. It was trust. And back then, she hadn't been ready to trust anyone.

"Sam, take off the coat."

She dipped her head again, her hair falling around her face. With his other hand he brushed it off her cheek and tucked it behind her ear. There was no hiding for her. Not in this.

He let go of her hand and took a step back. A signal he was ready for the show she'd obviously planned in her mind. Evan loved the idea of her fantasizing about them. Of her thinking about how the two of them might make love. About what it would feel like to strip for him.

"What did you think about when you put that coat on?" he said as he started walking around her. Looking at her from every angle. Taking in her bare legs, her feet still in those impossibly high heels. Thinking about what was under that coat. Thinking about where he would put his hands, his mouth first.

"I..." She took a deep breath. "I don't know."

"Yes, you do," he said, taking another lap around her, loving that she was for now the center of his little universe. "You were thinking about me and what would happen once you were naked. Me touching you, kissing you? Or did you think I would be too far gone for that. That once I saw you naked, standing in front of me, I would need to be inside you. Deep. Fast."

He could see her body react. The slightest tremble as she must have imagined what that was going to feel like. He could imagine it, too.

He stopped walking. Prowling, really. Like a cat cautiously stalking a frightened bird. He almost thought he should warn her that his plan, once she was naked, was to devour her.

"Take off the coat, Sam."

Her hands went to the belt. For a minute she played with the two straps as if she was attempting to see whether or not she had the courage to do the thing she wanted to do. Then she began to pull apart the knot and Evan wanted to applaud his brave girl.

The straps fell to her sides, and the coat opened. Evan's first thought was to put his hands inside the material until he found her soft skin. To claim her with his touch. But his next thought was that he wanted the show she had promised. He wanted to see her reveal herself to him. Completely baring herself to his gaze and touch.

No ice between them. Only heat.

"We should go upstairs," she said with a slight hitch in her breath.

"No. I want you here. I want to see you with the sunlight coming through the windows. No shadows. No secrets. Finish it, Sam. Take off the coat."

It was the most feminine thing he'd ever seen. The roll of her shoulders that made the material around her lose its grip on her body. The raincoat fell to her feet, and there she was before him, naked, as she had promised.

Evan had never felt anything like this before. He was a man; he'd had what he thought was plenty of sex in his life, but this was so completely different. She was his. To have. To hold.

"Say something," she whispered, as she dipped her head again, so that she wasn't looking at him.

"Beautiful." It was the only word that came to mind. He took a step toward her and cupped her face in his hands. Lifted it so he could see her eyes, so she could see his.

"Are you going to take off your clothes now?" she asked.

He smiled at her. "Eventually."

He wouldn't tell her what it was doing to him—the idea of her naked while he was dressed. It was utterly arousing. Instead he kissed her, loving the feel of her mouth moving under his, opening to his tongue. That feeling of wanting to devour her kicked in again, and he struggled for more self-control.

She was precious and soft, and he couldn't be rough with her. He'd never been rough with any woman, but there was something about Sam that made him fierce. Like he needed to hold her tighter and closer or she might get away.

He dropped his hands down her back and pulled her to him, loving the feel of her ass in his hands. Loving the press of her body against his. He dipped lower and lifted her leg around his waist, and he heard the faintest whimper as she wrapped her arms around his shoulders to hold on.

Breaking the kiss, he dipped his head to run his mouth along her neck. Tasting the soft flesh of her ear. He bent down even lower, until he had her pebbled nipple in his mouth.

"Evan," she whispered.

The thrill of that, of hearing his name on her lips, was just another layer of arousal. He had eight million ideas in his head of what he wanted to do to her. Where he wanted to suck and taste and touch. But that whisper of his name was more than he could handle.

"I can't wait," he muttered against the spot between her breasts. "Sam, you're so freaking beautiful, and I can't wait."

"Evan."

It was as if she had no other words, and it drove him crazy. He wanted to growl and snarl. He wanted to howl like a wolf. He wanted inside her. He stood and dropped her leg.

She teetered in her shoes, but she didn't take them off, and he liked that, too. That their bodies were aligned. He moved her with his hands on her waist, walking her back to the couch.

A nice couch with two round arms on each end.

"Like this," he told her, even as he turned her around and positioned her over the couch facedown with her ass raised in the air. "Yes? Hard and deep."

She nodded. "Evan," she whimpered. "Please. I don't want to wait, either. I need you inside me."

He pulled off his shirt and dropped it and then reached for the wallet in his back pocket. His hands were shaking as he pulled out the condom, and the urgency to be inside her was like nothing he'd ever known.

There was no time to take off his shoes or his pants. Just the sound of his zipper coming down was enough to unravel him. He was lucky he still had the wherewithal to know he needed the condom.

Once it was on, he ran his hand down her back, marveling at how soft she was, how the lines of her body curved and dipped. He smoothed his hand over her ass, and he thought how all of this was different with her. Like he'd waited his whole life to experience what this was. Not his body reacting to her body, but his being reacting to her being.

He dipped his hand down lower and found the center of her, wet and lush, and this time he didn't hold back on the growl that was in his throat.

"Evan!"

Yes, he thought. Knowing what she needed. Knowing what he needed. He positioned his cock, and with one hard thrust he was deep inside her. Together they groaned. For a moment he didn't want to move. He just held her hips in his hands and stayed pressed against her as if he could fuse their bodies together indefinitely. She was so tight all around him. He felt her trying to take him deeper inside opening herself to him.

Then suddenly she was moving, pushing herself back against his hips, creating the friction she craved. It was impossible not to give her whatever she wanted. Everything she wanted. He pulled out and thrust deeper. Again and again. Until there was nothing left of him. Until his only thought was her. Was them. He didn't stop when she cried out his name, when her body convulsed around him. He didn't stop until she did it again.

Only then did he allow himself to let go, and by doing so he knew he'd been transformed into something else. Someone else. He wasn't Evan Tanner anymore.

He was Sam's.

EVENTUALLY THEY FOUND their way on to the couch itself. Evan removed his clothes, and Sam finally lost her shoes. He covered them with a throw blanket, and Sam nestled into his body like he was one large life-sized pillow. To say she was content didn't even begin to cover what she felt. Happy and scared. Thrilled and terrified.

Physically spent.

She'd never been more vulnerable in her life than when she'd taken off that coat, but because it was for Evan, that had made it okay. She hadn't realized what her lack of trust had done to her. How much it closed her off from people outside her family.

"Have there been any men since the asshole?"

The question jarred her out of her contentedness. It was another layer of exposure. Another piece of herself she had to be willing to offer up to Evan. The asshole was years ago. Many years ago. So many, he'd found and been engaged to two other women in that time. Obviously Donald didn't have a problem moving on.

"No."

"Honey," he said softly, running his hand down her back. "What did that douche bag do to you?"

"Was it that obvious... I mean the sex?" Could a man really tell that she hadn't had a lover in years? What gave it away? Was it her desperation or her lack of finesse?

"Only that you seemed rather...needy. Don't get me wrong—I thought it was hotter than hell. Am I going to get hit for saying that?"

She smiled against his chest. "There's nothing wrong with being a little needy. So I'll accept that."

"Talk to me, Sam. Tell me what power he held over you that made you lock yourself away for years. Give me a reason to go hit him, assault charges or not. I'm starting not to care."

Sam sighed. "Please, don't. I'm serious. Donald actually is a very good lawyer. I don't want the next time I sleep with you to be a conjugal visit. I don't know why I reacted the way I did. I mean, it was one bad night. But I… I just completely shut down after that. I could tell myself over and over again that he was a jerk. He slapped me across the face, I did the smart thing, ended the relationship and never looked back. End of story." Sam lifted her head off his chest and faced him directly. "I'm not totally sure why I'm risking myself being vulnerable with you, but I can't seem to help it."

"It's because I'm very charming." He smiled at her.

"You didn't want me two weeks ago. What changed?"

He shook his head. "Correction. I wanted you very much two weeks ago, but I wanted to make sure there was enough of me to offer you."

"Is there?"

He lifted his hand and ran it through his hair. "I hope so. Because there's no going back now. We're doing this, Sam. You and me. I don't care who knows it, either."

"Unfortunately, I have to care. If we continue this, we have to be discreet. No one can know."

She could feel his body tense underneath her.

"Why? We're two single people. Who cares what we do in or out of bed?"

Sam sat up on the couch, taking the blanket with her, using it to shield herself. "Evan, my professional reputation is already in shreds. Being linked romantically to my only client is not going to look right. They'll think I slept with you to get your business."

"That's horseshit."

Sam shrugged. "Sometimes it's all about perception. I have to be worried about my image. And you have to be worried about your image."

Now Evan sat up. "This is about Kelly and Connor."

"What did you tell them when you left so suddenly?"

"That it was an agent emergency."

Sam laughed, but really there was nothing funny about it. "So you've moved them into your house?"

"For now."

"Does Nelson know?"

"No. Not that I'm hiding it. I just haven't talked to him. He'll freak out, but then eventually he'll figure it out. What I'm doing... it's what's best for Connor, and I can't *not* do what's right for that kid. I just can't."

Sam nodded. Of course he couldn't. She reached out and cupped his cheek, enjoying the feel of his scruff against the inside of her palm. But she had to remember, she was his agent first. She dropped her hand.

"It's going to confirm the suspicions about Connor. You might not think anyone is watching you, but trust me when I tell you that's not the case. You're a commodity right now."

"Don't do that," Evan said sharply. "Don't start thinking like an agent on me."

"Yet I am, in fact, your agent. While I know what kind of man you are, you need to be prepared for what other people are going to think about you. You've said it yourself, that you're a deadbeat dad, who ignored the fact he had a son for seven years. A son with a serious medical condition."

His jaw tightened, and she could see that she had hurt him. It wasn't intentional. It was just the brutal truth he'd once voiced, and she was repeating it back to him.

"Where does this go, Evan?"

"What do you mean?"

"She won't get the paternity test. You won't have any answers. Now you've got him living under your roof. Have you ever considered what Connor is thinking about this? About who you really are?"

She could see that he hadn't by the confusion in his eyes.

"He knows I'm an old friend of his mother's. I don't think a kid his age is really going to leap to ideas. He'll believe what the adults in his life tell him."

"And he also knows that you and Kelly aren't really very fond of each other. You can't help it. Your suspicion is always right there on your face. A kid his age might not theorize about what's happening, but he'll pick up on the tension and know that you two aren't friends. It has to confuse him."

Evan got off the couch and started searching the floor for his clothes.

"You don't like what I'm saying," Sam said, feeling his tension as he dressed.

"No, I don't. What the hell am I supposed to do, Sam? Tell me what the answer is here. What if he's my kid?"

"What if he's not?"

Evan tugged on his jeans. "Doesn't matter. I'm giving her the money."

"What money? I haven't negotiated anything for you yet."

"Why are you doing this?" he asked angrily, even as she shrank farther down into the couch. They had been so content a few minutes ago.

"Telling you the truth?" she replied tightly.

"No, putting up those walls again. It took a hell of lot to shake them down, enough to the point where you were willing to come to my house wearing only a damn coat, and now there they are again. Right back in place. You're not Sam my lover now, you're Sam my agent. You want to be upset that my ex-girlfriend is living with me, fine. You being upset about the perception people are going to have about me because I'm a commodity… that's not cool. Not after what we shared."

She felt the blow directly. He was right. As soon as the moment was over. As soon as the real world intruded, she felt like she needed that layer of protection. Evan wasn't hers. Evan belonged to a little boy, and while she knew it was so wrong to be jealous, she couldn't help it. No, Kelly didn't bother her. Connor was the one she was worried about.

"It's why you pay me," she said coldly. Ruthlessly. It was better this way, she thought.

He barked out a humorless laugh as he stood, now fully dressed and seething with anger.

"I have feelings for you. Serious feelings. But this has to work both ways, Sam. You can't shut me out."

"I'm trying to protect you," she said, attempting to defend herself. Pretending that she wasn't wishing he would leave now. That he would be gone and she wouldn't have to think about why she couldn't just let herself be with him.

The woman, not the agent.

"No, you are not. You're trying to protect yourself. I won't have it."

She bristled at that. He couldn't just demand that she be fixed. That she not be the person she was even if that person was messed up. "What's that supposed to mean?"

"If I only get one of you… Sam the woman or Sam the agent…"

"Don't say it," she warned him, sensing what was coming. "Don't you dare say it."

He didn't even wait a beat. "Then, Sam… you're fired."

CHAPTER FIFTEEN

"MAKE WAY, MAKE WAY, make way," Scout shouted as she ran like a blur through the house.

"And hello to you, too," Sam said as she held the door open. Given that the downstairs bathroom was just off the living room, and Scout hadn't had enough time to shut the door behind her, the sound of profound vomiting soon filled the house.

Jayson followed carrying two suitcases and wearing a sheepish smile. Like he was sorry and not so sorry that his wife was vomiting right now. He leaned in to give Sam a kiss on the cheek.

"Is it always this bad?" Sam asked.

"No," he answered earnestly. "Sometimes it's worse. But once she's had a bout, she's usually good for about two hours. I'll just take these up to her room."

Vomiting every two hours. Sam reconsidered those pangs she was having and her desire to have a baby of her own. A baby, maybe with Evan's eyes....

Do not go there!

"Oh, yeah, that did the trick," Scout said as she emerged from the bathroom. She plunked down on the couch and let her head fall back on the cushions. "There we go. Now I get to be nausea-free for the next few hours."

"Way to be positive."

Scout lifted her head to look at Sam. "All I've got to say is I really better like this kid. Because right now it's kicking my ass."

Sam smiled. "Of course you're going to love it." That's just how it worked with a family.

Jayson came down the stairs with his car keys in hand. "I'm going to run to the grocery store and get your supplies."

"I need..."

"Fresca. I know."

"And..."

"Peanut butter and Ritz crackers. I know. I'll be back in a bit. Sam, do you need anything while I'm out?"

"No, I'm good."

As soon as the door shut behind him, Scout dropped her head back against the cushions. "Man, this whole pregnancy thing is for the birds. I don't like to say that too much in front of Jayson because I think he's afraid I'll never agree to do this again, and he's really got his heart set on two kids. But if I'm not eating something, then I'm throwing it up."

Sam sat down next to her and patted her leg sympathetically. "Welcome home, sis."

Scout smiled. "It is nice be back. Driving through the streets, it made me glad we didn't sell this house. That, just by having it here, I'm still connected to the town. To Duff. It helps me to be more nostalgic and less weepy, you know what I mean?"

Sam nodded. Then a thought occurred to her. "Please, don't tell me, if you have a boy, you're going to name him Duff."

"What's wrong with Duff as a name?"

"It's not a real name. It's a nickname, and you shouldn't do that to your kid."

"Jayson and I are in negotiations, but it's a very strong possibility that Duff will be a middle name."

"Fine, that's acceptable for my nephew."

"Or niece. Listen to you. It's my kid. You know, just because you're older doesn't mean you get to be the boss of me."

"It means exactly that." Sam smiled. "When are Lane and Roy coming in?"

"Tomorrow early," Scout said. "Jocelyn timed the unveiling perfectly. With the All-Star game going on, we've got the next three days clear, but we will have to leave the next morning. There really is no such thing as personal time in the major leagues. Jayson and Roy need to make it back for a game that night. And Alice and Bob are coming, too?"

Sam smiled. There was a time when Scout would barely acknowledge she had a mother, let alone a stepfather. Thankfully those days were long behind them. "Yep. They're coming, too. It will be nice to have everyone here." Sam patted her sister's leg again. "Now, what can I get you? I think I already have peanut butter…"

"Nope. It's got to be chunky. You're a smooth girl."

Sam was a smooth girl. She stood, thinking about what else was in the kitchen. "Fine, then let me make you something… like toast."

"Because toast is the only thing you can make." Scout smiled. "No, I'm good for now. So, come on, while Jayson's gone. Give me the girl dirt. What's going on with you and Evan?"

The fact that Sam wanted to burst into tears right at that moment was probably not a good sign.

"Whoa," Scout said, clearly reacting to Sam's expression. "Obviously not good. When I find him, I'm going to break both his knees."

"Not until after I get him signed to a long-term deal," Sam said automatically. Then she reminded herself that, technically, she might not even be his agent anymore. After all, the last words he'd said to her were "You're fired."

That was two days ago, and she hadn't heard a word from him since. In truth, that was on her. She was the one who'd told him they had to be discreet, essentially communicating she was ashamed of their relationship.

Then she had called him a commodity after making love to him.

Finally, she was the one who'd pushed him back over the wall because she'd been too scared to deal with how she was feeling. And at the time, that had been blissfully happy.

She should have called him. But she didn't. She was an idiot.

"What happened?"

"I did what you told me to do and seduced him. You were right. Getting naked worked."

"Like it does every time."

"Then he fired me."

Scout tapped the center of her right palm with her left fingers. "Time out. Why do I think there's a lot of stuff in the middle you're leaving out?"

Sam winced. "Okay, fine, I might have told him that we can sleep together, but no one can know because it would hurt my reputation as an agent."

"You made Evan Tanner your dirty little secret? Ouch."

"No surprise he didn't like the idea. Then there's the fact he's moved his ex-girlfriend and her son into his house. And when his father finds out, he's going to blame me for letting it happen. I was supposed to be getting Evan out of this mess, not watching him get deeper into it. But he can be so stubborn, especially when he knows he's doing the right thing."

"Oh, my."

"Yes." Sam was now pacing back and

forth in front of the couch. "Like I'm just supposed to be okay with that. And of course I can't say that I'm not, because he's doing all of this for a sick little boy! A boy who may not be his. Do you know what that's going to do to him if it turns out not to be true? If she's been lying this whole time? He should be putting as much space as possible between himself and her until he has a definitive answer. Instead she's living in his house making him sandwiches for lunch. And I can't do anything about it!"

Scout blinked. Then blinked again. "I'm sorry, did you just say you couldn't do anything about it? You're Samantha Baker. Remember her? Badass agent extraordinaire. That Samantha Baker does whatever the hell she wants to get the results she wants for her client."

Sam looked at her sister, and it was odd, but it was like she was suddenly just remembering that, too. When did she become powerless in this situation? She was never powerless, not when it came to fighting on her client's behalf. And for better or worse, regardless of what Evan might think, he was still her client.

She owed him her best.

Sam stopped pacing and put her hands on her hips. "What a jackass I've been. This whole time I've been upset for him and worried for what he's feeling for this little boy. I've been jealous and angry without an outlet, which has nothing to do with our professional relationship. What I haven't been doing is fighting for him. That's what I do. I fight for my clients."

"And she's back, ladies and gentlemen," Scout said, clearly pleased with the effect of her pep talk. "You have to find out what she wants and give it to her. It's the only way she might be willing to tell the truth."

"She wants money," Sam said.

"You have money. Gobs and gobs of it. Hello, have you seen your shoe closet?"

"No," Sam said as she thought about it more carefully. "She doesn't want money. She wants a cure for her son. Which means she wants a doctor. The best doctor."

Sam instantly reached for her phone. The one she'd purposely left on the coffee table so that she would hear it from anywhere in the house in case Evan called her. He hadn't.

She dialed a number and waited for the one person she knew could help to answer.

"Jocelyn, it's Sam. Remember when you did me that really big favor with the jet?"

"Hey, that's not fair," Scout shouted from the couch. "She got you a jet? I'm her actual friend."

Sam waved at Scout to be quiet. "Well, it looks like I'm going to need another favor."

It took exactly four calls, the last one sealing the deal. Sam closed her hand around her phone and finally felt like she had some control back in her life. Now it was just a question of getting Kelly onboard.

KELLY CAUTIOUSLY ANSWERED the knock at the front door. It felt weird. This wasn't her house, but what was she supposed to do, pretend like she wasn't here? Connor was outside playing on the swing set, and it wasn't as if she would have left him alone.

When she did open it, she realized she wasn't necessarily surprised.

"Oh, it's you," Kelly said, looking at Sam and wondering how she always got her hair to fall so perfectly even around her face. The woman always looked so damn…collected. It made Kelly self-conscious. "Evan isn't here."

"I know. He's got a game in an hour. I

didn't come here to talk to him. I want to talk to you, if you have a few minutes."

Kelly shook her head. "I think we've said everything we need to say to each other. Look, I get it. I know you hate me. I know why. I'm not an idiot. I know what's happening between you two. I saw the look on Evan's face when he left to follow you home the other day. I'm sure you're not happy I'm here, but this is what's best for Connor so…"

"I don't hate you, Kelly," Sam interrupted her. "I'm here because I want to help you."

Right. As if she might believe that. This woman only wanted one thing and that was for Kelly and Connor to be gone. "You want to help me? You get Evan the biggest contract there is—that will help me."

"I can do better than that," Sam said. "What if I told you I made an appointment for Connor in two days with one of the country's leading asthma specialists?"

Kelly crossed her arms over her chest. "I would say you are full of shit. How would you even know who that is?"

"Dr. Stan Whitman. Google him. He works out of Children's Hospital in Philadelphia. He's made serious progress in the treatment of severe adolescent asthma. You think you want money. But money won't get you access. You have to know someone, which I do."

Kelly didn't need to Google Dr. Whitman. She knew exactly who he was. He was exactly the person she wanted to treat Connor. She'd even gone so far as to see what might be involved in getting an appointment. They had told her there was a waiting list of over seven thousand children trying to see him. Seven thousand, and now she had an appointment in two days.

"How?" Kelly asked, her voice breaking as tears welled in her eyes. Two days. Connor was going to see Dr. Whitman in two days.

"That's not your concern," Sam said. "Just say yes, Kelly. For Connor."

Of course she was going to say yes. The word was on the tip of her tongue when suddenly she stopped herself. "Wait a minute. You didn't do this for nothing. You're an agent. It's all about negotiations with you. What do you want in exchange?"

"Just the truth, Kelly. What you're doing

to Evan is not right. Now you're in his house. You're making your son part of his life. If you're not being honest with him, how do you think that is going to make him feel? Connor, too, for that matter. The closer they get, the more difficult all of this becomes. You wanted Connor to see the best doctors. I'm giving that to you. Agree to the paternity test."

"And if I say no?" Kelly challenged.

Sam held up her hands. "Then nothing. You still keep the appointment because Connor should be seen by the best if he has that opportunity. You might think I'm a cold, ruthless bitch, but this is a little boy we're talking about. A little boy Evan cares about. I'm going to do whatever I can for him."

"I don't trust you," Kelly told her.

Sam smiled. "I don't trust you, either. Should make for an interesting road trip. If we leave first thing in the morning two days from now we should get to Philadelphia by noon. The appointment is for two in the afternoon. Then we come back here. There's nothing to lose out of this deal."

"What should I tell Evan?"

"Tell him his agent is finally doing her job."

SAM HEARD THE knock on the front door, and her body actually trembled. It was late. Scout and Jayson had long since gone to bed, but she hadn't been able to sleep, so she was attempting to solve the problem with caffeine-free tea. She checked the clock and saw that it was after midnight and knew there was only one person it might be.

She opened the door and smiled. She couldn't not smile when she saw him.

"Hi."

"Hi," Evan said back. "I know it's late. But I wanted to see you. Can I come in?"

Sam stepped back and let him inside. "I couldn't sleep, so I was making tea."

"Tea sounds amazing."

He followed her into the kitchen, and Sam took an old, cow themed teakettle and filled it with water. Evan sat at the kitchen table, and Sam couldn't help but think how nice it was that he was here. Late at night when she was tired and weary from a long day. He settled her. Made her more peaceful, even though she had no idea what was going through his head.

Then suddenly he wasn't sitting but was instead closing his arms around her from behind. He tucked his face into her neck and breathed deeply.

"It's only been a few days, but I've missed you."

Sam shut her eyes. She had missed him, too. Two stupid days of not talking to him and she'd missed him. A sign of how gone she was. She couldn't make herself say the words back to him. They would reveal too much.

Instead she turned in his arms, and instantly his mouth came crashing down on hers. It was as if neither of them had taken a breath since being apart, and now they could only breathe together.

Evan broke the kiss but rested his forehead against hers. For a time they stayed like that. Holding each other. Breathing the same air. Connected to each other.

"Just so we're super clear. I don't want the agent. I want the woman," he finally said.

"I think I'm better at the agent part." The truth in that made her heart break a little.

"Kelly told me what you did today. She's over-the-moon excited. Apparently, she did a lot of research on this Dr. Whitman."

That made sense, Sam thought. A woman with a son who has asthma would have done all the research she could. She must have known who Whitman was as soon as Sam mentioned the name.

"Why did you do this, Sam?"

"To help a sick boy. To help you."

Evan lifted his head and looked at her. "I don't need you to help me. I need you to love me."

The words crushed her. Mostly because she had this overwhelming urge to tell him that she already did. But she couldn't say it. It might only hurt him more when he realized she still wasn't ready to trust anyone fully with her heart.

Despite thinking she was in love with him, she was still afraid of it. Sam was pretty sure a person ready to be in a serious relationship wouldn't have this fear.

"I don't know what you expect me to say."

"That's not true. You know exactly what I want you to say. You're just afraid to say it."

"You're right. I am. So let me do my job instead. Kelly started this, because she wanted to get the best care for her son. I'm giving her an opportunity to have that. Once she sees this is not a trick or a scam, she might be willing to be completely transparent about Connor's parentage."

Evan sighed. "You really think she would keep a lie going this long?"

Sam didn't know how to say this gently. "I think you're too trusting."

Evan's expression tightened. "And you don't trust enough. What a fine couple we make."

"Evan…"

He took a step back from her. "No. I get it. You were okay letting me in so far. You were okay having sex with me, but that's as far as it was going to get, wasn't it?"

Again Sam had to bite down on the words. It had been more than just sex. Way more with Evan, but if she told him that, then he would want even more. He would want all of her.

"More silence," he said like accusation. "I can't go to that appointment. The unveiling of Duff's statue is tomorrow, but then we go on the road for a three-game stretch."

"I know."

"Right," Evan snapped. "Because you're my agent, and you know these things. Just don't give Kelly too hard a time. She's already nervous, which is making Connor nervous."

He was trying to protect Kelly from her.

That hurt, too. "I'm not the bad guy in this story, Evan," Sam said. "All I wanted was the truth of a paternity test. That really isn't a lot to ask when you're claiming you're entitled to part of a person's salary."

"I didn't say you were. I just…"

"No. I get it. I can be pretty cold sometimes," Sam said, feeling a lump in her throat. Hating the idea that Evan thought like so many others did when she'd shown him a different view. "That's what everyone tells me anyway."

"Sam," he said, reaching for her again, pulling her close.

She tried to wiggle out of his arms, but it was too late. The tears fell, and she could feel them on her cheek. Evan wouldn't let her go, and then she could feel his fingers brushing the tears away.

"Not cold at all," he muttered. He kissed her cheek, and it was breaking her heart.

"Evan, just leave. This isn't going to work. I'm not capable of making this work. You have to know that."

"No. I'm a stubborn son of a bitch, Samantha Baker, and I'm not ready to give up on us yet."

"There is no us."

"There sure as shit was an us two days ago on that couch."

Sam blushed, thinking about it. About what it felt like to have him deep inside of her. Connected to her. Surrounding her. "That was sex," she said lamely, as if it hadn't meant everything to her. "Isn't that what you said?"

His mouth tightened, and she knew he wasn't happy with what she said, but then his intent seemed to change.

"Fine. Then this will just be sex, too."

Again his mouth was on hers, and the feel of his tongue dancing over hers was intoxicating until she remembered they were in her kitchen.

"Scout and Jayson are upstairs. They came in today for the unveiling of Duff's statue."

"Upstairs asleep?"

"Yes."

"Then you'll have to be real quiet." With that he lifted her on to the counter. She'd been wearing a simple tank top and pajama pants, and with hardly any effort he'd pulled the tank top up and over her head. She couldn't manage a gasp before he'd cupped her breast and was rubbing his thumb over her nipple until it hardened under his command.

"Evan…what if they…oh, my."

His other hand had dipped into the pajama bottoms and caused a wave of heat to rush between her legs.

"Nope, not cold at all," he muttered against her neck. "In fact, you're scorching hot."

She could feel his touch everywhere. His lips kissing her along her collarbone. His fingers playing with her nipple, his other finger between her legs pushing inside her, teasing her in a display of what was to come. Two days ago it had happened so fast. One moment she was naked, and the next he was inside her. She'd forgotten about this part. About how she liked to be touched and teased and played with. Her head fell back against the cabinet and she let out a low, deep moan.

Then Evan was kissing her again until he pulled away. "I said…quiet."

Quiet? Why did they have to be…

Then nothing mattered, because Evan was tugging off her pajama bottoms so that she was completely naked in his arms. Then he lifted her and moved them both until he was sitting on one of her kitchen chairs, and she was straddling his thighs. Before Sam could even process her position, Evan was pulling a condom out of his wallet.

"You came over here to seduce me," she said.

Evan chuckled as he was undoing his pants. "Not exactly. It's just, since seeing you again, I've thought it was a smart idea to carry a condom everywhere I go. Call me a hopeless romantic. Help me here, love."

It was a throwaway word. Him calling her his love, but still Sam felt it down to her toes. She wanted to give him something back. She wanted him to have all the power of her emotions without actually saying the words he wanted to hear.

Her hands went to his pants, and she worked at the jean button and zipper until she was able to free his erection. She stroked him in her hands until he was the one groaning.

She bent down and kissed him. "Remember, quiet."

"You're killing me."

No, Sam thought. He was undoing her.

With the condom in place, he lifted her and positioned her all so easily until she found herself sliding down on his cock, letting it fill her. This time they both groaned.

"Quiet," they whispered together.

It was an effort for them both as the pleasure overtook them. Sam rocked her body against his while Evan's hands cupped her ass, so that he could thrust into her hard. She felt the material of his jeans against her inner thighs, his T-shirt in her hands where she had grabbed it behind his back as a way to anchor herself to him.

She thought how again she was naked in his arms while he was still dressed and decided that one day she was going to reverse that, and he was going to get naked for her while she watched. But for now all she could think about was how this felt. How good and amazing it was to be in his arms. To be filled with his body. To be connected to him in a way she never thought she would be again to another man.

The pleasure when it hit her was intense. She bit down hard on her lip not to make a sound and wrapped her arms so tightly around him, so that she didn't think she would ever be able to let go.

She felt the jerk of his hips, the soft groan in his throat, and for a second, one fleeting second, she wished there was no condom between them. Wished that he might be giving her more than just himself.

A little girl with Evan's eyes.

When he relaxed she cupped his face in her hands and kissed him. "Thank you," she said. "You were beautiful."

"No, Sam. That's what I'm trying to tell you. That was us. We're beautiful together."

Us. If only she could believe in that word again.

CHAPTER SIXTEEN

"O'ER THE LAND of the free and the home of the brave!"

The stadium burst into applause at the anthem's end, and Sam squeezed both of her sisters' hands before letting them go. They were standing in the tunnel, and the next part of the night's ceremony was about to begin. Just the three of them would be on the field for the unveiling. Lane's husband, Roy, and Jayson, along with their mother and Bob, were in the stadium sitting behind home plate. After the game the plan was to all go back to Duff's house for a barbecue and family celebration.

Sam had wanted to ask Evan to come. To really get to know her family. But that had seemed so real. So formal. Evan meeting her parents. Her parents meeting him again in an entirely different context. It was a stupid little step in a relationship, and she couldn't even take that. She wanted it too much.

"Sam, is everything okay with you? I know this is going to sound crazy, but since I got here this morning and every hour after that, you look like you've wanted to cry," Lane asked her.

"Yeah, go right ahead and start crying, Sam," Scout said, the sarcasm heavy in her voice. "Because that's not wrong at all in a baseball stadium."

Sam sniffed a few times. She had no idea what was wrong with her. It was something about the way Evan had left her last night. A simple kiss to her forehead. A soft goodnight. A sad smile on his face as he walked out the door.

She hadn't wanted him to leave. She'd wanted instead to take him up to her room, sleep with him in her bed and wake up with him this morning. She wanted him there tonight with her family.

Only none of that was going to happen because she was too afraid to ask for what she wanted.

In fact, she had been the one to tell him to go. Realistically she told herself it was all part of being discreet. Not that she thought reporters were lurking outside her bushes waiting to take pictures, but still, no one needed to see Evan leaving his agent's house in the morning wearing the same clothes he'd worn the night before. Or see his truck parked outside her house all night.

Truly, that was only part of it. The real reason she made him go was because she couldn't handle a conversation about *us*. Didn't want to think about what *us* would look like and feel like. *Us* scared the crap out of her, and more and more she was realizing that a decision was going to need to be made.

Sex with Evan was too earth-shattering to think she could do that, and that was all she could do. She could still feel him and smell him in every single one of her pores. The longer they went on, the more invested she would be. The more she would be expected to give back.

So, yes, with all of that on her mind, not to mention this night was all about remembering Duff, naturally the singing of the national anthem was going to be enough to bring her to tears.

"I'm feeling overly patriotic today," she said in lieu of a real explanation.

"Wow, I'm not buying that at all," Lane said and looked over at Scout.

"It's man problems," Scout told her. "More specifically, Evan Tanner problems."

"Evan Tanner? Isn't he the guy you went out on a date with to make Jayson jealous?"

Scout shook her head. "I didn't do it to make Jayson jealous, but it did have a nice effect. Remember when he sent the other players from the team to chaperone me? That was so sweet."

"Hey, just a thought," Sam interjected. "Could we maybe not reminisce about your date with Evan?"

"Relax, I told you we didn't kiss or anything. Although I have to say I might regret that. Now that I'm married and knocked up, that might have been my last chance to kiss someone other than Jayson. It might have been good to have a comparison. Not that I think anyone could ever kiss better than Jayson. Still, Evan does have a fine set of lips..."

Sam shuddered. "Also, can we not talk about you kissing Evan?"

Lane nodded. "Ah, so this is serious. Good. It's about damn time you got over what that jerk Donald did. He must be some man if the icy and indomitable Samantha Baker can be brought to tears over him."

Sam turned on Lane. "Did it ever occur to you, to either of you, that calling me icy hurts? You're basically saying I'm a cold-hearted bitch, and frankly I'm sick of it."

Lane's eyes widened. "Sam... I would never... First, I don't think you're a bitch. That is unless you're fighting my jerk of an ex-husband in court. Then you were a perfect bitch. The icy... I'm sorry. It's just sometimes that's the way you come across, but I know you. You're fierce and loyal, sometimes to a fault. You would do anything for someone you cared about, and that's a pretty bold claim, because when Samantha Baker wants something done, it gets done. You know I love you."

"Ditto," Scout said, reaching for her hand again. "Just because I think you're more Kim Basinger then Glenn Close doesn't mean I don't love you."

"I am not Kim Basinger. Oh, for heaven's sake, can we stop with the movie references?" Sam growled. "Look, I'm sorry I snapped. It's just... I've been having a hard time processing everything that's happening with Evan, and I'm really not sure what's going to happen next."

Lane reached over and rubbed her back.

"Honey, you don't process it. You just feel it. Let it warm you up from the inside. You'll see. It's a good feeling."

"Oh, right, like love is that easy."

"Whoa," Scout interjected. "Did you say love? For real, love?"

Sam wasn't sure. It could be. It might be.

Oh, hell, who was she kidding? Again she had to force away tears. They were about to be called out on to the field in front of ten thousand people at any moment.

"I just can't... If I try again with Evan, and it doesn't work I couldn't handle it. So it's better to not try, right? I mean, that's why it's easier to be cold. I don't want to have to deal with any ridiculous emotions that do nothing but make you want to cry. Look at me. I'm Samantha Baker. This is ridiculous!"

Lane and Scout looked at her like she was the biggest idiot in the world.

"Sam," Lane said gently. "The answer to your question goes back to the love thing. If you do really love him, then there's no such thing as not trying. You're already there."

"But that's what I'm saying. I don't want to be *there*. It's too freaking scary."

"Yes, but it's also pretty awesome," Scout told her. "Look at me. I'm hacking up peanut butter and Ritz crackers practically every hour on the hour. I should be miserable and cranky. Instead I'm walking around with this goofy smile on my face all the time, because I'm so damn happy. With Jayson, with the baby. Don't you want all that?"

"Yes, I want a baby!" Sam shouted. "There, I said it. I didn't think I did, or I didn't think I could, but now I do, and that scares the crap out of me, too. I want it all. I just don't have it in me to trust that he is never going to hurt me, or lie to me or betray me."

"I had to trust Roy again, after he set me up so I would catch my husband cheating on me. That was a big deal," Lane reminded her.

"And I had to trust Jayson again, even though he broke my heart when he left Minotaur Falls the first time. Not easy. But again, totally worth it."

Sam looked at her sisters and thought about what they'd overcome to find happiness. Real happiness.

"I'm not as strong or courageous as you two," she said solemnly.

Lane and Scout looked at each other, then burst out laughing.

"What?" Sam asked. "This is serious."

"Honey," Lane said, "trust us. Of the three of us, it goes without saying you are the strongest and most courageous one by far."

Scout patted her on the shoulder. "If it makes you feel any better, you're the scariest one, too."

That melted her heart, the awareness that these women, her sisters, knew her at her core. "I really love you guys."

"Back at you," Scout said. "Wait a minute. Are we going to do some sloppy sister hug now? I have to say I've gotten way more sentimental with all these hormones in me now, so I would not be one hundred percent against that."

"Yes," Lane said. "When your sister is having a crisis of love, it's important to surround her with sloppy sister hugs."

So they did, and once more Sam started to cry.

THE PHONE RANG as Evan walked in the door. He was tired after the game, and he was still pissed off that Sam hadn't invited him to come over and meet her family. He knew Scout, obviously, and had met Sam's parents briefly a few years ago, but it would have been a different thing altogether to go over there for a barbecue after the game. To present themselves as a couple.

But did she say anything about it to him? No.

Scout had been the one to ask him to come over, and because she had to be the one to do it, he couldn't actually go. Not when Sam should have asked him herself.

So instead, he was home and in a mood to brood, which he couldn't do with these two other people in his house.

"H-hello?" He heard Connor answer the phone, while he put his equipment bag down by the door. Evan wondered if he should tell him not to do that. It wasn't likely, but it could be a reporter. A reporter who might have grown curious why Evan would move his ex-girlfriend and her son into his house.

Then again, telling a kid not to answer a ringing phone because he was supposed to be secret seemed like a crappy thing to do. None of this was Connor's fault.

Hell, none of it was his fault, either.

"Uh… Connor…h-he j-hust got h-home."

Evan rounded the corner into the kitchen where the phone was and reached his hand out for it. The boy seemed relieved to turn it over. It wasn't lost on Evan that Connor was wheezing again pretty badly and probably needed his inhaler. "I got it. Go have your mom check to see if you need your inhaler."

Connor nodded. Then left the room in search of his medicine.

"Evan speaking."

"What in the hell are you doing?"

It was not hard to identify the shouting man on the other end of the phone. "Relax, Dad."

"Relax! Now the boy is in your house? Where is the mother? Let me guess. You've got them both there with you."

She wasn't even Kelly any longer. She was *the mother.* "That would be correct. She's in the room right next to Connor's. Dad, I didn't have any choice."

"That's not true. You had plenty of choices. Your problem is you're too damn soft. I mean, what's next, Evan? Are you going to marry this girl?"

"Of course I'm not going to marry her. But I had to get Connor out of that motel room, and she's not going anywhere. So, this is where it stands. You said you weren't going to lecture me."

"I said I was done telling you to try and keep your distance. Now you've gone ahead and done the opposite. What does Sam have to say about this? I'm sure she's not happy. Hell, son, are you trying to ruin that relationship, too?"

That caught him off guard. "What are you talking about?"

"Well, you obviously have feelings for the woman. She must share those feelings, or she wouldn't have sat up all night with you in a hospital. But before you can get that relationship off the ground, you're moving your ex-girlfriend into your house. How the hell do you think she's going to interpret that?"

Considering what had happened between them—twice—since the move, Evan hoped Sam understood there was nothing going on between him and Kelly.

No, Sam's not understanding how much he felt for her, wasn't their problem.

It was her lack of faith in him that was their problem.

Even after the amazing sex, even after the sweet moment in her kitchen when she'd collapsed against him and then cuddled into him like a satisfied kitten, even after that,

she still had asked him to leave. He got it.
It could have been a little awkward the next
morning with Scout and Jayson, but still it
had hurt almost physically to walk away
from her.

"Sam knows how I feel about her, Dad.
That isn't our problem."

"Everyone is always talking about their
issues and their problems. Back in my day,
you fell in love and you got married. Then
you went to bed. If people started getting
that right again, they would stop talking
about all their problems. Sex complicates
things."

Evan stood in his kitchen listening to his
father give him sex advice. This was truly
a bizarre day.

"You've got to fix this, Evan. You've got
to send her back to where she belongs, in Arizona. Tell her she wants anything from you,
she's got to take a paternity test. And as hard
as it is, you've got to let that boy go. Until a
DNA test proves it, he is *not* your son."

Evan closed his eyes, trying to hear what
his father was saying. Intellectually he got
it, but he cared about Connor.

"Dad, I get where you're coming from…"

"I don't think you do. Have you ever considered this is less about that boy and more about you wanting to have kids of your own?"

Evan glanced over at the kitchen doorway at the sound of footsteps in the hallway. Kelly was following Connor. She opened the freezer and handed him some kind of pop she must have bought.

Was this really what he wanted? A woman in his house, raising his child, being part of a family?

Yeah. It was exactly what he wanted.

Except Kelly wasn't the woman he wanted any of that with.

"Maybe. Maybe it was because I had such a good family growing up. I had a great childhood, Dad. I probably don't thank you enough for that."

"Well, you're welcome. Truth be told, you were a pretty damn easy kid to raise. But I liked it better when you always did what I told you to do. Things were much simpler back then."

Evan smiled. "I've heard everything you've had to say, and I'll think it over. But, no, that doesn't mean that I'm just going to do what you want."

"Understood. You know I say all of this because I worry about you."

"I know."

"Sometimes I worry that you're too trusting."

Sam had said the same thing last night. Maybe she had a good reason to be less trusting. Between her jerk fiancé hitting her and her jerk client lying to her and making her lie for him, he could tell why she might be gun-shy. But if she didn't overcome that, then they would both lose out on something amazing.

"Maybe I am, Dad, but I would rather think the best of people than the worst."

"All right. I'm still coming to your game as soon as you get called up. No word yet?"

"No, but they said after the All-Star break, which is happening now."

"What about the statue unveiling for Duff Baker? How did that go?"

It went with Scout, instead of his lover, asking him to come to a family barbecue.

"Very nice. It's a great resemblance. I think the Baker girls are very happy."

Not that Evan would know, since he wasn't at the party asking Sam how she felt. If she was missing her father a little more tonight. If she was sad or happy that Duff had been recognized.

Maybe he'd gone about this all wrong. Maybe the thing to do was to force her hand. He had to remind himself with Sam this wasn't just a single battle he was engaged in; he was out to win the war.

"Okay. Well, think about what I said, and hopefully I'll see you soon."

"Yep. Got it."

Evan hung up the phone and turned to see Kelly still standing near the doorway of the kitchen. Connor must have been back in his room with the ice pop.

"I can tell him not to answer the phone," she said. "He probably didn't know what was happening. All I have for a phone is my cell."

"My dad still insists on calling my home phone first. Says it's clearer, although I've never noticed a difference."

"What you said about thinking the best instead of the worst in people. I assume he was talking about me. I guess he's not happy that we're living here now."

"It's not his call," Evan told her. "It's mine. But at some point we're going to have to figure this out. Hopefully, you can see the doctor tomorrow, and we can start working on a plan."

"Not *we*," Kelly said sharply. "I have to start working on a plan. All you have to do is…"

"Pay up. I know." Evan sighed. "Kelly, Connor and I are connected now, and how far we take that connection is up to you."

Kelly crossed her arms over her chest. "I just want to see him get better. So that he can be a normal boy who runs and plays and has friends. That's all I want for him. A normal happy and healthy life."

"I understand, but this is my life, too."

She shook her head. "I can't talk about this right now. I can only worry about tomorrow."

"Right. What time is Sam coming to get you?"

"Six in the morning. The appointment is at two o'clock, which should give us more than enough time."

"Good. Call me after."

"If that's what you want," she said.

"If that's what I want?" Evan asked incredulously. "Of course that's what I want. I'm his father. Kelly, am I his father?"

"That's what I told you," she snapped.

He closed his eyes. "Then I guess that's what I have to believe."

Evan turned and left the kitchen, heading for the front door.

"Where are you going? I thought you just came home."

Evan didn't turn around as he reached for the door. "I was invited to a barbecue, and I've decided I'm going to go."

Kelly snorted. "Why do I get the feeling the barbecue sounds more like a mission?"

Evan smiled as he stepped outside. "Because it is. Tell Connor I said good-night and don't wait up."

CHAPTER SEVENTEEN

"DAMN IT," SCOUT MUTTERED.

"What's the matter?" Sam asked as they sat looking up at the stars. She and Scout had wandered outside while the family was gathered in the house in various stages of eating, drinking and catching up. "You're not going to get sick again, are you?"

"No, I'm actually feeling pretty good right now. That will last, you know, for about another hour. I'm going to enjoy it while I can. No, I'm upset because it's almost ten-thirty. He has to have been done showering after the game by now. I had hoped he would be here already."

Sam stiffened. "Scout, you didn't. Please tell me you didn't invite Evan."

"Of course I told him to come. A, he's my friend. B, you're in love with him, so the rest of the family should get to know him more."

Sam stood up, ready to scream and shake her sister, only she couldn't scream and shake her sister because now she was pregnant. Very good timing on Scout's part.

"Scout!" she hissed. "You idiot. *I* didn't invite him."

"I know. That was really stupid of you, since you're in love with him and deep down want a relationship with him. He's probably really pissed at you right now. I know I would be. So, you're going to have to work hard to make that up to him when he gets here."

"Seriously, if you weren't pregnant," Sam growled, "I would punch you in the face to give you a matching black eye like the one you gave me two years ago."

"Hey, remember that?" Scout smiled. "That night was crazy. I was so drunk. But then Jayson came and bailed me out of jail, so it ended up pretty well. That's why I'm doing this for you, Sam. I'm trying to help you get to your happy ending. You deserve it, finally."

"It's not like I didn't want him here," Sam said, twisting her hands together. "I did. I do. I want everyone to get to know him and see how amazing he is… I just didn't know…"

"What? You didn't know what, Sam?"

Sam turned at the sound of his voice behind her.

"Evan," she breathed.

"Sorry to interrupt, but I heard you two talking out here, so I came around the back. Is it okay if I come in?" He was standing just outside the fence.

Sam nodded, and he stepped inside.

"Awesome, you came," Scout said as she jumped up and then walked around Sam to hug him. "Now Sam can start making it up to you for being such a jackass. What can I get you? A beer? A burger?"

"He doesn't drink alcohol during the season," Sam said.

"Unless it's cold sour water," Evan reminded her with a twist of his lips.

Scout looked between the two of them. "Right. I'll let you two figure it out. I'll let everyone inside know you're here. Bob is definitely going to want to meet you, but don't be scared of him. Really, he's just a big teddy bear. A teddy bear who can kick ass, but a teddy bear, nonetheless."

Scout left them alone in awkward silence. How was that possible when last night she'd been sprawled naked against his body so utterly and thoroughly content?

Content until she'd told him that he had to leave. Then, of course, there was the small issue of not inviting him to the barbecue.

"I told you I'm a stubborn son of a bitch, Sam. I came here tonight knowing you didn't ask me. That wasn't cool. You should have asked me to come and meet your family."

"I know. I'm sorry. I wanted you to come," she said as she walked toward him. "I was just…"

"Afraid of taking that step. I know. That's the thing, Sam. I understand you're afraid. What I want to know is how we get past that. What do we have to do to get you over that fear?"

Sam wished it was that easy. Like there was some plan they could come up with that would fix her inside. "Does it count for anything that I'm trying? If you only knew how hard I was trying. I…want this, Evan. I want *us*. Please, you have to know that."

He opened his arms to her. "Okay. You're trying. Yeah, that counts."

She walked into those arms, and being held by him was so amazing. There was no other way to describe it. He warmed her up from the inside, just like Lane said. And for a moment, standing there in his embrace, she had a thought that they could be happy. Really happy.

"I'm glad you're here," she whispered.

"Not afraid of someone snapping our picture while we're in your backyard?"

"Nope."

"Not afraid your family might be peeking out the window and seeing us in a very non-agent/client way."

She smiled and shook her head. "Nope. In fact, how about you come inside and meet the folks?"

"Let's do it."

Sam took his hand and led him inside to the kitchen. It was hard not to blush, thinking what they had been doing just last night in this same kitchen, now filled with her family.

Alice and Bob were sitting at the table. Scout and Jayson were missing, which might have meant a return of the nausea, or they went to make out. Roy was leaning on the counter with Lane tucked in between his legs, and her back against his chest.

"Everyone...you remember Evan."

Bob stood to shake his hand. "Heard you're about to be the next big thing in baseball. Looks like Scout was right about you."

Evan shook his head. "Thanks. Hey, could you let all the major league pitchers know that? It might help if they were all intimidated by me instead of the other way around."

Everyone laughed, and some of the weird tension dissipated. Evan shook Roy's hand, and the conversation naturally fell to baseball.

Scout and Jayson returned and joined in the conversation while Sam got Evan a soda and filled up a plate of food for him. She watched him sit at the table with her mom and Bob, and she held her breath waiting to see how they would interact.

This was the first man she had introduced to her parents since Donald. They must know he was important to her.

Not that she was really worried about how they'd take to him. Of course they would like him. Evan Tanner was a completely amiable person, and anyone would like him. Beyond that, it really didn't matter what her family thought of him; it only mattered what she thought of him.

Then she remembered that Bob had never really warmed up to Donald. The two men had been cordial but never friendly. Bob had only told her after the broken engagement that something about Donald hadn't sat well with him. Which only went to show that her family was a better judge of character than she was.

No, there was no way they wouldn't like Evan. But if Sam had to guess, she imagined they might be more cautious with him. In a way, that was sad. One more thing Donald had done to impact her life.

"Come, sit outside with me again. The fresh air helps," Scout said, grabbing her by the arm. Sam resisted, though. Bob was targeting Evan with some direct questions. The former Navy Seal had experience interrogating people. Bob could be very intimidating when he wanted to be.

"But Evan…"

"Is a big boy who can handle conversing with other adults and will come find you when he needs you."

Sam resisted a second tug, then finally relented. It was hard to say no to something her pregnant sister wanted, and besides, the point of Evan being here was for her family to get to know him.

"Evan," she told him and watched him

turn his focus on her again. "I'm going out-side with Scout again. Okay?"

He reached for her hand and kissed the back of it. "Have fun."

Once they were outside, the cooler air was refreshing. Scout took a deep breath, and the two of them found their way back to the deck chairs they had been sitting in before Evan showed up. Sam got another glass of wine and thought how different it felt now. Earlier she'd been guilt-ridden, confused, angry at herself. Now that Evan was here, inside with her family, it felt right. This was where he was supposed to be, and now she could relax.

"So, what time do you pick up the ex?" Scout asked.

"First thing in the morning, so this is my last glass of wine."

"That's a pretty cool thing you did. And pretty smart to think of it. And can I just say it is way cool having Jocelyn as a billionaire friend who knows everybody and can pull those kinds of strings?"

Sam smiled. "Actually, she couldn't help me out this time. She didn't have any con-tacts who knew anyone in the medical com-munity who could get me in the door."

"Then how did you get the appointment so fast with the big-deal doctor?"

Sam took a sip of her wine before she confessed. "I remembered Richard Stanson has a younger brother who has problems with asthma. I figured, given all his money, he would make sure he had nothing but the best care for his brother."

"You called Dickhead Stanson? For real?" Scout asked, clearly shocked.

"Yep. I told him he owed me, and it was time to cash in."

Scout smirked. "Did you also tell him to stop hitting his wife?"

"Apparently they're in counseling," Sam said. "Anyway, that isn't my concern anymore. I did what I had to do for the sake of the child and Evan. Kelly didn't agree to the paternity test, but I think if she gets what she wants, she'll see there's no reason not to do it."

Scout smiled and rubbed her belly. "See, now that's some serious hard-core Samantha Baker badass. You know that's what we really mean when we say you're cool or frosty. It's because you have this way about you that says you can shut your emotions down and do the thing you need to do. Not everyone works that way. You've always been like that. Even before Donald."

Sam smiled. "Evan wants to hit him. He almost did."

"Shut up!"

"We were in Boston having lunch with Reuben—"

"Another dickhead. Sorry, continue."

"Donald came over to say hello, not realizing I was there, and flipped out on me for telling his fiancées about how our engagement ended. Evan got in his face and wouldn't let him near me. It felt good. It felt even better knowing he made Donald look like a fool."

"Seriously, I like that boy more and more. I like him for you."

That was interesting, Sam thought. Given all her issues, someone as open and as trusting as Evan was probably the worst sort of match.

"What do you mean by that?"

"You balance each other. I mean, look at what's been done for this kid who he doesn't even know is his son. He's a total softie. He needs someone who's a little badass to have his back. And you need someone who doesn't look at the world as suspiciously as you do, to show you there's some good out there, too."

Scout bumped her shoulder against Sam's, and Sam returned the gesture.

"When did you get to be so smart?" Sam wondered.

"Uh…like almost two years ago when I finally got my head out of my ass and realized that Jayson was it for me. When you're in love with a good man, it helps you to see things differently."

Sam could only hope. "Thanks."

The back door opened, and Evan walked out. Scout got up and walked toward him. "Hey, you remember when I punched Sam in the face and gave her that killer black eye?"

"I do," Evan answered.

"I like you, Evan, but you hurt her… I'll punch you that hard in the dick."

"Scout!" Sam shouted.

Evan smiled. "Got it."

"More importantly," Scout told him, "when they call you up—"

"If they call me up," Evan said. "I've been hitting better over these last few weeks, but I'm still not where I want to be."

"You'll recover. You're a pure hitter. So when they call you up, never ever take the first pitch. It will give you time to let the nerves settle. I would even say don't take the first two, but you're on your own with that. A pitcher will know you're a rookie. They will paint corners and try to dazzle you with curves and sliders. No one will want to send heat straight down the middle out of the gate against a power hitter, unless they've thrown balls instead of strikes. You got that?"

"Yes, ma'am."

"What do I know?" Scout asked him.

"You know baseball," Evan replied.

"That's right. Now I need to go throw up again. Geesh, kid, you're killing me."

Evan sat in the chair vacated by Scout and stretched out next to Sam.

"She's impossible," Sam muttered.

"She's Scout."

"Don't give her that excuse. Now that she's pregnant, it's like Scout times two."

"So, I assume you know Bob was a Navy Seal, right?" Evan said.

"You already knew that!" Sam closed her eyes. "Did he threaten you, too?"

Even held up his fingers pinched together. "Maybe just this much."

Sam closed her eyes on a groan. "I'm sorry."

"Don't be," Evan said, even as he reached

over to take her hand. "Your family loves you. That's why it's important for them to get to know me. For me to get to know them."

Sam looked down at their linked hands. Felt the connection to him. She wanted to lie back and look at the stars and just be happy. Instead, all she could think about was how sometimes he was too good to be true.

"I'm thirty-four," she blurted out.

Evan immediately stood up. "What? Are you serious? How could you?"

Sam glared at him, and he sat back down with a chuckle.

"Why was I supposed to care about that?"

"I know it's only a five-year difference between us, but if we go down this road…"

"Sam, we're already like a mile *down this road.*"

"I'm just saying we might be in two different places in our life. I'm thinking about a relationship that ends in marriage with…with babies. You're twenty-nine, you're about to be a millionaire. Most likely a baseball superstar. How do I know you're not going to want to bang as many baseball bunnies as you can?"

His jaw tightened, and she could see that she had upset him.

"You think I'm the type to have indiscriminate sex with women I don't know?"

No. He was absolutely not that type. Baseball bunnies would do nothing for a man like Evan. He was too grounded. The guys who did that always seemed like they had something to prove.

Evan didn't have anything to prove to anyone.

"I'm sorry," she said. "Again. Why do I have to keep saying that to you? I'm a jerk. You're not a baseball bunny type of guy."

"No, I'm not. You know how I know that? I've only been thinking about one woman for the last two years. I started dating another woman to try and forget you, and that didn't work at all. I ended it after three dates."

"I bet you're regretting that now," Sam said sheepishly. "You're stuck with me."

Hell, even she was getting tired of her insecurities and suspicions.

Evan looked at her, his expression intent. "You're not the easiest woman to be around I've ever known, Sam, but you're worth it."

"You can't stay over tonight." Again, she wasn't sure why she felt the need to tell him that. Maybe because she wanted him to stay over but knew for so many reasons why he couldn't.

"You seriously think I would have sex with you under the same roof with Bob?"

Sam chuckled. "Right. That probably wouldn't be the best idea, all things considered. Not until he gets to know you a little more."

"I'll take your word for that, but truly we could be married for ten years with five kids, and I would still not have sex with you in the same house as him. That is how scary that man is."

"I only meant to say that I have to get up super early tomorrow."

"Right. The appointment. Kelly said you're picking her up at six."

Sam could see by his expression he wasn't happy. "What?"

He shook his head. "Nothing. My dad called earlier tonight, and Connor answered the phone."

"Uh-oh."

"Right. He flipped out. He thinks, like you do, that I'm too trusting."

Sam had to bite her lip. He was too trusting, but she was starting to realize that's what made Evan who he was. It was also something she didn't want to change about him. It was like Scout said, she just needed to be the one who had his back.

"He also thinks this might be about me wanting a family. I thought he was crazy for saying it. All I'm trying to do is the right thing. But thinking about it, I realized for the longest time it was just him and me. The idea of a house with a woman and children… I'm not going to lie, it's appealing. So when you talk about our stages in life, I think we might be in the same place. I know Kelly isn't a part of that. But Connor…he's just a kid who didn't ask for any of this. I very much want to make a place for him in my life. How do you feel about that?"

Sam squeezed his hand. "I feel like I would be very lucky to have such a sweet kid in my life. Even if it was only part-time. I would also do anything to get him the care he needs. If this doctor isn't the answer, we'll find another one."

"You mean that."

Sam straightened her shoulders. "I've been reminded recently I'm a badass agent who has the power to get what she wants. Yes. I do mean it."

Evan leaned over and kissed her softly. "I'm glad you're my badass agent."

Sam smiled. "Me, too."

Just then the back door opened, and everyone poured out of the house.

"We want to all be together," Lane explained, "so we can toast Duff. After all, it's really his night, isn't it?"

Sam smiled. Duff would have loved to have been here. He would have loved to meet Evan. He definitely would have loved to watch him play baseball. She could only hope that somehow he was out there in the universe. Watching over all of them.

You're going to be a granddad, Duff, Sam prayed to him silently.

She hoped somehow he knew that. That somewhere he was beaming with joy.

"Everyone, raise your glasses," Scout said. "To Duff. One of the greats. We miss you like crazy."

"To Duff," everyone echoed.

Like crazy, Sam thought.

CHAPTER EIGHTEEN

SAM SAT IN the lobby of the doctor's office tapping her foot to the steady beat of the so-called music that served as background noise. Kelly and Connor were in with the doctor now. It had been over thirty minutes, which was all the time they'd been allotted for the appointment.

She wished she had some indication of how much longer it would be. Or how it was going. Evan had already texted her three times for updates. Making her even more anxious.

The long car ride had been a strain on everybody's nerves. Sam had attempted to make small talk, but it had been obvious Kelly was too nervous to hold up a conversation about something as simple as the weather.

Connor only wanted to know if they were going to take blood. He apparently wasn't a big fan of needles and had come to associate doctors with them. Sam didn't blame him. She wasn't a fan herself.

Her phone started buzzing in her purse. No doubt Evan had resorted to calling instead of texting, as if that might help give him the answers he was looking for. When she took her phone out, though, she was surprised to see it was Reuben calling.

"Reuben, hello."

"Sam, glad I caught you. Do you have some time?"

Sam had nothing but time. "A few minutes. What's up?"

"I want to talk turkey about your boy. I think it's time we made a deal. I'm offering three years at eight million a year."

Sam blinked. She thought about what Evan might say. Twenty-four million dollars guaranteed. More money than he probably ever imagined having in his lifetime. Certainly enough money to pay any doctor Connor needed to see.

He would no doubt take it on the spot. And that was why he needed an agent.

"That's a solid opening offer, Reuben," Sam said calmly. "I'll think about it and let you know. I've got to run now."

"Sam, wait…"

But it was too late. Sam had already disconnected the call. Reuben didn't call suddenly with an offer like that in the middle of the day without a reason. She immediately ran a search for the New England Rebels.

It was the first story that popped in Google. All-Star right outfielder Sergio Vasquez, one of the Rebels' best hitters, had ruptured his Achilles tendon last night rounding third base.

"Solid offer, Reuben," Sam muttered to herself. This meant that Evan was going to be called up. Probably as soon as tomorrow. And, given an Achilles could take up to a year to heal, Reuben obviously wanted to lock Evan up tight going into next year, as well.

While he wasn't hitting what he had been before Connor came into his life, he had definitely turned the corner on his slump.

Reuben knew exactly what he was doing.

The door to the doctor's office opened, and Connor came out first, sucking on a lollipop. He didn't seem the worse for wear, but Kelly had a tissue in her hand and was wiping away tears.

However, she was smiling. Sam stood and walked over to them.

"You really think he could see that much improvement?" Kelly was asking the doctor.

"I do. But again, we're talking about an aggressive treatment program that would need to be sustained over a longer period of time than you're used to now with his sporadic attacks."

"Understood. I know what I need to do. Thank you. Thank you so much."

"You're welcome."

"I take it things went well," Sam asked.

"I didn't have to give blood," Connor announced.

"Awesome," Sam replied and ruffled his hair. "And you got a lollipop, which is also awesome."

"It's grape," he said, confirming it by pulling it out of his mouth.

"Dr. Whitman is going to continue treating Connor," Kelly said. "He thinks Connor can see major improvement over the next year with fewer severe attacks."

"That's great." Sam smiled. "I'm really happy for you both."

"Oh, Connor." Kelly groaned, looking down at him. "You've got that lollipop all over your hands. Let me take you to wash up before we head back."

Kelly whisked Connor to the nearest wash-room, and Sam shook hands with the doctor. "Dr. Whitman, I can't thank you enough for seeing us on such short notice. I know I was calling in a favor, but I had to do what I could for him."

The doctor nodded. He was younger than Sam expected but with a long and serious face. "It's hard. I wish I could see every child who needed me. Connor has a real chance of turning the corner. His condition isn't that uncommon, given his premature birth."

"Premature?"

"At thirty-two weeks those lungs just weren't fully developed, but if Kelly and Connor follow the program, we can work to strengthen them."

Sam's smile faltered. "Well, again, thank you for your time."

The doctor turned and headed back into his office, and Sam waited by the bathroom doors. Connor was in the men's room washing his hands while Kelly waited outside the door for him.

"He says he's big enough to go in by himself now," Kelly said. "I know he is, but it's funny, I still worry."

"Connor was premature," Sam said. It was all she said. It was all she had to say.

Kelly looked at her but had no reply.

Connor bounced out of the bathroom and showed his mother his clean hands.

"Hey, so how about we stop for ice cream? I think that is very well earned before we drive back," Sam announced.

"Ice cream!"

"I'll take that as a yes." Sam laughed, although it was forced. She wasn't going to show Connor one ounce of her fury. This day was about him. Sam was just going to have to park her anger with his mother somewhere else.

Kelly nodded. "Yes, that's fine. Sure. Why not ice cream?"

"And then later, we'll talk," Sam said softly.

IT WAS CLOSE to nine when Sam pulled up in front of Evan's house. He was on a road trip, so the house was dark. Connor was dead asleep in the back seat. Sam could hear the slight wheeze in his steady breathing. A wheeze, hopefully, Dr. Whitman could improve.

"You're going to tell him," Kelly said. It

was the first sentence she had uttered in the four-hour drive from Philadelphia.

"Of course I'm going to tell him. I didn't want to text him or do it over the phone. I only told him the appointment was a success. This is going to hurt him, Kelly. Badly. But you knew that, didn't you?"

Kelly nodded. "I'll have us packed up and gone before he gets back from his trip. It will be easier for him that way. No difficult goodbyes."

Sam couldn't argue with that. Having to say goodbye to Connor when all this time Evan had been thinking of him as his son… it would crush him.

"I think that would be best."

"Yeah. In order to have Connor go through this program at the Children's Hospital, we're going to need to find a place to live in Philadelphia. Connor won't like it. Changing schools. But this is his best chance of getting better, so I'm going to take it."

Sam didn't have anything to say.

"You think I'm a horrible person."

Sam sighed. "Kelly, I get it. Or at least I almost get it. You were desperate to help your son. But telling a man he's the father of your child when he isn't… I think that's a horrible thing to do. Does Connor's actual father know about him?"

Kelly snorted. "Oh, yeah, he knew. He wanted me to get an abortion. He wasn't going to take any responsibility, and the truth was I really didn't care. All I cared about was the life growing inside me. Connor was mine. I never saw the father again after I told him I was keeping the baby."

"What are you going to tell Connor?"

"That we had a nice visit with my old friend, but now we need to go home and figure out how we're going to move to Philadelphia. What are you going to tell Evan?"

"The truth. But he has your number. He's going to want to at least say goodbye to Connor."

"He has my number, but I doubt he'll use it. He might be hurt initially, but in the end he'll be happy to have us gone and out of his life."

Sam looked in the backseat at the sleeping little boy. She thought about what Evan had said about wanting a family. A family that, if Connor had been his, would have included him.

"I don't think Evan will be happy at all."

Evan pulled his truck into the hotel parking lot and hopped out. These last two games had put him right back on track with his swing. Though it was awful to think, no doubt being away from Kelly and Connor had helped him to keep his focus solely on the game.

He thought about the text he'd gotten from Kelly late last night.

The doctor was amazing. Can really help Connor. Thank you for everything.

Sam had already let him know the same. He wanted a little more of a breakdown of everything the doctor had said, but when he'd called Kelly this morning she hadn't answered her phone. That hadn't worried him until he walked into the lobby of the hotel where the team was staying to see Sam there waiting for him.

A surge of fear gripped him. He practically ran to her. "What's wrong? Is it Connor? Is he in the hospital again?"

"No, nothing like that."

Evan took a deep breath. "Okay, well, not that I'm not happy to see you, but what brings you here? I know you like watching me play, but going on the road for me...that's a whole new level of dedication."

Sam didn't smile. "Can we talk in your room?"

Again Evan was gripped by fear. "I hate conversations that start with *Can we talk?*"

Sam winced. "Well, you're not going to like this one. We should do it in private."

Evan didn't say another word. He hitched his equipment bag over his shoulder, and Sam followed him to the elevators. They rode up in silence, which told him how serious this conversation was going to get. She didn't want to even start it until they were behind closed doors.

They reached his room, and he took out his key. He let Sam go in first and then dumped his bag on the floor.

As soon as the door closed shut behind him, he said, "Okay, we're alone. Let me have it."

Sam took a deep breath. "Connor was born at thirty-two weeks. That's the cause of his asthma. His lungs weren't fully developed when he was born."

Evan tried to think about what that meant.

"He was born two months early."

Evan understood what she was trying to tell him.

"Sam…"

"I'm sorry," she jumped in, cutting him off. "I didn't really know what to say. If you were going to be relieved or sad. Or worse, devastated. I know what he's come to mean to you in a short time…"

"Sam," Evan stopped her. "I already knew he wasn't my son."

He could see her confusion. He should have shared with her what he knew, but he hadn't because it had taken a while for him to face the truth.

"The night of the barbecue, I asked Kelly one more time if he was my son. She didn't say that he was. She said that was what she told me. I knew then she was lying to me. Or at least, I strongly suspected it."

"Oh. You didn't say. In fact, you asked me if I could make room in my life for him."

"That still applies. Whether he was my son or not, it was too late. I was going to do anything I could to help the kid. I'm going to do everything I can to maintain a friendship with him. How could I not, when I'm going to have all this money? All this money that I could do something good with."

He tried to read Sam's expression. Right now he would have called it bewilderment. "I don't understand you. That woman used her child to extort money out of you. She made you worry about him, put you through all of that. Why aren't you angrier?"

"I'm not going to say Kelly is one of my favorite people on the planet, but she did what she did for her kid. The lying is over, at least. I'm not sure what her plan is now, but we'll still come up with some kind of agreement to help her pay this Dr. Whitman guy."

"Kelly and Connor are gone. She packed up and left the next morning."

Evan's eyes narrowed. "Sam, please, tell me you didn't make that happen."

Sam shook her head. "No. It was her idea. Once I called her out on her lie, she knew what she had to do. But I knew you would want to say goodbye to Connor."

"That must be why she didn't answer my call this morning. She thought I was going to rail on her."

"You should be railing on her. What she did was awful. Why she did it we both understand. But can't you see this is exactly the reason why you can't trust people? The way she lied to you, the way Richard lied to me."

Evan put his hands on her shoulders. "You're mad at her for me. Don't be."

"I'm furious with her for you. I was there

when you got the call that Connor was in the hospital. She made you feel that fear, and it wasn't right."

"Yes, she did. But for the first time, she didn't have to go through that experience alone. I'm not sorry I was there. For her or Connor."

"So that's it," Sam said, clearly frustrated with him. "You just look at everything through rose-colored glasses. Everyone gets a pass. That's a little naïve, isn't it?"

Evan dropped his hands and took a step back. "Okay. That hurt."

She frowned. "I didn't mean to say it that way."

"No," Evan charged. "What you probably meant to say was that you think I'm some kind of idiot. I'm sorry if I don't follow the Samantha Baker model of not trusting anyone about anything. News flash. It's not going to change, either."

"How can you say that? My *model* was completely warranted in this case. I mean, really, Evan, how long would you have dragged this out if I hadn't discovered the truth? Were you going to pay for his college, too, maybe buy them a nice home to live in?"

"I don't know. But it would have been my call, Sam. Not yours."

She crossed her arms over her chest. "Why do I feel like I'm being cast as the bad guy again?"

"You're not the bad guy, Sam. But you and I both know that if we're going to have a chance at a relationship, then you have to get over that fear you have of everyone in your life being one second away from betraying you. It makes me wonder, too…what if it's not about you not trusting people, but you not trusting yourself?"

"What's that supposed to mean?"

"You dated a creep who turned on you. I get it. It sucks, but you did the right thing by ending the relationship. I have the feeling you still blame yourself for that."

Sam's eyes lifted. "I blame myself for Donald? For getting hit?"

"Not for him hitting you," Evan clarified. "For not knowing he was the type of guy who would do that. Yet you couldn't know that until you saw for yourself what he was capable of. Same deal with Richard. *He* lied to *you*. You couldn't have known he would do that. You couldn't have known he would be the type of person to send you out in front of a room full of reporters to lie for him. They were the assholes. Not you. Until you understand that, the mistrust you have for people, including me, is never going to go away."

"Don't say that," she whispered, looking like he'd just sentenced her to live in her own personal Siberia.

Evan hated to hurt her, but he needed her to see the truth about herself if things were ever really going to change between them.

"Well, isn't it true? Tell me, Sam. Why do you really want to keep our relationship private?"

"I told you, my reputation as a professional agent…"

"Bullshit," Evan snapped. "I don't think it's about that at all. It's about denial. You've opened yourself up enough to be in a relationship, which is great, but you've also spent this whole time waiting for me to disappoint you. Haven't you?"

"No, that's not true," Sam said, even as the color faded from her cheeks.

"Isn't it? So, when I do—because that's how you think, isn't it, *when*, not if—so, when I do, you can pretend we were never re-

ally together and that the indomitable Samantha Baker didn't make yet another mistake."

"That's what you think of me?" Sam whispered. "Then, why do you even want a relationship with me? Why not just leave me
alone and let me do my job? You started this.
You pushed me to this place."

Evan closed his eyes. "Sam, don't you get
it? I love you. I love you, and it kills me that
the things that were done to you have hurt
you so much you can't let yourself love me
back."

"Evan, I do—"

"No, don't say it. To tell you the truth, I
don't think I would believe it."

Any color that had been left in her face
was now gone. She looked like an ice princess, her skin was so pale.

He'd delivered another blow. Another one
that crushed him, too.

His cell phone rang, and Evan pulled it
out of his back pocket. It was just a number
listed with no name, so he turned it off.

"Who was it?"

"Just a number. They can leave a voice
mail."

"No, you need to call them back."

Evan frowned. "Why?"

"That's the other reason I came down here. The Rebels' right outfielder got hurt playing in the All-Star game. They're calling you up, and Reuben's made an offer on your contract."

"Sam, we don't have to talk about this now," Evan said quietly. He could see she was practically shaking. "We need to settle this between us."

"No, we do have to talk about this!" Sam shouted. "Because you want me to change who I am. For you. Like it's easy!"

Evan tried to walk toward her, but she retreated with every step. "Sam, calm down, love."

"No, I will not calm down! I hadn't been with a man in three years until you. I hadn't gone on a date or, hell, even smiled at a man in the grocery store. I was ready to write off being a mother! A mother, which is something I've always wanted to be. Then you made me feel things and want things I didn't think I ever would again…"

Her voice cracked, and Evan took another step toward her, but again she backed away. "Sam…"

"No, stay away. You have the audacity to tell me you don't believe what I'm feeling? You think I'm really that cold, I could lie about something as important as love? So, no, we're not going to talk about us anymore. I can't."

She took a moment and gathered herself. Took a few deep breaths. She smoothed her hair. She straightened the silk top she was wearing.

"We are, however, going to talk about baseball," she finally said in a very cool tone. "Because I'm a coldhearted badass agent. Let me be what I am."

The two of them stared at each other, but Evan could see just by the way she was holding herself together she had dug her heels in on this. He'd hurt her and he hadn't meant to. But he did want to help her get past the trust issues. Not just for them. For her, too.

A single ding announced a voice mail.

"Listen to it."

Evan hit the button on his phone to play the message and held it to his ear.

"Well?" Sam asked as soon as he put the phone away.

"Well, it looks like I'll be starting in to-morrow night's game for the Rebels."

She nodded tightly. "Now, we talk about our counteroffer to Reuben."

CHAPTER NINETEEN

"So, how do I look?" Evan asked his father.

They only had a few minutes before Evan needed to be on the field for batting practice, but Nelson had wanted a chance to see him before the game. After suiting up, Evan had left the locker room where he'd gotten one of the team's security people to escort his father down to the players' level in the stadium.

Nelson clapped his hands once in excitement. "You look like you're in the major leagues."

Evan laughed. "Well, that's good. Looking the part might be all I can do right now."

"You'll be fine. You're not one to let the big stage rattle you."

"No, it's not that. Sam and I got into it yesterday, and I just… I don't know. I don't know where we stand. We went from talking about me being in love with her to contract negotiations with Reuben. She completely shut me down. Wouldn't even consider discussing it further."

Nelson nodded. "Your mother used to be the same way. She decided when the fight was over. It took me six or seven years, though, to figure that out. Spare yourself the agony and learn to accept it now. When she's ready to talk again, you'll know it."

"If she's ever ready to talk again. I don't know what I'm going to do," Evan said, running his hand through his hair. "I truly don't know if she can do it. If she can let go of her fear of being betrayed. If she can find a way to believe in us. Because if I can't believe that, how am I going to know if she means it when she says she loves me?"

"Hmm." Nelson snorted. "You really do love this girl?"

Evan sighed. "I really do. It's going to sound crazy, but I honestly think I fell in love with her the moment I laid eyes on her. All this time I've been waiting to get to her. Only she's not completely there yet."

"Then, you wait a little longer," Nelson said.

"Dad, it's not that easy."

"It's exactly that easy if you love her. You can't tell a person who's hurting inside when that hurting should stop. If you love her like you say you do, then you should be willing to hang on as long as it takes. You should also do everything you can to let her know you're there for her. You keep telling me you don't know what *she* can or can't do. Have you thought that maybe *you* should be helping her do that? Son, you're the reason she's taking a chance on you despite her fear. Which means you need to do *your* part to help her."

Evan remembered how upset she'd been last night. How she'd yelled at him that he thought it was easy to just fix herself. This whole time he'd put the burden squarely on her to deal with her issues. Because, for him, it was easy. So easy to love Sam.

His father was right. The burden should have been on both of them. He needed to prove every day that he was trustworthy. That he would never hurt her.

It was as if a bomb exploded in his head.

"I screwed up," Evan admitted.

"We're men, we usually do. But you can fix that."

"How?" Evan wanted to know. "She's not exactly talking to me right now."

Nelson laughed. "Well, if I were a professional baseball player making my big league debut, I would probably try and show off to her."

Evan didn't buy it. "You think a home run will impress Sam? Not happening."

"No. A home run will make me happy. You want to woo a woman? This woman you claim to love? Hell, something that big… you're going to have to hit the cycle."

Evan laughed outright. Right. A home run, a triple, a double and a single…in his first game against major league pitching.

"Are you kidding me? Do you know who's on the mound tonight for the other team?"

"Hey." Nelson chuckled, patting Evan on the shoulder, "I didn't say it was going to be easy. Good luck, son."

SAM SAT IN the ballpark and took in the size of the crowd around her. She'd gotten so used to the attendance for the Minotaurs, she'd forgotten how impressive a major league stadium could be. Everything was bigger: the fans, the food, the spectacle.

The money.

All for being able to throw and hit a small white ball. It really was a crazy game.

"Is this seat taken?"

Sam turned and smiled up at Nelson. "It happens to belong to the father of Evan Tanner, who is making his first start for the New England Rebels tonight."

"Well, excellent, then, because that's me."

Nelson sat down and handed Sam a beer. "I figured we could do with a little alcohol to settle our nerves."

She took it, grateful for something to help calm her down. "It's crazy. I've been in this situation with maybe thirty or forty clients, but I've never been this nervous."

"That's because you're not looking at him as a client."

Sam shifted in her seat and sipped her beer. "Uh… Nelson… I should probably tell you we had a pretty bad fight. I think the only way he sees me right now is exactly as his agent and nothing else."

"You young people. You get so excitable. You fight. Then you make up. That's the way it works."

"It's not that easy," she muttered.

Nelson laughed. "I'll tell you what I told him. It's exactly that easy if you love him."

"He thinks there's something wrong with me—psychologically. That I don't trust him. He could be right. I don't know."

"Okay," Nelson said. "Then don't trust him. Trust me. I know my boy, and he would never intentionally hurt you. He would never cheat on you or lie to you unless to tell you you look beautiful in a dress when you really don't. He would also match your fierce loyalty. You need someone exactly like that."

Sam smiled. Then she leaned over and kissed him on the cheek. "I know one thing for certain."

"What's that?"

"I'm definitely falling in love with you," Sam told him.

Nelson chuckled. "Sorry, my dear, a woman stole my heart thirty-one years ago and I've never gotten it back. But I'll tell you this…you remind me of her. A lot."

Sam smiled and drank her beer and settled in to see her client… Evan…play ball. They put him fifth in the lineup, which was high, considering this was his debut, and given the ace pitcher he was facing. Sam held her breath when he came up to the plate the first time and smiled when he let the first pitch sail by.

The low curve ball was called a ball.

The next pitch he hit for a double. Both Nelson and Sam were on their feet. They added hot dogs and more beer to their evening and waited until Evan came to the plate again.

He did his due diligence this time, watching and letting the first two pitches go by.

"Good eye, son. Good eye," Nelson said as he clapped. "That's the only baseball vocabulary I know."

Sam smiled. "You've got a long time of watching him to get there."

Evan swung at the next pitch, and Sam could hear the contact before she saw it. A sharp hit well into right field. She watched as the fielder misjudged the distance, and it sailed over his head and rattled along the track.

"Go, Evan!" Sam shouted, standing as she watched the third base coach wave him past second. The throw, when it came from the outfield, was like a cannon, but Evan had already slid safely into third.

"Holy cow. This is crazy!"

Sam kept clapping. "A double and a triple, which is almost impossible, in his first outing. Reuben is probably having a fit."

"That's not what's crazy," Nelson said with a smile.

"What do you mean?" Sam asked. "It's an amazing debut."

"Yes, but he's not done yet. I told him if he really wanted to impress you, he was going to have to hit for the cycle. Another baseball term I learned."

Sam's jaw dropped. "Nelson. The cycle is one of the hardest things in baseball. It's like pitching a no-hitter or, even harder, a prefect game."

"You might already know this about Evan, but he's stubborn, and when he sets his mind to something, he usually gets it."

Sam looked at Nelson, then out at the field. The next batter up had just knocked Evan in for the run.

"You think he's doing this for me?"

"Partly for you," Nelson said. "He promised me the home run, but the rest is…yep… all you."

Sam sat down, amazed. Practically, she knew it couldn't be true. A player didn't try to hit for the cycle. It was just one of those happenstance things that could unfold over a long game.

The sixth inning rolled around, and Evan came up to the plate again. Sam held her breath. She had to force herself to watch.

When she heard the sound of the hit, she jumped up in her seat. A Seeing Eye dog that sped right past the pitcher and bounced past the short stop.

A single.

"Yes, my boy sure is stubborn, and when he wants something, he usually finds a way to get it."

Sam heard what Nelson was saying, but she couldn't believe it. It wasn't possible to make something like this happen in an attempt to impress her. To win her. To show her how he felt about her through baseball? It was lunacy.

It was a baseball movie!

The buzz in the stadium changed immediately once Evan hit his single. Now everyone knew what was at stake. Sam had been to enough big sporting events to know when the crowd's attention was suddenly piqued, and the tension would only increase from here.

"He's still got to hit the home run," Sam whispered. They had just started the seventh inning. He might get another chance in the eighth, if the other players started getting on base, but the most likely outcome was that he would have his last chance to bat in the ninth.

One last chance at a home run. One last chance to hit the cycle in his debut start in the major leagues.

Sam pulled her phone out of her pocket and dialed Reuben's number.

"Yeah, yeah, Sam," he said immediately upon answering the phone. "I'm watching it."

"He's going to do it, Reuben."

"At best he's got one last shot at bat."

"He's going to do it." Sam could just feel it. Like this was fate and it was happening to her. To both of them.

"You want to bet?"

Sam smiled. "Make me an offer."

"Four years, ten million if he makes it. My original offer if he doesn't."

Sam chuckled. "Reuben, that's so funny. You think I would risk my client's livelihood on something as difficult as hitting a home run. You're going to give me the four years at twelve million, because you're lucky enough to have traded for one of the best hitters in baseball right now. That's a given. We'll work out the specific terms in your office next week. However, for a bet… I don't know. I was thinking more along the lines of a dollar?"

Sam heard him chuckle and then sigh. "All right, Sam. One dollar he doesn't hit the cycle. I know where to find you to pay up."

"Not going to happen, Reuben. He's going to do it."

"If he does, he knows the drill, right? He stays for everyone to interview him."

"He knows the drill."

Sam disconnected the call and smiled—rather smugly, she imagined—because that's how she was feeling right about now.

Nelson just whistled. "Did I hear that right? Are they going to pay my son forty-eight million dollars to play this game?"

"They are, and if he continues to pull stunts like these, the sky's the limit."

Nelson shook his head. "It's really sort of crazy when you think about it."

Sam patted his knee and smiled. "It probably is, but you raised a fine man. And a fine man will put a lot of that money to good use."

"You think he might send me on a cruise for Christmas?" Nelson smiled. "I've always wanted to go on a cruise."

Sam laughed. "Nelson, you can go on all the cruises you like."

They continued to watch the game as the Rebels' pitcher gave up a bunch of runs. Despite Evan's offense as they entered the bottom of the ninth, the game was tied. Given the order, Evan would be batting fourth, but that meant at least one of the batters in front of him had to get on base.

Sam nearly came out of her skin when the first two batters struck out. The people in the ball park were on the edge of their seats, all of them willing the batter who was hitting third—the man who had once been the team's star for so many years—to get on base.

He did it with a walk.

At that point the pitching coach came out of the dugout, and Sam watched as he jogged out to the mound.

It was a tie game, so it was the other team's closer on the mound right now.

"What do you think?" Nelson asked.

"The smart thing to do would be to pitch around him," Sam muttered, sitting on her hands to keep from wringing them. "He's obviously on fire, but…"

"But?"

"That's Applebaum on the mound," Sam told him. "I met him once, and he's a real jerk. Cocky son of a bitch, too. He's not going to want to pitch around Evan in this situation. Especially knowing he's a rookie. He won't like the way it makes him look. Like he's scared of giving up the home run."

"That doesn't sound like he's playing the game with his head."

"You're assuming Applebaum's got any room left in his head after his ego has sucked up all the space. Look at him shaking off the pitching coach. Unbelievable."

The pitching coach jogged back to the dugout, and Sam waited to see if the manager might follow. The goal was to win the game, and any manager with an ounce of sense wouldn't let a pitcher throw a ball near Evan.

But it seemed like this manager either didn't care, or maybe he was hoping to teach Applebaum a lesson in humility.

Applebaum threw the ball over the plate, and Evan watched it fly past.

Strike one.

The second blew by him, too. Another strike. Applebaum could throw mid-nineties, which was no joke.

Sam looked over at Nelson, who seemed so completely calm while she wanted to run screaming up and down the rows.

He turned to her and smiled easily. "Just watch, honey. Just watch."

She did. She turned her head to the stadium and watched Applebaum wind up.

It seemed like it was happening in slow motion. The windup, the pitch. The ball flying through the air and then that sound.

The crack of the bat, making pure contact with the ball.

Hear that, Sammy. You can always tell by the sound of the crack when the ball is going yard.

She could feel the tears streaming down her cheeks. They all rose as one to watch as the ball went back, back, back and finally over the fence.

Not only had Evan hit the cycle. He'd just done it with a walk-off home run to win the game.

She plunked down in her seat while the crowd around her erupted. A stadium full of people shouting "Tanner" as Evan rounded the bases with his head down, no emotion. Just a humble guy doing his thing until the team was there to meet him at home plate.

She watched as man after man piled on him, and she thought he would probably be sore the next day. He was the old guy, after all.

But she could give him a massage, and that would make him feel better.

That's when it clicked. When she knew deep in her heart she trusted Evan. Trusted him to do the right thing when confronted with a bad situation. Trusted him to behave professionally when he hit a walk-off home run. Trusted him with her heart when she was vulnerable to him.

Because she loved him. It really was as simple as Nelson said it would be.

Sam could feel her phone buzzing immediately. She pulled it out to see the first text from Reuben.

You win.

No, you win, Sam replied and hit Send.

Then Roy and Lane texted, telling her to pass on their congratulations, but when the phone rang, she knew it was Scout.

She put her finger in one ear to drown out the crowd. They'd linger, no doubt, to watch the traditional shaving cream face-plant which was a time-honored ritual any player had to undergo after winning the game with a walk-off home run.

"Am I good or what?" Scout asked. "The flipping cycle right out of the gate."

"Scout," Sam shouted into the phone over the noise, no longer really caring about his baseball accomplishments. "I love him. What should I do now?"

Because, while the love was overwhelming, so was the fear. Fear she had fought him too much and too hard.

She needed to prove to him in a way as tangible as hitting a cycle that she loved him.

"Go tell him," Scout said into her ear. "Now."

Sam nodded. That was it. She needed to tell him. She put the phone in her back pocket and looked at Nelson. "I'm going to go find him."

He nodded, and she could see he had wiped a tear from his cheek. A very proud father.

"We'll meet you back at the car," Sam said. "And then we'll celebrate together at dinner."

"I like the sound of that."

"What?"

"We," Nelson said. "Now go get him."

Sam climbed over Nelson to get into the aisle. She had to fight the people who were finally now just filing out of the stadium as they were moving upstream while she was moving down. They had seats just a few rows up from first base line in the players' section, but Sam was going to need to get over a few rows to get closer to him. She wore agent credentials, which should get her by the security guarding the field, but if not, she was just going to have to make a run for it.

Hell, she'd seen a hundred baseball movies with happy endings. She could do this.

"Evan, can you tell us how you feel right now?" It was a local reporter from one of the news stations, the first in a line of them who were probably all going to ask him the same question, but he didn't care.

Evan smiled into the camera. He couldn't say how he felt. Because how he felt right now was pure joy. Joy in doing something he loved for the two people he loved most in the world.

He wanted Sam. He wanted to tell her he was sorry. He wanted to tell her that he would wait ten years for her if that's what she needed. He wanted to tell her that she had been with him in his heart the whole day and it made everything crystal clear.

It made focusing on a small white ball seem like a very easy thing to do.

"Well, right now I feel like I've got shaving cream up my nose, but all things considered, I'll take that."

The reporter laughed.

"This was your debut appearance in the major leagues. Did you imagine having a day like the one you had?"

The first answer that leaped to his mind was yes. Yes, he'd wanted to do this for Sam, for his father. Yes, he'd wanted to have this kind of day. But of course he couldn't say that.

"Uh… I don't think anyone expects to hit the cycle their first day up. I think today I got real lucky."

"Evan!"

Evan turned at the sound of her voice. There she was in the stands right over the dugout. She was waving to him as she tried to negotiate around stadium security.

"Looks like you've got a fan," the reporter said.

"That's my agent," Evan said carefully, hoping for all the world the truth didn't show on his face. He knew how Sam felt about disclosing their relationship, and he was on camera. He didn't want everyone watching to know what a goner he was.

Then something remarkable happened that both he, the reporter and the cameras that were on him all turned to watch.

Sam, who had been trying to get around security by showing her credentials, hauled off and kicked the guy in the shin, causing him to reach for his leg.

Evan's jaw dropped as he watched Sam jump over the rail and on to the dugout roof, which was about a three-foot drop. Then another four-foot drop took her to the field.

She was wearing capris and sandals, something that should have looked casual at a baseball game, but on her looked sleek and elegant.

At full speed she ran toward him, shouting his name, until he realized unequivocally what she meant to do. He opened his arms, and in the last second she leaped into him, wrapping her legs around his waist and holding on to him for dear life.

She cupped his face in her hands and forced him to look at her, not that it was any hardship. His beautiful, beautiful Sam.

"I love you."

The words went right through him and filled him with a certainty they were true.

"I love you back," he whispered against her lips.

The reporter who still held his microphone, in front of a camera that was still rolling, said, "That's not like any client-agent relationship I've ever seen."

Sam turned to him and smiled. Then she smiled back at Evan.

"That's because I'm not just his agent. I'm also his girlfriend. And guess what? My boyfriend hit the cycle just for me."

"For you," Evan repeated. "All for you."

He hugged her, and she hugged him back. Then she carefully kissed him on the lips in a way to avoid any of the shaving cream that was still slathered about his face in spots.

She unwound her legs until she was back

on solid ground. Then she spanked him on the ass. "Now, finish these interviews, baby. I've got some sponsors to line up."

"Now, that sounds like an agent," the reporter said, and everyone around them laughed.

CHAPTER TWENTY

SAM SAT NEXT to Evan in his truck as they made their way through the narrow streets of Philadelphia. It was early October, and while Evan had provided a boost of offense for the Rebels, they had failed to win their play-in game to get into the next round of the play-offs. Which meant this was his first day of the off-season.

However, the team was confident, with a full season under his belt, the sky was the limit for both Evan and the Rebels. He'd ended the season batting .343, which was amazing for a rookie. In addition, he'd managed to knock in seventeen home runs and over ninety RBIs in half a season. Not to mention he'd been named the National League rookie of the year.

He'd been on the cover of *Sports Illustrated* with the caption underneath: *Over the Hill?*

And Sam, being Sam, had gotten him a

number of endorsements to augment the already ridiculous money he was making.

Like she told him, she had to earn a living, too.

The more people got to know Evan through his interviews and through his baseball contacts, the more they understood he wouldn't allow someone to represent him who wasn't one hundred percent aboveboard.

He sure as hell wouldn't be dating her.

Sam's phone had been ringing steadily ever since Evan's success, with athletes who wanted her representation. A small boutique agency where Sam felt fully confident in everyone on her list. As fully confident as she could be, that was, as Evan would casually remind her that she couldn't foresee what might happen in the future. Or what trouble her clients might get into.

She was learning she had to accept that. People weren't perfect, and you couldn't always know that in advance of signing them.

"Okay, turn down this street and find someplace to park. According to the GPS, it's that building," Sam told Evan.

It wasn't the easiest thing, but Evan managed to find a place to park his truck between the rows of cars. He looked at it warily, sticking out into the narrow city street.

"Someone's going to hit it," he told Sam as she came around to his side. He held out his hand, and she reached for it easily. This was something else that had taken her time to get accustomed to: being able to show anybody watching how she felt about this man just by holding his hand.

Then again, purposefully outing herself as his girlfriend on television had been a nice ice breaker.

"No one's going to hit it. Everyone knows how to drive around here so as to not hit big trucks. Besides, you're the one who insists on only having the truck. You could buy something smaller that would be easier to get around in the city. We do live in Boston now."

Evan frowned even as he pulled a wrapped box out of the cab seat. "It just seems weird for one guy to have two cars."

Sam smiled and reached up to stroke his cheek. "It's so cute that you don't know how to spend your money. Especially when I keep making more of it for you."

"Hey, I spent money. I sent Dad on a cruise."

Sam smiled. Nelson had been thrilled with

what Sam imagined would be the first of many trips Evan would send his father on. In the off-season, of course. Nelson made every attempt to follow his son around, watching him play baseball.

They walked up to the apartment building, and Evan searched the printed names to find the right button to get through the security door. As luck would have it, an elderly couple was coming out, and they were able to get inside without announcing their presence.

"This might be better," Sam said. "This way, she'll have to talk to us."

"You're sure she's home."

"No, but I checked with her manager at the restaurant, and she's not working this afternoon. The weather is kind of lousy, not a good day to take Connor to a park. Let's hope we get lucky."

Kelly's address was listed as Suite 315B, and it appeared that the numbers lined up with the floors of the building. Sam and Evan took the elevator up to the third floor and found 315B on their left.

"You're sure about this?" Evan asked. Sam wasn't sure if he was questioning his decision or their welcome.

"It's not for me to be sure. It's for you to be sure. It's your money."

Evan frowned.

"I'm sure," he said finally.

He knocked on the door, and they heard a scramble inside. The door swung open, and Connor's expression was a combination of surprise and awe.

"Connor, how many times have I told you, you can't just answer—" Kelly stopped talking when she saw who was standing in her doorway.

"Mom! It's Evan. And he's like a real professional now and everything."

Kelly pulled back her hair and worried her lip with her teeth.

"Can we come in?" Evan asked her.

"Uh…sure."

Connor stepped back, and Evan and Sam entered the apartment. It was small. A living room and a kitchen that was separated by an island counter. There was a small neat couch and a leather chair that looked like it had seen better days.

"I…don't really have a bunch of places to sit," Kelly said, gesturing to everything they could see.

"That's fine. We're not staying long. Connor, I wanted to bring you this in person."

Connor took the box and unwrapped it. "Wow!" he exclaimed, pulling out the baseball mitt. "Look, Mom, it's signed."

"I got the team to sign one. Don't know if you're a Rebels fan…"

"I am! I tell everyone how you're my mom's friend and how we hung out together this summer. Now they will totally believe me."

"Not just your mom's friend. Your friend, too," Evan said. "Kelly, I was hoping we could talk. Alone."

"Oh. Sure. Connor, why don't you take your mitt in your room and check out all the signatures? The adults want to talk for a minute."

He shrugged like a typical kid who didn't necessarily understand what "adult" talking was but acknowledged it as a serious thing.

Once his door was closed, Kelly folded her arms over her chest.

"Evan, I told you on the phone. I was sorry to just take off like that, but really it was for the best. I told Connor you had to go to Boston, and we had to go back to Tucson. It was no big deal. You called to say you'd be in touch. He thought that was great. He didn't think anything of it. You didn't have to come all this way."

"I wanted to," Sam interjected. "Making you feel as if you needed to leave this past summer, that was my fault. I got in the middle of something between you and Evan, and I shouldn't have. I wanted to apologize in person."

Kelly nodded. "Okay. Fine. But we all know I was the one who did something wrong. I just want to put it behind me. You came, you apologized. Was that it?"

"How is the treatment going?" Evan asked.

"It's good. He's still adjusting to the new city and the new school. But he hasn't had an attack since we've started the treatment, and that's like…amazing."

"We called Children's Hospital," Sam announced, figuring it was best to be as upfront as they could, not really knowing how Kelly was going to react to any of what Evan planned to do.

"Why? It's not like they could tell you anything about his condition. It's protected information."

"We weren't asking about his condition.

Only the general cost of care," Evan told her. He reached inside the light jacket he wore and pulled out an envelope.

Kelly took it, and Sam could see that her hands were trembling.

Then she handed it back. "No, I can't. I'm making it work on my own. I've got two different waitressing jobs. I've taken a loan through the hospital to pay for the treatments. What I did by coming to you was desperate. I was looking for something to be easy in my life. Just this one time. It was wrong. I can't raise Connor like that."

Sam smiled. "I bet it's amazing what some real sleep—now that you're no longer in constant fear of your son's condition—can do to your thinking."

Kelly shook her head. "You're giving me an out, and I appreciate that, but I did a shitty thing."

"You did," Evan told her. "You got me invested in Connor's life. You can't really do that and turn around now and say 'stay out of it.' I want this for him. I want to know that I was able to help."

Evan put the envelope on the small coffee table next to the couch.

"It's important to me," he told her. "The

truth is, I don't know what the hell to do with it all."

Kelly stared at the envelope and eventually nodded. "Okay. For Connor."

"We thought we could take you and Connor out for lunch or something," Sam suggested.

"Really? You seriously want us to be, like what, friends?"

"I would like to think I could check in on Connor from time to time," Evan said. "So, yeah, that would be easier if we were friends, don't you think?"

Kelly seemed to consider that. "You know, Evan, sometimes you're a little too good to be true. I don't know how you put up with it, Sam. Okay. You win. I'll go get him and his coat. And Evan, Sam...thank you both. Evan, for your being so accepting of all of it, and, Sam, for reminding me what kind of person I want to be. Even though at times you're a little scary."

Sam wiggled her eyebrows. "Everyone says that about me, but I have no idea why."

Kelly smiled, an actual smile without any nervousness behind it. "I'll be back in a second."

When it was just the two of them alone

in the living room, Sam looked at Evan and wrapped her arm around his waist.

"She's wrong. You're not too good to be true. You just really are one of the good guys, Evan Tanner."

He gave her a peck on the lips, and a knowing smile teased his mouth.

"Are you sure about that?"

"One hundred percent certain," Sam said, amazed at how certain she was. She believed in Evan. She trusted him. Most importantly, she loved him, and she felt confident he loved her back.

"Excellent, because after lunch I have a surprise for you."

Maybe now was the time to tell him that, as a natural control freak, Sam wasn't all that crazy about surprises. But his eyes were twinkling and his lips were doing that funny thing they did when he tried not to smile too big, and she decided maybe this one time she could let him have his way.

Connor came racing out of the room with his arm in one sleeve of a jacket but his hand still stuck in the mitt.

Kelly followed behind with a look of both exasperation and love. She pulled the mitt off and tucked his loose arm into his coat.

"The mitt stays in the apartment."

"Ah, Mom."

"No 'ah, Mom.' You want it to stay nice, don't you?"

"But I can take it to school," Connor insisted. "You said."

"Yes, I said."

Satisfied with that, he turned to Evan. "Hey, so now that you're rich, can we eat at a fancy place?"

Sam chuckled as Kelly groaned. "Connor!"

Evan smiled. "Kid, we can eat at the fanciest place."

"Let's go for cheesesteaks, then! Pat's is the best."

"Ah," Evan said. "You mean really fancy. Okay, let's go."

THE SURPRISE, WHEN Sam was allowed to take the blindfold off, was a small private airport.

"You're giving me flying lessons?" she asked. She got out of the truck and saw the jet on the runway. The steps to the door were down.

"Nope."

"You bought your own plane. We talked about this, Evan. You don't really want to buy these types of high-ticket items. Not when you can lease or become part of a co-op..."

"I didn't buy a plane, either."

"Evan, then what are we doing at a private airport somewhere in New York, which I only know because I could tell, based on the position of the sun, that we were driving north from Philadelphia for the last four hours."

Evan came around the truck and took her hand, pulling her toward the plane. He stopped as soon as they were at the bottom of the steps.

"You're taking me on a trip," she guessed.

"Yes, if it's a journey you're willing to go on with me."

"Of course. Anywhere you want. I'll need to call my clients, though. You have to remember you're not my one and only anymore. But I could try and arrange a few days..."

Sam stopped talking when she saw Evan get down on one knee. Her heart lurched into her throat, and her natural reaction was to hold her breath, which probably wasn't the best idea because she already felt on the verge of fainting.

"When I got that first check there were only two things I wanted to spend it on. Helping Connor get better, and this."

Sam watched as he pulled a tiny box from his pocket and opened it.

The solitaire diamond ring sat nestled in black velvet.

"When the season ended, there were only two things I wanted to do. Give Kelly that money for Connor and give you this."

"Oh, Evan."

"Sam, if I didn't fall in love with you at first sight, then I sure as hell fell into something. You have been in my head and in my heart ever since. I want to marry you and make babies with you, and I don't want to wait. This plane is fueled up and ready to fly us to Las Vegas. I want to be married to you tonight. I want to be in our bed together tonight. I want to be a legal us tonight. I waited two years for you, Samantha Baker, and I don't want to wait one more day. Not without you being my wife. Will you marry me?"

Sam waited for the slightest hesitation. A resurgence of that old fear. She'd been proposed to twice in her life now. The first man had nearly destroyed her trust in people. The second man had restored it.

"Yes, Evan. I will marry you. Tonight."

Evan got up and slid the ring on her finger. He cupped her face in his hands and kissed her, and she thought she had never felt so much love in her life. From him, from herself.

Then, like two school children, they started to run up the steps.

"But what about a dress or clothes?" she asked him.

"We'll buy what we need when we get there," he told her.

"Oh, sure, now you have no problem spending money."

They got on the jet, and Sam could see he was prepared with a bottle of champagne already on ice. "Spending money on you is easy."

Sam and Evan took their seats while the flight attendant congratulated them on their engagement.

Minutes after liftoff and when the pilot had removed the seat belt restriction, Sam was sitting in Evan's lap, a glass of champagne in her hand, and they were on the way to Vegas.

"But what about our families?" Sam said as the first doubt crept in. Not about marrying Evan. Never that. Just about how they were doing it. "Don't you think they'll be upset with us?"

Evan shook his head. "I told Dad what I wanted to do, and he agreed the faster, the better. I told Bob what I wanted to do…and that was a little awkward."

Sam thought about why Bob might have a problem with them getting married. The two of them had seemed to get along great any time they were together. Bob had already told her that this time she did well for herself. He trusted Evan completely.

"What was his problem?" Sam asked.

"He said I should have already married you, since we've been living together for a few weeks. Then he said…he wanted to walk you down the aisle. He missed a lot of moments in your life as you grew up, and he was hoping he would get to have that one."

Sam thought she could actually feel her heart swelling. "That's so sweet."

"Please." Evan snorted. "Do not ever put 'Bob' and 'sweet' in the same sentence. That man is scary. Anyway, I offered him a compromise. He lets me do this now in Vegas, then you get to plan whatever you want back in Boston. Just as long as there's an aisle long enough to satisfy Bob."

That made Sam very, very happy. "Deal. I love you, Evan Tanner."

"I love you, soon-to-be Samantha Tanner."

"Oh, wow. That will be it, then."

Evan frowned. "What?"

"Well, for so long, it was always the three of us. The Baker Girls of Baseball. Now, none of us are left. Lane married a pitcher. Scout married a coach, and I married a hitter, each of us blissfully in love. You know what I'm thinking, though?" Sam smiled.

"What?" Evan said as he dipped his head again to kiss her.

"I bet Duff wouldn't have it any other way."

EPILOGUE

"AH! OH, FLIPPING mother of…"

"Scout, your language," Alice said as she walked next to the wheelchair Sam was pushing toward the maternity ward. The task was made slightly more difficult by three-inch heels and a Vera Wang wedding dress with a short but elegant train.

"Seriously? I can't swear while I'm in labor?"

Alice raised a single eyebrow and looked down at her daughter. "Is that really the first thing you want your baby to hear coming out of your mouth?"

Scout started to go into contractions again. "Ahhh, this hurts!"

"Hey, hold it. I'm here. I've got it." Lane was running up behind them with the baby bag. "Jayson said you're supposed to be listening to soothing music."

"Oh, like that's going to do it! What the

hell was I thinking, soothing music? Where the hell is he, anyway?"

"Evan and Roy are driving him. Evan's parking the truck now."

"Can you believe he fainted? I am so going to hold that over his head for the rest of his life."

Sam smiled. "It did make for a pretty interesting end to my wedding. Evan kisses the bride, your water breaks, and Jayson passes out."

Alice patted Sam's hand. "At least Scout held out until Bob got to walk you down the aisle. That's all that matters."

"I mean, I didn't want to steal all of your thunder, but let's face it, it's not like this was the real wedding."

No, she and Evan had been happily married for months, but still, this was the wedding where she got to wear her fancy dress.

Not that the birth of her niece or nephew wasn't way more important.

"I can't believe we still don't know if it's a girl or a boy," Lane muttered. "It's 2016 for Pete's sake. Everybody knows."

"I wanted it to be a surprise," Scout muttered as another contraction squeezed her body. "Now I just want it to be over. Oh,

Sam, you should probably not watch this. Lane, you either, if you ever plan on doing this."

Lane smiled. "Well…actually…it looks like in another seven months, we'll all be back here again."

Alice beamed. "Oh, Lane, that's wonderful."

"Seriously?" Sam asked. "I mean, the two of you are messing with my big moments. First, Scout has the baby on my wedding day, and now Lane is going to have her kid probably right before me."

All eyes turned to her.

"You, too?"

Sam just smiled, not really miffed at all about the wedding or Lane being pregnant at the same time she was. How could anyone be miffed when they were so filled with joy?

"Oh, Sam. We're going to be preggers together."

"Yeah, and I'm not. I'm going to laugh my ass off watching you have to go through what I just did."

Alice patted her daughter on the shoulder. "And I'll be laughing my ass off while you see what being a mother is like. Say good-bye to sleep, Scout."

"I'll take it as long as this pain stops! Ahhh."

Sam and Lane looked at each other. "Maybe we shouldn't be watching this?" Sam suggested.

"Oh, no. You two are not leaving my side. Not until Jayson gets here."

"We're here!" Jayson said, running up behind them. "Sam, I can push her. I should really be the one to take her to the room."

Sam took one look at her chalky white brother-in-law and shook her head. "I don't want you throwing up on her."

"Ew, gross," Scout cried. "Jayson, go get some ginger ale and then meet me in the room."

He nodded and tried to breathe through his nose. "That might be a good idea. Then I'll be fine, Scout. I'll be good. I'll be ready to go."

The three sisters, along with their mother, watched him weave his way down the hall like he was drunk, when they all knew he'd been stone-cold sober for the past month in the event Scout went into labor, and he would have to drive her.

"Somehow I'm guessing he's not going to be able to watch his child being born," Alice mused.

"Not without fainting," Scout concurred. "He can hold my hand. That's all I need."

Roy and Evan caught up with them, too.

Evan, Sam thought, looked deliciously handsome in his tux. It was a shame she wasn't going to get to dance with him tonight, but, really, there was nowhere else she would rather be than with her family. With him.

"Nelson and Bob are heading over to the reception. They're going to see that everything is set up and the guests are having a good time without us before they come."

"There should be plenty of time," Alice said. "Having a baby takes hours. Now, come here you two and give your mother-in-law a kiss on the cheek for giving me two more grandchildren."

Evan's eyes shot to Sam. "We said we were going to wait," he muttered under his breath.

"Until after the wedding," Sam agreed. "I did."

Evan looked to Alice. "I don't suppose we could wait a few more days to tell Bob.

I know we've already been married for months, but I can't help think he would not be happy knowing I knocked up his daughter before he walked her down the aisle. Not going to lie, love the guy, but he still scares me sometimes."

"Trust me," Alice said, patting Evan on the cheek. "He'll simply be thrilled he's going to be a grandfather."

Roy patted Evan on the back. "So glad he's Sam's dad and not Lane's."

"Thanks," Evan muttered.

"Okay," Scout said as she doubled over again. "Now that we've got all the happy-happy stuff out of the way. I've got some work to do."

Three hours and ten minutes later, Grace Duff LeBec came into this world screaming, surrounded by a family that adored her.

Her dad didn't even faint.

Duff would have been thrilled. Because, they all agreed, she looked like she was going to be a hell of a baseball player.

* * * * *